HEARTBEATS & STETHOSCOPE

SNEHA SENGUPTA

ISBN 979-8-89632-723-3

PROLOGUE

Jessica

When I think of Dev, it's the fire in his eyes that comes back to me first. We were teenagers, caught in that reckless, defiant phase where everything felt like a challenge. Dev Mukherjee wasn't quiet or awkward to me—he was infuriating. Always ready with a sharp retort or a smug smile whenever I tried to outsmart him in chess or prove my monologues were better than his verses. We were rivals, the kind who lived to argue, to one-up each other in the small, passionate world of our college's literary society. And yet, in between those arguments, I began to see him differently—not just as someone I had to beat, but someone I couldn't help but admire.

There was a brilliance to Dev, this maddening mix of arrogance and vulnerability that made him impossible to ignore. He had a way of making everything he touched—words, ideas, moments—feel like they mattered. But there were times when the bravado slipped, and in those rare, unguarded moments, I'd catch a glimpse of something raw and tender beneath his competitive edge. Those moments always disarmed me and made me forget what I was even fighting him for.

Looking back, maybe we weren't rivals at all. Maybe we were two kids too afraid to admit how much we understood each other. Dev was the first person who made me feel like love could be as sharp and exhilarating as a debate, as heartbreaking as a loss. And when he walked away, I realized he wasn't just someone I wanted to beat—he was someone I wanted to keep.

Sarah

Dev was magnetic in a way that didn't make sense. We met in the heart of Mumbai, in that glittering whirlwind of a lit fest, and he was... different. He carried himself like someone who had weathered more storms than he let on like he wore every scar under his skin. He was intense, almost painfully so. There was a rawness to him, this unhealed part that drew me in, like he was both broken and beautiful all at once. I remember watching him at a café one night, just observing the way he'd get lost in his thoughts, his fingers drumming on his notebook, barely aware of the world around him. With Dev, it always felt like you were orbiting something deeper, something beyond what he was willing to share. He'd smile and say something charming, but there was always this sadness, buried just beneath the surface. I thought I could reach him, that maybe I'd be the one to finally pull him back to shore. But I was wrong. I was just another passing wave on his endless ocean.

Ahaana

Dev was never meant to be understood. Even as kids, he was an enigma—my best friend, my anchor, and yet someone whose mind was always elsewhere. Our lives were so intertwined it felt like we shared the same pulse, but there was a part of him that belonged to something greater, something I could never touch. At 17, I'd find him on the school rooftop, not just staring into the horizon but losing himself in it, like the world around him wasn't big enough to hold his thoughts.

His warmth could light up anyone's life, but it was his obsession with creating—writing, imagining, bringing something intangible to life—that consumed him. There was a restlessness in him, a need to find meaning in things most of us take for granted. Years later, when our paths crossed again, I saw a man who had given everything to his art, even parts of himself he couldn't afford to lose. His fire burned brighter than ever, but it carried the weight of sacrifice—the people, the moments, the love left behind in its wake.

And yet, in his eyes, I caught glimpses of the boy I had loved—a boy whose heart beat for both me and the endless stories he longed to tell. A part of him still clung to those dreams, but the rest had surrendered to the pull of a world only he could see. I was part of that world once, but in the end, it was his art that truly owned him.

1

As I walked down the streets, the cold breeze brushed against my nose, while the warmth of my sweater offered a fleeting sense of comfort. Winter had arrived, yet it felt as though it was just yesterday I'd returned from a vacation. It's been over nine months since I came back to this town from the city, and everything here feels different—heavier. The town, once familiar, now feels like a cage. The memories, the ones that used to bring joy, now suffocate me. I can still see them, like old photographs, but they're stained and faded. It's hard to ignore the weight they carry.

Holding a flask of alcohol, trying to drown the noise in my head, I dialed a number. But even that didn't stop the endless thoughts racing through my mind. *"An acclaimed writer,"* I think to myself. *"So why does it feel like I've failed at this?"*

I've won awards and been recognized, and my books have been read and praised. But that doesn't change the feeling. The feeling that the stories I write no longer mean anything. That the words on the page aren't as raw as they used to be. I still get calls from my publishers, but it feels like they're talking to someone else. Someone they've created. Not me.

They don't see me—they see the success, the name, the next bestseller. But all of that feels distant as if it belongs to someone else. And here I am, standing at the edge of this place, chasing after a version of myself that seems to have disappeared.

I used to find solace in these familiar streets—the street vendors packing up for the night, the quiet hum of the pharmacy where I'd see the same old attendant handling the same old crowd. The beggar who sat on the same corner for years, unchanged. I used to see comfort in that repetition. But now, it feels hollow. *"Nothing's the same anymore,"* I mutter to myself. Even the stray dogs, once playful, have become something else—grown up, hardened, more like me.

I try to find meaning in these things, try to make them fit into the story I'm supposed to tell, but it all falls apart in my hands. The world is no longer the story I thought it was. It's a blur. A constant reminder that nothing will make sense. That I'll never be the man I once was. I don't even know who I am now.

"What's the point of writing anyway?" I ask aloud, even though I know no one's listening. *"Is it the words that matter, or the silence they fill?"*

I write because I have to. Not because anyone cares, not because it will change anything. Maybe it's the only thing that keeps me tethered to some semblance of reality in this speeding world. But I'll tell you something—being a writer isn't glamorous. You think success will fill the void, but it only makes it bigger. You stand on a stage in front of thousands, but all you hear is the echo of your own thoughts. You give interviews, sign books, sell copies, and yet you still come home to an empty apartment, to silence. And that silence? It's louder than any applause.

I used to dream about this life. I used to believe that writing the right story would make everything finally click. But then I realized—the world doesn't care about your story.

It moves on, indifferent to everything you've put into it. And you're left there, still chasing after the version of yourself that no longer exists.

I used to believe in love too. I thought love could save me, could fix all the broken pieces. But love doesn't save you. It breaks you. You fall into it, and it pulls you under. And yet, like a fool, I keep chasing it. I've chased it in all the wrong places. In all the wrong people. Maybe that's the real story I'm telling now. Not the books I've written, not the fame, or the accolades. No, it's the pieces of myself I lost along the way. The parts that will never come back.

"I should have known better," I whisper to the empty street. But knowing better doesn't change anything. It doesn't undo the damage. And now, I'm just here—wandering, lost, trying to figure out how to write myself back into something that feels real again.

Cell phone buzzed.

"Can we catch up later tonight?"

Receiver: "Yeah! Sure, when do you want to meet me? Dinner?"

"Sounds fair enough."

Call disconnected.

It's strange, really, how life works. At the moment, everything seems so ordinary, so unremarkable. But now, looking back from where I stand in 2026, I realize that night, that call, was the beginning of everything I'd been avoiding for so long. It had been five years since I'd last seen her. Five years—yet the weight of those years didn't feel like a stretch of time, just a collection of moments stuck together, like pages of a book I kept reading over and over, hoping to understand what the story was about.

We had been best friends back in school. But now? Strangers, I guess. Strangers, with a few familiar memories scattered between us. She was back in town for her. And in the background, the world was crumbling under the weight of a pandemic. The country was locked down, people were wearing masks, standing six feet apart, and sanitizing every surface they touched. It felt unreal. The government had implemented strict guidelines, and everyone, including me, was forced into this new, disconnected rhythm of life.

The town had changed. I had changed. The streets were quieter now, almost like ghosts of what they once were. After 6:00 p.m., they felt like a deserted island, as though no one lived here anymore. I walked back home, a flask of alcohol in hand—something that had become a constant companion over the past months, almost like a self-inflicted numbness.

I passed by the ice cream parlor. It used to be my escape, a place where the world felt lighter and simpler. I could sit there with her, share an ice cream sandwich, and talk about everything and nothing. That place is now empty, just like my memories of it. I lit a cigarette, inhaling the smoke as the cold winter air settled around me. Funny how memories work. You think you know a place or a person, but in the end, it's time that leaves the deepest mark.

As I stood there, my mind drifting through all the things that had changed, the phone rang again.

"Hello, Jacob?"

"So, I wanted to know what about the other pages you were going to send me, Dev?"

I didn't have the energy to deal with Jacob. My publisher, always breathing down my neck. And yet, here I was, still trying to make sense of it all.

"Yeah, about that... Just give me some time. I'll try to get it done soon."

"You can't be so irresponsible, can you?"

"I know, I just need some time."

"The publishers are waiting to hear from you. They've released the dates already.

Don't push this. Don't make things difficult for yourself. Got it?"

"Okay, I'll talk to them. Thanks, Jacob."

Click

And that's where I found myself—trapped in a loop, tethered to a past that refused to let me go, with a future that felt like a shadow I couldn't step into. I had nothing left but words—words that seemed to mean less with each passing day, words I wasn't sure anyone still cared to hear. But those words? They were all I had. And so, this story—my story— begins with them. Whether you believe in it or not, whether it matters or not, I'm going to tell you what happened. Because, in the end, it's all I've got.

"Where were you?" (I threw the cigarette immediately on the ground and crushed it.) *"You already reached my place?"* *"Of course. Have you looked at your watch?"*

"Ugh... yeah! I'll be there in a while. Can you ask Ma to switch on the geyser?" *"Sure! Also, I can't wait—Aunty cooked your favorite mutton curry and paneer for me. Now will you come fast? I'm dying to taste it."* *"Yeah, I'm on my way."*

I disconnected the call and walked as quickly as I could, realizing how certain things we never think of holding onto sometimes hit us square in the face at the most unexpected hours. The memory of having mutton curry and rice at the dinner table with her for the last time before she left for Delhi flashed in my mind.

She had said to me, in a very non-Bengali accent, *"Babai, toke khub miss korbo."* To this day, I don't know if she really meant it for the *"Babai"* she had grown up with or the neighbor her mum had forced her to be friends with because I was the Bengali kid—innocent, played cricket, good at art and music.

Back then, I had no idea how to say goodbye to someone who had been my whole world. It wasn't just a *"click, unfriend, and block"* kind of situation. Watching her walk away was like standing still while the world kept spinning around me, and facing life without her felt like a cold, unfamiliar reality— scary and yet, strangely liberating. It was bittersweet, really, because, in a way, we were both finding our own paths, thriving in our own separate lives. But anyone who knew me could see it—you were the one I turned to when the weight of the world felt too heavy. The one I'd call if I needed to cry or rant about the latest movie that just hit the theaters, or when I needed someone to listen to my play-by-play breakdown of a cricket match.

Back then, as I waved you off with that half-hearted *goodbye,* I didn't look back. I didn't have the luxury of time to dwell on those memories. Maybe I didn't even want to.

It was a chilly evening, the kind that made you pull your collar up and bury your hands deep in your pockets. The streets were eerily quiet, the air crisp with the scent of distant rain. As I walked toward home, the familiar hum of the town seemed muted, as if everything was holding its breath. I could hear my footsteps echoing in the stillness, my mind a tangled mess of thoughts.

I had just received a message on my phone.

Message popped in "Where are you, Dev? We're waiting to start dinner!"

I picked up the pace, half-jogging, half-stumbling toward home, feeling a weird mix of excitement and dread. There was something about seeing her after all these years that made my heart race in ways I couldn't explain. I was panting by the time I reached the door—definitely not the most dignified entrance.

"Can you believe we're finally doing this?" Ma asked, her voice too loud for the quiet room. I knew Ma was excited, probably more than I was.

I dropped my bag by the door and grabbed a seat. *"How's everything, Ma?"* I asked, trying to settle into the normalcy of the situation, though my chest still felt tight. She was setting down the last of the dishes, and I couldn't help but glance over at the mutton curry Ma had cooked. It smelled delicious, but the absurd feeling in my chest made me question if I'd ever taste it without thinking of the past.

The dining table was set, just as it always had been. Ma was busy in the kitchen, making sure everything was just right. The smell of mutton curry filled the room, and I couldn't help but feel a strange nostalgia hit me.

Ma, glancing up from the stove, asked, *"Has your family had their dinner?"*

I shrugged with a smirk. *"Yeah, I'm sure they've already eaten. You know how it is with them."*

Ma waved it off, a little too eagerly. *"Alright, you two start then. Must be starving!"*

I couldn't help but chuckle at her impatience. It was comforting, in a way—those little familiar moments that made everything feel just a bit more like it used to be before everything changed.

And just like that, the conversation drifted, flowing between us, picking up right where we left off. It felt strange but comforting. There we were, eating dinner as if no time had passed. Her eyes sparkled as she began teasing Ma about her cooking, asking how she managed to make everything taste like it came straight from a five-star restaurant. I smiled, feeling the warmth of familiarity settle over me.

All I could be happy about was seeing them get along as gossip buddies, catching up after years. If I had the energy to recall the past, I'd mention how they used to gossip at our place, sharing every little detail about the neighbors. *The Banerjees*, of course, were a favorite topic. The only thing that ever seemed to concern them was the *Banerjees'* daughter— *Nandita*—and her dating life. Apparently, she was considered the most flirtatious beauty in the neighborhood, always the talk of the town.

For some reason, Nandita was never an interesting subject for me. But for her, she always was. I remember how she'd joke about her latest crush or the guy she was seeing like it was the most pressing news of the day.

I smiled at the thought, though I couldn't help but wonder if it was time to stop thinking about all that old gossip. But of course, she had always found it fascinating, probably more than I did.

Nandita had changed over the years, like most people did. She was now a mother of two, happily married, and had settled in the same city as mine. Life had taken her down a path far removed from the one we once shared, and though we had never been close, there were moments when I remembered her fondly.

I still recall how, about a year ago, Ma had insisted that I go meet Nandita. She was pregnant again, Ma had said, and it seemed like the right thing to do. But my response had been blunt—something that I had never really thought much of until later.

"Ma, seriously? Why would I go and meet her? We aren't even friends," I had said, more out of reflex than anything else.

Ma, in her usual calm tone, had brushed it off. *"Babai, think of her like your sister. Can't you?"* she had suggested, as if that would make everything simpler.

"Sister?" I asked, my tone rising in confusion. It didn't make sense to me.

"Yes, sister," Ma had replied, her voice steady and patient.

And after a pause, I sighed. *"Yeah, fine. I'll go see her."*

I hadn't gone, though. Time passed, and the idea of reconnecting with Nandita lingered in the back of my mind, something I never really followed through with.

Nandita Banerjee was one of those girls who seemed to live in the spotlight, and not just because of her good looks. Back in school, she had the kind of allure that drew attention without even trying. She was the one all the guys talked about, mostly because of her flirtatious nature and her ever-growing list of boyfriends. It was almost like a new name was added to that list every week, and no one could quite keep up. It was part of her charm, or maybe part of the mystery that surrounded her. Her father was a wealthy businessman in town, and it seemed like money was never an issue for her. While most of us were stuck in our little corner of the world, Nandita spent her summers jet-setting around the globe, as if she had a frequent flyer miles card to every luxury destination.

But there was more to Nandita than just her pretty face and fancy trips. She wasn't one of those super-studious types who always had their nose in a book, nor was she the athletic one scoring goals in gym class. No, Nandita was an enigma—fascinating, but in a way that had nothing to do with what you were supposed to be good at. I remember she danced exceptionally well, always the one to lead the moves at school events. And somehow, she managed to make it into our drama group for the annual play in 11th grade. It was as if Nandita lived for the spotlight, not just in the classroom or on the sports field, but wherever she went, even in the most unexpected places.

As I recalled '*Miss Nandita,*' the phone rang, snapping me out of my thoughts.

Mobile phone buzzed.

She picked up the call, and a voice on the other end asked where she was. She replied nonchalantly, "*Yeah, I'm having my dinner. Is it something very important?*"

The voice, sounding professional, responded, "*Ma'am, Dr. Ahuja was expecting you here with him. All the interns are expected to report to the hospital in an hour.*"

"*Oh, okay! Sure... um... I'll be there in 15 minutes, hopefully.*" Her voice had a slight tremble, and I could tell she was tense; it was one of those odd-hour phone calls that always carried a sense of urgency.

As soon as she hung up, she informed us that she had to leave. Without wasting a moment, she quickly finished her dinner, rushed to the sink to clean up, and began preparing to leave for work. Before heading out, she hugged Ma and thanked her for the meal. She smiled and said, *"I loved it, Aunty."*

Ma, the ever-helpful one, asked me to drop her off at the hospital. She had been mentioning her internship there for quite some time now, and I had grown accustomed to hearing about it. I drove her to the hospital while she gathered her essentials—a stethoscope, gloves, and a mask.

When we reached the hospital, she asked politely, *"Do you want to wait for me?"*

I shrugged, *"Do I want to? I don't really have any story to fill my papers with. So, I guess I can wait here until you're done with your work."*

I sat on the worn-out bench outside the local hospital, my thoughts drifting between the cold air and the buzz of activity around me. A woman, adorned in her surgical apron, walked past. Her wrist gleamed as she adjusted the antique 'Fastrack' watch that had become a part of her—its old model telling a different story. She was joined by other interns, all dressed in the same uniform, entering the operating theater.

Then, as if something nudged her in my direction, she walked up to me, her hurried steps quickening.

"Dev," she said, her voice warm but edged with urgency. *"Thank you so much for dropping me off on time. You don't need to wait here for me. I've got to assist a senior doctor with an operation, and it's going to take a while. I'll probably ask Papa to pick me up later. You should head home and rest."*

Before I could respond, a nurse hurried over, calling her name. *"Dr. Ahaana... Dr. Ahuja is looking for you in the OT."*

"Yeah, I'm coming." She waved at me quickly, her face a mix of focus and concern, then turned and rushed toward the operating theater.

As I made my way home, I stopped in the quiet corner of the street, lighting a cigarette. In that stillness, memories I'd tried to bury began flooding back. Before me stood a young boy, innocent and wide-eyed, lost in the maze of his own emotions—his heart scattered across this town. And then there was the man I had become, trying to pick up the broken pieces of what once were. A heavy weight, as thick and suffocating as a blanket, settled over me on a frigid winter night.

The wristwatch. The spectacles. The way she'd bite her lips when she was lost in thought. I could see it all in front of me, but it felt like I had already lost it, even though it was right there in my memory.

I inhaled deeply from the cigarette, my fingers unsteady as I fished my phone out of my pocket. A few quick swipes, and there it was—the picture of her. Time seemed to stall. The world around me blurred, leaving only that moment frozen. A deep quiet settled over me, the kind that had been absent for years as if all the noise in my life had been muted.

2

What does it feel like to be friends with a failed author? That thought kept gnawing at me. I wondered if Sarah would ever think of me that way. The questions tangled in my mind, slipping over one another like a mess of jumbled words. I hadn't dropped anyone off at the hospital before and never had the chance to stick around for long, either. The last time I'd been in a hospital was two years ago after I collapsed from a reckless binge. The publisher's nincompoops had found me face down in my own mess and patched me up while I regained my senses after a full day.

All I remembered after waking was the sharp sting of stitches on my forehead and the acrid scent of antiseptic—except there was something else, something sweeter. It lingered in my nose, mixing with the sterile smell. The familiar scent of Chanel No. 5. Funny, I'd never associated perfumes with hospital rooms.

I drifted in and out of hazy thoughts until I heard a voice. Faint at first, but unmistakable.

"Was that Sarah?"

Of course, it was. Only Sarah would show up this early, her Starbucks cup in hand, looking like she'd just stepped out of a business meeting. She didn't give a damn about me, or about anything, really. But there she was, in a crisp, premium Ralph Lauren shirt and her signature black straight-leg pants, the look of someone who'd conquered the world before breakfast. Her black hair was pulled back in that perfect, effortless way, the strands held in place, but there was always one rebellious piece that fell just so.

She leaned against the window, sipping her Americano as if it were a normal morning, while a strand of her hair fell over the small mole beneath her lip. I stared at it for a moment, remembering how many times I'd kissed that spot. How could I forget this left profile?

"God, how many times have I kissed that mole?" I muttered to myself.

She walked up to the bed, tossing the empty Starbucks cup into the trash. I could barely move with the bandages and stitches, but I still couldn't help but notice how she commanded the room. She picked up her phone, tapping away, making a few calls with a quick, decisive tone—business as usual, even in a hospital room.

I couldn't remember the last time anyone had done that for me—sat in the chaos of my mess, taking control of it all. But she didn't even flinch. Sarah was always a force. Too much of a force sometimes, but I could never quite decide whether I was drawn to it or suffocated by it.

As she turned back toward me, her gaze softened just a bit. But only just. *"You really are a disaster,"* she said, shaking her head. *"What the hell were you thinking?"*

I couldn't tell if it was concern behind her words or just the usual indifference. Either way, it didn't matter. I was in no place to question her or anyone else. All I could focus on was how everything had changed. How I'd let the city change me. And now, with her standing there, everything felt more distant than it ever had before.

She walked up to my bed as I lay there with a couple of stitches on my forehead and a sprained arm covered in a bandage. She threw the Starbucks paper cup and made a few calls.

"Hey, how are you feeling now?" Sarah asked as she stepped into the room, her voice carrying a warmth I hadn't heard in a long time.

"Much better... I think," I muttered, my voice still shaky. *"I don't even know how I got here, honestly. I must've just... dozed off from too much alcohol."* I tried to shrug it off, though my head was pounding. *"So, uh... are they discharging me soon?"*

She hesitated, her eyes clouding over with concern. *"Dev, you weren't okay at all,"* she said softly, looking at me like she was seeing a stranger. *"They found you with... drugs, and, well... you created a huge scene at the office."* Her tone was serious, almost disappointed. *"You even tried to hit the staff."*

I winced. *"Sarah, I... I guess I did. But I was out of it. Completely out of my senses. Do you think this'll affect my job?"* My voice faltered, trying to cover up the panic. I'd really managed to mess things up this time.

She exhaled, as though she'd already gone over this a hundred times in her head. *"Look, for now, don't worry. They're not filing a case. I've cleared things up with the staff, and they're going to discharge you in an hour. I'll be waiting outside, okay?"*

"Thanks for covering for me," I mumbled, feeling a mix of guilt and relief. *"I'll... try not to pull something like this again."*

She smirked, a hint of irony in her gaze as she turned to leave. *"You always say that, Dev."*

As she walked out, I watched her through the door's glass panel, catching her in conversation with the doctor. A nurse entered, carefully removing the IV from my arm. My head was spinning, and the doctor insisted on wheeling me out, considering the state I was still in. I didn't argue. I wasn't in any shape to.

Sarah Qureshi. She wasn't just my boss's daughter. She was the heiress to the publishing house I worked for, the one who'd invested in me, cleaned up my mess, and now, for better or worse, was tangled up in my life. I'd gotten into fights with her employees, caused scenes, and written the most self-indulgent garbage that somehow kept getting published. Yet there she was, still willing to be there for me.

Yes, Sarah was my girlfriend. Not because she pitied me, but because we'd met at a writing workshop before everything went downhill. We'd worked on a novel that somehow turned into a bestseller, and I think she fell for me there. *"It's your eyes,"* she'd once said, tracing a finger over my cheek. *"This whiskered beard, the way your eyes look so dark like they're hiding something... what are you running from, Dev?"*

Our story was unconventional. She cared about me deeply—maybe too deeply, like a child clinging to her favorite toy. But I, on the other hand? I was beginning to feel trapped. I craved freedom, writing, and whatever substances could keep me from feeling anything for too long. She saw love, commitment, and something to build on. I saw an escape hatch I kept ignoring.

Growing up, Ahaana was always the one to pull me through dark times, holding my hand, and helping me find a way out of my own mind. But when adulthood hit and I needed that support again, she was gone. Sarah tried to fill that void in her own way, but she was loving someone who had already drifted beyond reach. She was trying to save me, and I was dragging her down, knowing she'd do anything to keep me afloat.

Maybe she saw me as her biggest project, her broken masterpiece. And maybe, in some twisted way, I wanted her to believe she could fix me. But I knew better. I wasn't looking to be saved. I was looking to burn it all down.

After the book launch party of a colleague, I stumbled out, buzzing with a few too many drinks. The alcohol burned, filling a hollow space inside me, though even I knew it was only temporary. When the sting faded, I was left with an ache I couldn't shake, a dark pull that drew me to Sarah's door. I banged on it hard, loud enough to wake the floor, calling her name again and again, louder each time. She didn't answer. Not even a whisper.

A familiar frustration simmered, turning bitter as her words from earlier echoed in my head, every syllable sharp and unforgiving. *"Can you ever just be a good boyfriend, Dev?"* It was the look in her eyes when she'd said it, that edge of weariness, the last thread of patience slipping. She was tired of me. Tired of fixing my messes, tired of lying to her father, her colleagues, and anyone who still had enough faith to believe in me.

And maybe... maybe I was tired too. Tired of pretending I was worth saving. Of being the reason she lost pieces of herself.

Standing in that hallway, the cold air pressing against my skin, I felt something deeper than anger—a vulnerability that I rarely let myself feel. It made me want to break something, to crush the ache in my chest with force. Growing up, vulnerability meant weakness. It was something to bury, to hide. I had become an expert at numbing myself, at ignoring every tender part of me. But now, with nothing but silence between us, I wondered if maybe I was wrong.

Films make it look easy—this idea of love, this notion that a woman could walk into a man's life and save him, soften his edges, and help him change. They sell it like a promise. But was that true? Was that why Sarah kept giving me chances? Or was it just another lie to comfort people like us, the ones who are too far gone to believe they can change on their own?

I wasn't born with this darkness. I think it grew inside me, year after year until it was all I had. My father was a man who thought he could shape me through sheer force; his way of love was nothing more than criticism and hard lessons. He was rarely around, busy with his own life, his work, and his disappointments. And when he was home, he was just a voice in the shadows, whispering to my mother, blaming her for every flaw I had. *"If you'd raised him better, he wouldn't be like this,"* he'd say as if I was a problem to fix, a mistake they both regretted.

My mother never argued back. She just took it, her silence heavy, her eyes dull. She endured, and in her endurance, she taught me to do the same. I was home, yet I never felt like I belonged. I learned to ignore the emptiness, to push it down, to live around it like a scar. And for a long time, I believed that was just life.

But then Ahaana walked into my world, and for a while, it felt like there was more. She was the only one who seemed to see past the walls I'd built and who didn't shy away from the darkness. With her, I didn't feel the need to pretend. She held my hand through the worst of it, listened without judgment, and gave me a taste of something I didn't know I needed. Ahaana had been a refuge, but that was a lifetime ago.

Now there was only Sarah—the one who tried to hold me together even when I gave her every reason to leave. And there I was, breaking her down, draining her piece by piece, turning us into something toxic and twisted. We were becoming my parents. And maybe I was becoming my father.

I banged on the door one last time, my knuckles bruising against the hardwood. But the door stayed closed. Maybe she was standing just on the other side, hesitating, deciding if I was worth the trouble. But deep down, I knew I wasn't. I didn't deserve her patience, her care. I didn't deserve her love.

So, I turned and walked away, letting the cold wrap around me as I stepped back into the night. I didn't look back, even as the emptiness swallowed me whole.

"What do you want, Dev?" Her voice was sharp, cutting through the tension in the air.

I ran a hand over my face, sighing. *"Look, can we just not go over what happened after the party?"*

Sarah's eyes narrowed, arms folded across her chest. *"Dev, I don't want to talk about anything that happened at the party... or after. It's better if you leave."* Her tone was firm, but I could see the exhaustion in her eyes. She was holding back more than anger—there was hurt there, too.

I leaned against the doorframe, trying to steady myself. *"You're really asking me to leave? Over this?"*

"Yes, Dev," she replied, exasperated. *"I am. Just sober up, get some clarity, and maybe we'll talk."* She was barely looking at me now, her eyes fixed somewhere in the distance as if she'd already checked out of the conversation.

I leaned closer, dropping my voice. *"Sarah, I know I messed up. I got into it with the editor, and I said I was sorry. But can't you just... handle this for me? One last time?"*

She let out a bitter laugh, shaking her head. *"One last time? After everything I've done for you, that's what you have to say?"*

My face fell, and a faint panic flickered through me. *"What...?"* I mumbled, stumbling over my words. *"I thought it was just the editor."*

Her eyes flashed with anger. *"No, Dev. You didn't just 'get into it with the editor. You made a scene in front of our investors. And you expect me to clean it up, like always?"*

The weight of her words sank in, and I opened my mouth to speak, but she cut me off, her voice rising, almost desperate. *"Do you even realize how much I've risked for you? For us?"*

I forced a shaky laugh. *"Sarah... come on. I know you're upset, but you don't have to make this sound like the end of the world."*

She stepped closer, her eyes blazing, unflinching. *"You think this is a joke? You're ruining everything, Dev. And I can't keep doing this."*

I tried to reach for her, my hand almost brushing her arm. *"Just listen—"*

"Enough." Her voice was cold, final. She looked at me one last time, her expression unreadable. *"Leave, Dev. Or I swear I'll call security."*

For a moment, I just stood there, staring at her, the impact of her words settling in. She wasn't bluffing. She was tired, maybe even done. And in that silence, something in me broke.

"Fine," my voice was low, almost bitter. I turned and walked away, the door clicking shut behind me, leaving me alone in the dim hallway, with nothing but the reality I'd been too stubborn to face.

The next morning, the tension was thick. The publishing office buzzed as usual, yet it felt colder, a silent pressure hovering above us. I'd stormed in without warning, still reeling from the previous night. The sting of my own regrets mixed with the rage simmering inside me.

Sarah stood at her desk, organizing a pile of manuscripts, as if putting the pieces of her life back together. When she looked up and saw me, her face betrayed a flicker of surprise, quickly replaced by a hardened stare.

"Dev... um... the investors have decided on your book," she said, her voice low and reluctant as if she were forcing each word out.

I already knew what was coming, but hearing it still cut deeper than I'd expected. *"Are they... planning to throw me out?"* My voice cracked with an almost desperate curiosity.

She nodded slowly. *"You could say that. They're pulling their investment. They'll be funding another writer's work instead."* She paused, her gaze wavering. *"And we think... you should get help. It's clear you're not stable enough to carry on like this. We can't keep investing in a trainwreck, Dev."*

I stood there, stunned, the word 'trainwreck' echoing in my mind. *"A trainwreck? That's what I am now?"* I laughed bitterly, a wave of anger building. *"I thought you were on my side, Sarah. I thought you of all people would stand by me, and try to handle this instead of throwing me to the wolves. But you didn't. You just—stood there and watched."*

She raised a hand, her voice pleading, almost cracking under the weight of the situation. *"Dev, please, don't make a scene here. It's over. Let's just leave it alone."*

"Oh, don't worry. I'm not falling for that pity routine again." I stepped closer, the words spilling out, too hot to hold back. *"You guys had the best. I was the one giving you real work, powerful writing. And now you're throwing me away like I'm nothing? You're withdrawing all my contracts?"*

She took a steadying breath, her eyes filled with something like genuine remorse. *"For now, yes. Until you're sober and can create the kind of work you used to. But I still believe in you, Dev. I know you can come back from this."*

Her words should have been comforting, but they only felt like salt in a wound. *"To hell with your contracts. To hell with the company."* I could feel the fire in my chest, burning brighter with every word. *"You just lost Dev Mukherjee and everything I could have created."*

She flinched as I took out a miniature bottle of alcohol from my pocket, defiantly taking a swig. Her face twisted in frustration. *"Dev... please, just stop it. You know you can't drink here. You know what's at stake."*

I sneered, the alcohol numbing my common sense. *"You know what? I'm done with this whole game. I was the one who made this place shine, not you. You're just the daughter of the man who built it. Nobody knew Sarah Qureshi before I made you famous."*

Her expression hardened, eyes flashing with hurt and anger. *"Shut the hell up, Dev. This isn't just some game. And for the record, I'm the one who's kept you afloat when no one else would. Now, get out of my office."*

"Oh, please. Without me, you'd still be the unknown daughter of a rich man. Let's not forget it's Dev Mukherjee they know you for." I could barely keep the bitterness from spilling out. *"If I hadn't stayed with you, no one would even care about 'Sarah Qureshi, the publisher.'"*

The words hung heavily in the air, and for a moment, everything stilled. Her face was tight, drawn with hurt and rage, her voice icy. *"Get out now. You're not the man I once admired, and you're not welcome here anymore."*

The silence that followed was louder than any words; her rejection was final and absolute. I walked out, feeling the weight of my own mistakes pressing down on me, my pride shattered, and the reality of who I'd become settling uncomfortably into place.

I barely pieced together fragments of memory from the last 48 hours when I opened my eyes, my head throbbing, vision blurred. There, sitting by my bed, was Sarah, eyes red and swollen, exhaustion etched across her face.

The sight of her stirred something unexpected in me—a tangled mix of shame and irritation. *"What... what are you doing here?"* I mumbled, my voice rough.

She let out a hollow laugh, her tone dripping with sarcasm. *"Right, Dev? What am I doing here?"* She shook her head, hurt and disbelief filling her voice. *"I should be at the office, shouldn't I? You know, dealing with the mess you left behind?"*

I rubbed my temples, looking around, confused. *"Wait... shouldn't you? Why are you here, Sarah?"*

Her eyes flashed with frustration. *"You were missing for two days, Dev. Forty-eight hours! I'm tired of this. We all are. You vanish, your friends are frantic, I'm trying to handle things, and you—"* She stopped, her voice cracking as she fought to stay calm. *"Do you even care?"*

I scoffed, leaning back into the pillow. *"Yeah, yeah. The same old drama. I was probably just at some bar in Mumbai. You're overreacting."*

She looked at me, a mix of hurt and disbelief. *"Overreacting? Dev, you don't even remember. The bar owner recognized you, thank God. He contacted your friends, and they brought you home before anything worse happened. I thought... I thought I might never see you again. Do you get that?"*

I rolled my eyes, letting sarcasm drip into my tone. *"Sarah, I'm fine. Nothing happened, all right? Why do you care so much?"*

Her face fell, her expression one of defeated love. *"Why do I care?"* she whispered, almost to herself. She looked away, swallowing her hurt before speaking again. *"You don't get it, do you? You never do."*

I laughed bitterly, crossing my arms. *"Maybe I don't want to get it. I'm done pretending that I need saving, Sarah. You think just because you pull me out of a ditch once in a while, I owe you some kind of undying gratitude?"*

She held back tears, exhaustion laced in her voice. *"No, Dev. I don't need your gratitude. But every time I try to help, every time I care, you push me away. What am I supposed to do? Just watch you self-destruct?"*

I shook my head, dismissive. *"I don't need saving, Sarah. Stop trying to play the hero. Maybe if you'd focus less on fixing me, you'd see that we're both better off without this."*

Her face twisted in pain, a tear slipping down her cheek as she whispered, *"Maybe you're right. Maybe I am just fooling myself. But every time I try to walk away, I can't. I care, Dev..., despite everything. And it kills me every time you look at me like I'm the enemy."*

Silence fell between us, heavy and raw. I turned away, staring blankly at the wall, unwilling or unable to give her the reassurance she so desperately needed.

And in that moment, I could feel her realization settling in. She knew I was already lost.

What I'd just thrown at Sarah was no ordinary cruelty. It was a blow aimed straight at the heart of someone who had held me together more times than I could count, someone who was still standing by me, even after every mess I'd pulled her into. But there I was, tossing her loyalty aside like it was nothing, challenging her care like it hadn't kept me afloat all this time. The look in her eyes—that stunned, hollow silence—spoke of shock, of a kind of hurt she hadn't prepared for, even after seeing me at my worst.

I'd been reckless, arrogant, and downright insufferable, but I'd never expected myself to be heartless. I'd never expected I could go so far as to question the one person who'd stayed, who'd fought, who'd covered for me when I didn't deserve it. She'd carried the weight of my messes with a grace I couldn't match, and there I was, tearing her down with a few heartless words.

But as I stood there, I realized I wasn't just hurting her—I was pushing away the last bit of love I hadn't yet managed to destroy. I was sabotaging the only person who still saw something left in me worth saving. The guilt sat heavily in my chest, but I was too stubborn, too far gone to let it show, to admit that beneath it all, I needed her.

And yet, even as she looked at me, bewildered, hurt, and speechless, I felt an emptiness rise within me—a darkness I didn't know how to fight. I'd created a chasm between us, one she might never cross again. But maybe that's what I wanted. Maybe I'd become so tangled in my own ruin that I was willing to let the one person who cared finally walk away, so I wouldn't have to face what I'd done to her—or to myself.

Sarah's voice cut through the silence like a blade. *"Really, Dev Mukherjee? You have the nerve to ask why I care?"* She looked at me, furious yet hurt, her voice shaking. *"I care because I love you. Because I thought—God, I thought we were building something real here. But you? You're so far gone you can't see it, can you?"*

I laughed bitterly, crossing my arms. *"Love? For whom, Sarah? Yourself? Everything you've done—every single thing— has been about you—about keeping up your image, protecting your precious company. And I'm done being part of it."*

Her eyes hardened, though I could see the hurt still lingering there. *"You know what? Maybe you're right. Maybe we're both done. Let's take that break you're so desperate for."* Without another word, she turned and slammed the door behind her.

The room fell silent, and I was left alone with the mess I'd made. Anger surged through me, and before I knew it, I'd picked up the glass from the table and hurled it at the wall, watching it shatter like everything else in my life.

Buzz.

Sarah Qureshi: "I don't know why you need to know this, but... I'm leaving for London today. I'll be there for a while."

Her message lit up the screen, and suddenly the noise around me blurred—the laughter and clinking glasses, all muffled against the weight of those words. Sarah was leaving for London, putting an ocean between us.

The party swirled around me, but all I could picture was her. The way she used to look at me when she thought I didn't notice, the sound of her laugh, even the way she walked away. If there were a way to turn back time, to fix all the ways I'd messed this up... would I even know how?

In a room full of people, I'd never felt more alone.

14th February 2015

Winter in Mumbai was a quiet kind of magic—mornings bathed in soft golden light, evenings laced with a sea-kissed breeze. The air no longer clung to the skin; instead, it carried the scent of something new, something waiting. Much like my career, the season unfolded with a quiet promise, steady and unhurried. I was still learning the rhythm of the city, the pulse of a writer's life, but February had given me a gentle beginning—one that felt like a whispered assurance that I was exactly where I was meant to be.

And, a girl who constantly lingered in my head, in my thoughts, ran like a steady stream, her presence flowing through every corner of my mind. Her laughter echoed in my thoughts, a melody that refused to fade.

The woman in her late twenties decked up in her *Gucci & Prada* and a man who had just celebrated his 24th birthday, wearing a funky *Batman* graphic printed t-shirt, a pair of ripped jeans, and worn-out *chappals*. The *Davidoff* lover was about to collide with a pro-*Gold-Flake* lover; things were about to change. But, both of us were unaware of the storm; the Gateway LitFest was going to blow everything off, especially ME.

The beauty had entered the room, and there sat a shabby-looking guy with his headphones on.

"Is this seat taken?" she asked.

"Does it look like it's taken?" I replied.

Those are expressions vividly imprinted on my mind—the raised eyebrows and a straight face.

"Okay! Rude boy... What arrogance!" she glared.

The LitFest was anything but interesting for the two of us—a guy new to the publishing world and a woman with big, bold eyes, pupils dilating on every speech that mentioned her favorite authors. Both of us had been sitting beside each other for an hour now, but what she had missed noticing was that someone else witnessed her happiness too. And, I couldn't make sense of why I was staring at this woman who had been nothing but an audience to one of the authors' workshops.

The workshop ended after a good hour. I got up and walked toward the restroom. I stood outside the restroom, a cigarette dangling between my fingers. I could still hear the low hum of the workshop chatter fading down the hall. My mind raced, replaying our brief encounter like a movie reel, one moment skipping into the next. She was bold-pretty—an odd, arresting blend of beauty and defiance. Her eyes—dark and fierce—had cut through the workshop's dimly lit room, leaving traces of curiosity that seemed to find me no matter where I sat.

The restroom door swung open, and there she was, silhouetted by the low bathroom lights, her features half in shadow. She smirked when she saw me, her gaze caught on the cigarette as if she had caught me doing something I shouldn't. She leaned against the doorframe, folding her arms, her hip cocked, amusement dancing on her lips.

She glanced at the cigarette, smirking. *"Bet you think that makes you look mysterious."*

I raised an eyebrow, holding her gaze as I took a slow drag. *"I don't have to try that hard."*

She laughed—low and smoky—and stepped closer, leaning against the wall beside me. *"So, are you actually writing anything, or just here to look bored and brooding?"*

I chuckled, exhaling smoke away from her. *"Trying to figure that out myself. But you, you don't look like the writing workshop type."*

She shrugged, looking down with a wry smile. *"Guess I'm just here to keep things interesting."*

I took one last drag and handed her the cigarette, our fingers brushed for a brief second that lingered just a bit too long. We slipped out of the building, ducking down a narrow alley with faded murals on the walls, escaping the half-hearted claps and critiques echoing from the workshop. She pulled her coat around her as they walked, the cigarette smoke curling in the night air between us.

"So, what's a guy like you writing about anyway?" she asked, taking a drag and passing it back.

I shrugged, keeping it vague. *"Mostly things I'm trying to figure out."*

She laughed, a soft, teasing sound. *"Cryptic. You do know they don't hand out awards for brooding, right?"*

I grinned, tilting my head as I exhaled. *"And you? You're clearly not here for the thrill of workshop critiques."*

"I just like showing up now and then and see if anyone's worth talking to." She flashed him a glance with a playful challenge. *"Frank Sinatra's kind of like that, you know? Classic, smooth... feels like he could charm anyone."*

I raised an eyebrow, surprised. *"You're a Sinatra fan?"*

"Of course," she said, rolling her eyes. *"Who doesn't appreciate a good Sinatra tune?"*

I let out a skeptical laugh. *"I don't know... you don't seem like the type who'd be into someone so polished."*

"Oh, come on. Sinatra was the real deal—the voice of a whole generation." She smirked at me. *"Let me guess, you think he's overrated?"*

I shrugged. *"It's not that. Just feels a bit too... easy. My music's almost too perfect like it's more about the image than anything real."*

She stopped, narrowing her eyes at me. *"You can't be serious. Sinatra's all heart. You think he's just an image?"*

I grinned, leaning in. *"All I'm saying is that if you're really into the gritty, real stuff, you don't reach for Sinatra. That's just style."*

"Oh, please," she laughed, shaking her head. *"Maybe you just don't get that real doesn't always have to mean, raw, and messy. Sometimes, real is just... honest. Like him."*

We stood there, the cigarette smoldering between us, and I realized she was looking at me like I was the one with something to prove.

She studied me for a moment, a playful glint in her eyes, then reached into her coat pocket and pulled out a sleek, black business card. She handed it to me with a smirk, her fingers brushing me as I took it.

I glanced down at the card. Her name, bold and clean, followed by a publishing house I recognize—small but reputable, the kind of place that took chances on writers with a little edge.

"Think you can keep up?" she asked, her voice low and daring, almost challenging me. *"We're always looking for writers who have something to say."*

I raised an eyebrow, slipping the card into my pocket, a small smile playing on my lips. *"I'll think about it."*

She gave me one last, lingering look before turning to leave. As she walked away, I could feel the thrill of her words, the taste of her offer hanging in the night air. The conversation, I know, isn't over yet.

3

Two people. Two different paths, yet somehow—against all odds—we met at one place, caught in circumstances we'd both set in motion without even realizing it. They say your actions always come back to you, but back then, I wasn't too concerned about what I'd done to Sarah. I thought I'd moved past it. But the truth was, the aftershocks hit me harder than I'd ever imagined. By the time I realized what I'd lost, she was gone, building a new life in London. And I was here, still in Mumbai, working for a publishing house that barely tolerated my presence, hoping I'd deliver something big enough to redeem myself.

For the first few months, I managed to get by. My work for their columns was solid and consistent enough to keep them from showing me the door. They still thought I had it in me to pull off a bestseller, and maybe, on my better days, so did I. But just as I started to get my footing again, the world shifted overnight. The pandemic swept in, freezing everything in place. Opportunities vanished as fast as they'd come. What little I'd saved for tomorrow suddenly didn't feel like enough.

Dev Mukherjee, the guy who once believed he'd make it big, was left standing in silence, trying to make sense of a world that was no longer the same.

For the first few weeks of the lockdown, I chose to stay put, buried in my work-from-home. My work hours stretched longer than my sleeping hours—each day blurring into the next. And for the first time in my life, I began to understand what Sarah must have felt like. The grind was relentless, and balancing everything on my own was becoming unbearable. The difference was that she had it together. Me? I was just clinging on.

It was Jacob. Of course. Always timing his calls at the worst possible moment.

"Bro! Did you hear the news?" he said, a mix of mockery and forced concern in his voice. *"Due to the economic crash, the company's cutting some percentage off the column writers' pay. Have you planned anything yet?"*

I could almost hear the smirk in his voice. Jacob had been an arsehole from the moment I joined the house. He couldn't write worth a damn, so they kept handing his columns to me— he was never shy about showing his jealousy.

"What? What the hell, man?" I muttered, frustration bubbling up. *"I was saving up for that trip to the book festival in London. Now this!"* My voice cracked with irritation, but I was powerless. The situation was out of my hands.

Jacob, of course, couldn't let go of his need to remind me of his perceived superiority. *"I know, right? At least I still have a job. Oh, and I heard that a few writers are getting axed too— apparently, the house can't afford to keep everyone. You heard about that, right?"*

The way he said it, dripping with insincerity, made my stomach turn. He wasn't concerned, not one bit. If anything, he'd be thrilled if I lost my job. He'd have one less person to compete with.

"No... I'm hearing it from you," I shot back, trying to keep my cool. *"I'll see if I'm going to be jobless soon or not. Thanks for*

the heads-up." My voice was colder than I meant it to be, but I wasn't about to thank someone who clearly wanted to see me fail, especially in the middle of a damn pandemic.

"Sure, buddy," he said, dragging the words out. "Let me know if you hear anything. Take care."

Click.

The call ended. Just like that.

Jacob was the kind of guy who thrived on other people's failures. He had no genuine care for my situation—he only found delight in seeing me struggle. The moment I'd moved to Mumbai, he'd been waiting for me to mess up, just so he could revel in it. His jealousy wasn't subtle. I remember him once dismissing my first book as something a kindergarten kid could have written. Ironically, it turned out to be a bestseller that year. Jacob didn't even have the decency to hide his disdain. He was a hack, the kind of guy who slacked off while still managing to cling to his job, throwing shade at anyone better than him. He had no talent and no humility, and that made him insufferable.

Back with Sarah, things had been different. Working for Sarah was a privilege, yes, but it also came with perks no one else could get. I had my own personal editor—someone assigned exclusively to me by Sarah's publishing house, a luxury most writers could only dream of. I never had to worry about competition or feeling small. They respected my work, maybe even more because of who I was to Sarah. No one questioned my words, and I had a certain freedom I now missed. Here, every little thing I did felt scrutinized. The rules were different, the pressures heavier. I wasn't just a writer anymore; I was someone who had to toe the line, follow the guidelines, and keep my head down.

Then came the news.

I had been drowning in deadlines, battling the mess my life had become, trying to stay afloat. Work was the only thing I had left to focus on, but even that seemed to be slipping through my fingers. Just when I thought things couldn't get worse, they did.

The phone call from Ma came late one evening, shattering whatever semblance of stability I had left. My grandfather— my confidant, the man who had been a constant in my life— had suffered a major stroke. I had barely processed what she was saying when she confirmed that they hadn't even informed me for the first few days. By the time I got the news, he had already been unconscious, and things had taken a sharp, uncertain turn.

Ma's voice trembled on the other end. *"Dev, I know you're far, but are you in the right state of mind to hear this? It's about Dadu."*

I felt the world freeze. Dadu, the man I looked up to more than anyone, was fighting for his life. It felt like everything was crashing down all at once.

"Dadu...? What happened? Is he okay? I'm going to figure out a way to get home. I heard flights are back on, but with all the quarantine rules, it's going to take time... Ma, don't worry, I'll be there soon." I tried to keep my voice steady, but inside, panic was rising.

Ma's voice on the other end cracked, and the weariness in her tone hit me hard. *"He... he had a stroke, Dev. But they say he'll be okay. He's stable now. They're planning to discharge him soon, but for now, he's still in the hospital. I just... I need you to be here, Dev. He needs to see you."*

Hearing that Dadu was stable helped, but my heart wouldn't stop racing. All I could think of was getting back to him. The feeling of helplessness—the fear of not making it in time—was suffocating.

Fortunately, by then, flights had resumed, and I was able to book one without delay. But it wasn't the logistics that were consuming me; it was the thought of Dadu—sick and fragile. As the flight soared through the sky, my mind wasn't on the safety measures or the new travel restrictions; I was only focused on getting home, on seeing Dadu, and on being there before it was too late.

I landed at Bagdogra, grabbed a cab, and the three-and-a-half-hour drive felt like an eternity. As soon as I stepped inside the house, I felt the weight of the situation sink in. The familiar walls of my childhood home, now more like a prison than a sanctuary, echoed with memories. And to make it worse, I was quarantined. I couldn't even see Dadu in person yet. I had to follow strict health protocols, just like everyone else.

But when Ma finally told me the good news—Dadu was well enough to be brought home—I felt a weight lift off my chest. I was able to video call him soon after, and even though we were miles apart, it felt like he was right there with me. Seeing him on the screen, smiling weakly but warmly, filled me with an overwhelming sense of relief.

"I'm here, Dadu," I said, my voice thick with emotion. *"I'm home."*

Dadu chuckled softly. *"Good, good... You're back. I was waiting to see you."*

It felt like a lifetime since I'd been home—truly home, not just a visitor. Growing up, Dadu had lived with my maternal uncles for much of the time. When he came to visit us, it was always something special, a mini-vacation. I remember how he'd sit in his old armchair, reading a book, his glasses perched on the edge of his nose, a small smile playing on his lips as he read me stories about the world. He had always believed that I was the one from the family who would go on to do something different, something special. He was the first one to see the spark in me—the way my love for writing had begun to take root.

I had inherited that love from him. I remember asking him once, back when I was younger, what made him so passionate about writing. His answer stayed with me:

"You'll understand soon enough, Dev. Writing is more than just words. It clears your head when everything else feels like too much. It was my escape from a life I didn't always love. Writing kept me going when everything else was falling apart."

I didn't realize it at the time, but those words stuck with me. When I first picked up a pen and began scribbling, it was as if I'd unlocked something inside me I never knew existed. The words just flowed, effortlessly, as if I had always known how to do it. Writing became my refuge—my escape, just like it had been for Dadu.

Now, with everything that had happened—Dadu's health, the chaos of the world outside, the mess of my own life—it felt like a full-circle moment. His legacy of writing was a torch I had taken up, not knowing how deeply it would shape my life.

It had been nearly six years since I'd last seen Dadu, and after 14 long days of quarantine and worry, we finally had our time together. When I saw him—frail but still carrying that wise—reassuring aura, I could hardly contain myself. My thoughts raced back to all the years I spent with him as a child, listening to his stories, and feeling the weight of his wisdom in every word. He had always been the one to push me to be different and to think beyond what was expected of me.

He knew about my first book—the one that hit the commercial market like a storm—and my second, which had failed spectacularly. But when I walked into the room, there was no judgment in his eyes, just pride. His hand gently landed on my back, and he spoke with the kind of warmth that only a grandfather could.

"I'm proud of you," he said, his voice steady, but with a kind of emotion I hadn't expected. *"You're doing what you've always wanted, no matter how many falls or slopes you climb. Just remember—always write for yourself first, and then for others. In the end, you're the creator."*

His words hit harder than I anticipated. They didn't just echo around the room; they reverberated deep within me, stirring things I thought I'd buried. Dadu had always known I would be the one to break the mold, the one to carve a different path from everyone else in the Mukherjee 'bari'. What he didn't know, though, was the price I was paying to be that person.

He knew about the failed book. He knew it had shaken me, but he didn't know the full extent of the destruction it caused inside me. He didn't know how I was sinking into something darker—how the man I had once been was slowly being devoured by the things I turned to for escape. Drugs. Alcohol. Obsessive indulgence that felt like both a crutch and a punishment. To him, I was just the ambitious kid, the 'unusual one', the dreamer. What he didn't realize was that I was slowly suffocating under the weight of it all.

My parents, too, remained oblivious to the depth of it. They had no idea how far I'd fallen. And Sarah—God, Sarah—

she had no clue either. I had purposely distanced myself from her, buried any hope of reconciling with her under the weight of my own decisions. I had dug the grave for us, and now I couldn't bear to look back and see if there was any way to climb out of it.

The only question that clung to me like a shadow, gnawing at my every thought was deceptively simple: *Was I even in love with her?*

But no matter how many times I turned it over in my mind, the answer remained elusive, slipping through my fingers like sand. It wasn't just a question about Sarah—it was about everything that had become tangled between us, about the versions of myself I had abandoned along the way. Love, in its purest form, had always felt like a distant memory, something I used to understand before I lost myself to the mess of my own making. Now, that question felt like an accusation, a judgment I couldn't escape.

It was certainly the kind of question I thought I'd have an answer to, but the truth was, I didn't. Because the moment I saw her again—Ahaana, standing there in that medical apron, her stethoscope hanging around her neck, and that old 2011 edition Fastrack watch on her wrist—it was as if everything else in my life had dissolved. The question I'd been tormenting myself with suddenly seemed insignificant. Was I in love with Sarah? No, not anymore. In that moment, it felt as if Sarah, my relationship, and even the pain I carried had never existed at all.

When I looked at Ahaana, everything shifted. I wasn't trying to find answers anymore. I didn't need them. Because in that one glance, I had found something more profound— something that made everything else fade into the background. And as the conversation unfolded, the tension I hadn't even realized I was holding onto melted away. A warmth spread through my chest, and in that instant, my heart whispered, *"Welcome back home."*

Funny, isn't it? (I laugh, almost bitterly).

We read about these things in rom-coms, right? The kind of stuff that feels like a distant, unrealistic fantasy, something that only happens to the overly dramatic leads in those movies. But then, bam! Life throws you a curveball and suddenly you're standing there, heart doing backflips, and you're thinking, *Wait a minute... this feels familiar.* But then again, *no, it doesn't. Not at all.* It was like a warm, gentle wave crashing into me, soft enough to make me feel all mushy inside, but unfamiliar enough to make me second-guess whether I'd ever really felt this before.

On my way home, my brain was buzzing with all the things I could have said to her. Oh, I made up entire conversations in my head—most of them didn't make sense, but who cares? I was living in a world of *what ifs* and *maybe next time.* My mind was playing a weird game of *"what would it be like to see her again?"* I could almost feel those damn butterflies in my stomach and those bursts of sudden happiness that felt like I was a teenager again. But, deep down, I knew better. Luck wasn't on my side; this wasn't going to be a rom-com where everything magically falls into place. Still, I kept hoping... maybe someday, sooner or later, I'd see her again.

At home, things were... well, *normal.* Ma was in her corner, happily reading some book like she always did. I plopped down on the couch with my laptop, convinced that today was the day I'd finally finish the work I'd been avoiding. And just as I was getting into my groove, a message popped up on my screen. My heart skipped a beat. Could it be? No... it wasn't her.

It was from someone at Sarah's publishing house.

The publishing house had, honestly, been really good to me—mostly because, you know, I was dating the boss. But still, my life had shifted because of her, and I'd started to understand the grind of working in a fast-paced city like Mumbai. I had once been all about passion, creating work I loved for no other reason than the joy it gave me. But now? It felt more like pressure. It wasn't the same.

Dadu, on the other hand, used to tell me stories about his days working for a local press back in the 1960s. He'd write children's stories for a ridiculously small sum, but he loved it. That was his passion. And somehow, I wondered if I had lost a bit of that spark along the way.

The phone buzzes and the screen lights up.

"Dear Mr Mukherjee,

Hope you're well. I'm reaching out on behalf of Sarah and the team. We would love to have you join us at the upcoming book launch in India. The investors are eager to meet with you at the event. We'll forward all the details shortly if you confirm your participation.

Warm regards,

— "Indigo Quill Publishing"

Life was offering me a strange twist—another shot with the publishing house that once defined me, this time with Sarah, the woman who once set my life on a different trajectory. The email had all the details: a book launch, a stage, and investors with expectations. This wasn't just an invitation; it felt like a final chance to prove myself, to resurrect the name and ambition I'd buried under frustration and poor choices. This was my ticket out of the creative limbo I'd been stuck in.

That night, the excitement mixed with old anxieties, and sleep barely brushed my mind before I passed out right there at my desk. My dreams were patchy, hazed over by stubborn restlessness. I didn't wake until a sharp thud of banging jolted me awake. Checking my watch, I saw it was barely 5:30 a.m. Curious, I stepped onto the balcony to find the source of the commotion.

Across the street, she stood outside her door, fumbling for her keys, half-asleep yet somehow still radiating that quiet energy she always carried. I pulled out a cigarette, lighting it carefully to avoid catching her attention, but part of me wanted her to notice, just to see her expression. And just like that, she looked up, catching the spark of my lighter, and the faintest scowl flickered over her face. It was that same familiar look—a mix of disappointment and irritation. She'd worn that expression a million times back in school whenever I'd done something stupid or reckless. I could almost hear her voice again: *"You realize everything you do somehow spirals into chaos, right? Seriously... what a disaster."*

As I exhaled a slow plume of smoke, a strange nostalgia washed over me. It was almost as if life, in its own cryptic way, was pushing me back to square one, daring me to finally rewrite the story I'd been avoiding for so long.

Every time she made that face, I'd just laugh awkwardly, hoping she wouldn't dig deeper and roast me. Just then, my phone buzzed.

The cell phone buzzes.

"Hey, Dev! Didn't expect to see you up this early. And for the record, you don't need to check on me. I'm not a kid! Just got back from my shift; was waiting for Mom to unlock the gate."

"Oh, no, no! I wasn't keeping tab on you or anything. Just woke up to the sound of your gate and thought I'd see what's up."

"Oops, sorry! Didn't mean to wake the neighborhood. Mum wasn't answering her phone, so... had to give the gate a little workout."

You still apologize for the smallest things, just like always.

"It's fine, honestly. Besides, now I'm awake, so maybe I'll finally get some writing done. So... thanks for the accidental wake-up call, I guess."

"Seriously? Are you thanking me for that? By the way, since when are you a smoker, Mr. Writer? I'll have to interrogate you about that next time. Anyway, go work. I'm crashing."

There it was, the classic ultimatum, straight from the person who was never fond of 'lousy habits'.

"Alright, alright. Catch you later. Good night, Ahaana."

Ahaana: *"Hahaha! Goodnight, Dev."*

Ahaana Bharadwaj—eldest of the Bharadwaj family, Abhay's smarter, cooler, and effortlessly charismatic older sister. Growing up, she was the perfect blend of best friend and bad influence, a girl who could pull off a prank one minute and ace a math test the next. Her sense of style was always ahead of everyone else's; she knew how to make the latest haircut or the trendiest accessory look like it was created just for her. The closest in her family to her father, a retired Indian Army officer with stories for days, she inherited his mix of discipline and adventure, and they shared a bond that most of us envied.

And of course, she was a legend in our batch—the only girl who'd show up to cheer us on at every football and cricket match, hollering louder than most of the boys. If there was a Bollywood movie worth watching, Ahaana was my go-to partner; she could convince me to tag along just by bribing me with a vanilla ice cream, and soon we'd be laughing through *Kal Ho Naa Ho* or dancing to *Pretty Woman* and *Maahi Ve* like it was second nature.

She was my personal hero, too—the only one who'd defend me against bullies, and the only girl I knew who could throw a punch and patch up a bruise just as quickly. Ahaana was magnetic; everyone wanted her around, but she was particular about her inner circle, always choosing me first and everyone else second. She dated about ten guys in high school, and half of them never even realized they'd been 'dumped' when she lost interest. Serious commitment wasn't her thing; she was too busy living in the moment, collecting small but meaningful treasures like her old Fastrack watch, a gift she received when she topped her boards in 12th grade—a symbol of pride and nostalgia wrapped into one.

Now, life had taken her somewhere unexpected: she'd become Dr. Ahaana Bharadwaj, a calm and focused doctor, treating patients with the same warmth and humor she'd once shown her friends. The same girl who'd sobbed over *Aman Mathur's* death in *Kal Ho Naa Ho* was now bringing others back from the brink, her familiar smile lighting up an unfamiliar white coat.

Time had shaped her into something remarkable, and though I could have sat there and reminisced about all she'd been to me, all she was now, I couldn't let myself get lost in that. Instead, I forced myself to focus on my work, letting her remain the memory I'd always find comfort in, the friend who felt like home even after all these years.

4

What do you do when you can't erase someone from your mind? There's no 'Delete' button, just memories, relentless and uninvited, circling back like echoes in an empty room. That's where I found myself—a man desperate to craft something extraordinary but trapped in the same story. And that story was Sarah.

Sarah, who once thrived in the chaos of my life, now lingered in the quiet corners of my writing. Every word I tried to escape through only pulled me closer to her shadow. When I think back, I see myself lost in a state of hiraeth—not just longing, but aching for a place that never existed.

Was it nostalgia or something darker? A drugless high, maybe, where the past felt more vivid than the present. I couldn't tell. All I knew was that she was everywhere, even when I tried so hard to write her away.

The first time I tried LSD was during a trip to Goa, right after the success party of my first book. It was meant to be a celebratory escape with friends—and Sarah. But I ruined it for her. While she wanted time for 'us', I found myself drawn into the pull of something else entirely.

LSD, a tiny square of paper dissolving on my tongue, unlocked a world far beyond our hotel room in Vagator. My first 'trip' was a good one—ten hours of floating, feeling like the universe was within reach. Sarah, meanwhile, sat beside me in a panic, trying to talk me back to earth with words that barely made sense to her, let alone me.

By the time I snapped out of it, it was past midnight, and we'd missed our flight back to Mumbai. Strangely, none of us cared. The high overshadowed the chaos. But what I didn't tell Sarah was that Goa wasn't the end of it.

Back in Mumbai, LSD became my quiet companion. On weekends, as I wrestled with the pressure of my second book, I'd slip into that altered state, locking myself away in my dark, chaotic apartment. Sarah—publisher by profession and caregiver by circumstance—spent her Sundays cleaning up my mess, cooking meals, and grounding the chaos I had become. She was my only tether, though I don't think I ever said it.

For me, the acid trips brought clarity and creation, but for Sarah, they must've felt like a slow descent—watching me chase brilliance while losing pieces of myself along the way.

November, 2018

I woke up to a sound in the hallway, unfamiliar and sharp, slicing through the silence. My chest tightened as panic took hold—panting, trembling, sweat soaking my skin. The shadows shifted, twisting into shapes that weren't there. Voices whispered, louder and louder, until I couldn't tell if they were in the room or in my head. For the first time, I felt the grip of what the drugs were doing to me—the hallucinations, the chaos, the unraveling.

But I couldn't tell Sarah. What would she do? Beg me to stop? Watch helplessly as I spiraled further? She knew I wouldn't listen.

The sound of shattering glass woke her. She called my name, only to find me crumpled in the hallway, unconscious, drenched in sweat, with my breath shallow and erratic.

For a moment, she froze. The man she loved was slipping away, swallowed by something she couldn't fight.

The night suffocated me with its silence, the kind that clings to your skin and makes your mind restless. My chest was tight and my breath, shallow and ragged. And then I saw it—something, someone, standing in the balcony shadows. The edges of my vision blurred; my heart raced uncontrollably.

Sarah stirred awake, startled by the sound of my pacing. Her voice cut through the tension, laced with both worry and irritation.

"Dev? What's wrong with you? Why are you panting?"

I could barely form the words, my gaze fixed on the balcony. *"I... I can see someone there,"* I whispered hoarsely, pointing a trembling finger toward the shadows. My voice cracked. *"Don't look back... please, don't."* My body moved before my mind caught up, and I clung to her, burying my face in her shoulder.

She stiffened but quickly tried to steady me, her hands brushing my damp hair. *"Dev, listen to me. Look at me. There's no one there,"* she said firmly, her voice teetering between calm and desperation. She glanced toward the balcony, her confusion evident. *"You're imagining things."*

"No, no, no," I stammered, shaking my head violently. *"You don't get it, Sarah. I see someone. They're there!"* My breathing turned erratic, each gasp louder than the last.

She placed both hands on my face, forcing me to meet her eyes. *"Dev, breathe. Trust me—there's no one there. Just calm down, okay?"*

Her steady gaze should have reassured me, but it only fueled my frustration. *"You don't get it!"* I snapped, pulling away from her touch. My voice cracked with fear and annoyance. *"You won't understand. Just... just get me a glass of water, will you?"*

Her lips tightened, the sting of my words flickering across her face. She didn't argue, just walked to the table and poured the water. *"Here,"* she said, her tone clipped, anger bubbling under the surface.

I reached for the glass, but my hand faltered. My legs buckled as I tried to stand, and I crumpled to the floor. Weakness overtook me, a weight dragging me down.

"Dev!" Sarah's voice cracked, the sharp edge of irritation melting into alarm. She dropped to her knees beside me, her arms wrapping firmly around mine as she tried to pull me upright. I leaned heavily against her, my body refusing to cooperate, each breath shallow and ragged.

"Come on," she said softly, her tone steady despite the tremble in her hands. *"Let's get you to bed."*

I let her guide me, barely aware of the way her fingers gripped my arm, her shoulder pressed against mine for balance. Each step to the bed felt like dragging dead weight, and by the time she eased me down onto the mattress, my chest still heaved as if I'd been running for miles.

"Dev, you're scaring me," she murmured as she knelt by the bed, brushing damp strands of hair from my forehead. Her touch was light and hesitant as if she feared I might shatter beneath it.

I didn't answer. I couldn't. The room still felt too heavy, the shadows too close. I shut my eyes, retreating from the world, but sleep wouldn't come. My body twisted. I was restless and desperate to escape from whatever had burrowed into my mind.

"*Stop,*" she said softly, her hand pressing against my shoulder to still me. "*You need to rest.*"

I opened my eyes then, just enough to catch the fear etched into her face—the tight line of her mouth, the furrow between her brows. It struck something deep in me, something I couldn't name, and I hated it. I hated myself for putting that look there.

"*I'm sorry,*" I whispered hoarsely, the words barely audible.

Sarah shook her head, blinking rapidly as though trying to hold something back. "*Don't,*" she said, her voice steady but quiet. "*Just stop. Don't apologize. Just... let me help you.*"

She shifted, climbing onto the bed beside me. I felt her arm slide under my shoulders, lifting me just enough so she could settle in and pull my head onto her lap. Her hand found its way to my hair, stroking gently, rhythmically, as her other hand rested on my chest, grounding me.

"*You're okay,*" she whispered, leaning over just enough so I could feel her breath against my temple. "*You're safe. I've got you.*"

The words felt fragile like they might crack under their own weight, but I clung to them. I clung to her.

Slowly, my breath began to even out, the tension in my body giving way to exhaustion. Her touch didn't falter; her fingers were tracing patterns I couldn't follow.

As I drifted, caught somewhere between fear and comfort, I felt the warmth of her presence seep into the hollow spaces inside me. And for the first time that night, the chaos receded, leaving only the quiet assurance of her hands and her whispered promises holding me together.

May, 2019

Sarah and I shared a peculiar bond—one that often baffled even us. After we started dating, the world around us seemed convinced we were perfect together, inseparable even. Friends teased, strangers admired, but deep down, we both knew better. It was casual—at least, that's what we told ourselves.

But everything shifted during our first trip to Goa. Amidst sunlit beaches and late-night parties, I stumbled upon acid—my initiation into the world of psychedelics. Rave parties blurred into exchanges of exotic, overpriced drugs, and by the end of the trip, we were all running on fumes.

Sarah hated it—hated how quickly I gravitated toward substances, how my casual drink turned into a habit, and how the occasional cigarette spiraled into a chain-smoking routine. She tried to argue, to reason, but I was too far gone. With a limitless credit card at my disposal and a recklessness I refused to rein in, her words felt like whispers against a storm.

Maybe I was just a spoiled jerk. Maybe we both saw the cracks in what we called *us* but didn't want to admit they were growing wider.

So, there I was—Dev Mukherjee, your average, small-town guy who once believed in the pure, noble cause of working for passion. You know, the kind of guy who dreamed of writing because he loved it, not because it would get him a column in every magazine or a book deal with all the bells and whistles. That was the old me. The one before fame came knocking before the first book hit the shelves and everyone suddenly cared.

And then? *Bam.* The first book was a mega success. I had a few columns under my belt, a stack of cash in my bank account, and a whole new personality. It was like switching clothes—one night, I was that humble, struggling writer; the next, I was this commercial success with a new ego and zero self-awareness. The market loved me, and, honestly, I loved the attention. But poor Sarah? She had no idea who she was dating anymore.

She met me at a writing workshop, right? That guy was still somewhere in me, I swear. But overnight, I became a walking cliché of success—flashing smiles, chain-smoking, downing shots like it was my new hobby, and I'm sure I laughed every time she tried to bring back the old Dev.

Eventually, she gave up trying to fix me. I mean, who could blame her? It was like trying to clean up a tornado. By the time she accepted it, I had descended into my own personal mess. But here's where it gets good: One afternoon, she found out about the darker side of me. The part I'd kept buried deep, even from myself. And trust me, it wasn't pretty.

It was 2:00 p.m., and I woke up with a throbbing headache, the remnants of another restless night still lingering in my mind. The Mumbai heat pressed through the cracked window as I sat up, the humidity sticking to my skin. May in this city wasn't kind—it felt like the air was trying to choke you, thick and suffocating, but without the storm of monsoon rains to wash it all away. The sun was relentless, pressing against the walls, baking everything in its path.

I rubbed my face and glanced around the room, the mess as usual, the chaos I'd grown accustomed to. I had unfinished columns, and deadlines looming like dark clouds over my head, but the clutter around me was a more immediate concern.

I called out, *"Sarah, can you clean up my room, as always?"*

Her voice hit me first, sharp and annoyed. She'd been holding it in for a while, but today it was too much to keep quiet. *"Dev... How many times have I told you to keep the room* clean? At least try, for once! And why not let Meena clean it like the rest of the house?"

I winced as I stood up, my body feeling heavier than usual, and my voice a little too high as I responded from the bathroom, hoping to avoid her gaze. *"You know how I am... I don't like anyone touching my stuff except you. Please, just clean up and order something to eat. I'm starving."*

I could hear the irritation in her voice as she paused. Then, a small sigh of resignation. *"Okay... get out of the shower. I'll order something,"* her voice softened.

I was already halfway to the bathroom, but her tone caught me—calm and resigned like this was just another one of those days. Little did she know, today would be different.

As I took my shower, the sound of her moving around the room, the shuffle of the broom and dustpan, and the soft rustle of fabric as she cleaned, filled the air. But it wasn't long before everything changed.

I was finishing up in the shower when I heard her stop. A long, drawn-out silence that had me instinctively tensing. Then I heard it: the unmistakable sound of something being shifted around, a mattress being lifted. Her footsteps came closer, slow but deliberate. She was holding her breath, and I could feel it—the shift in the air around me.

"Dev..." Her voice was tight, her words laced with a fear I'd never heard before.

I stepped out of the shower, my towel hanging loosely around my waist. My heart was already pounding. *"What?"*

She didn't answer right away. Her gaze was fixed on something in her hands, her fingers trembling ever so slightly as she looked at me. *"What is this?"* she asked, almost too calmly.

I followed her eyes to the joints, barely visible in her hand—hidden under the mattress, tucked away like they didn't belong. But that wasn't all. Her fingers shook again, and her eyes flicked back to me, her voice quieter now, sharp with disbelief. *"And this?"*

She held up the *blotter* paper, the tiny squares of it almost mocking her confusion. The familiar dread rolled in my stomach. She was connecting the dots. I could see it in her eyes—the realization dawning too quickly.

I was already backing away, avoiding her stare. *"It's nothing,"* I muttered, but the words felt hollow, even to me.

But Sarah wasn't having it. She was on a mission now, her movements fast and precise as she searched through the room, pulling apart corners and lifting cushions, almost frantic. It was a game of cat and mouse, but the roles had switched. She wasn't the one hiding anymore.

I could hear her voice, softer now, edged with something dangerous. *"How long, Dev? How long were you planning to hide this from me?"*

I tried to speak, tried to explain, but nothing came out. There was nothing to say.

Her hands stopped moving, and she froze, staring down at the paper in her hand. LSD. The words I'd been too scared to utter aloud, even to myself. And now, here they were, sitting in her palms like a verdict. She had Googled it, I knew that. She didn't need to ask anymore. She knew.

I stood there, watching her, feeling the walls of the room close in around me, suffocating me just as much as the heat outside. I could feel her eyes burning into me, searching for answers I didn't have.

For a long moment, we stood like that—her eyes wide, filled with hurt and confusion, and me, unable to speak, unable to justify any of it. This was the moment I had been dreading, the moment Sarah would finally see the man I had become. The man I didn't recognize anymore.

Finally, she exhaled with a small, broken sound. *"I didn't sign up for this, Dev."*

Her words cut deep, deeper than anything else she could have said. She didn't need to shout. She didn't need to throw things. All she had to do was look at me.

I was caught. Trapped in my own web, and I didn't know how to untangle myself.

"What the hell, Sarah?" I barked, jolted upright as she shoved me lightly. My voice came out rough, groggy. *"Why would you push me? Ugh, what's wrong now?"*

Sarah stood at the edge of the room, arms crossed tightly. Her face carried an expression I'd grown used to—a mix of irritation and something deeper, something I couldn't quite bring myself to name. She didn't answer me, not right away. Instead, her eyes flicked toward the study table, where a small box sat slightly ajar.

"Dev, no. Not right now." Her voice was low, clipped. She walked to the table with slow, deliberate steps, pointing at the box as though it were some kind of explosive.

"What is this? What the hell are you getting into?"

My stomach sank. I knew I was screwed. The confidence I'd had about keeping things hidden from her dissolved in an instant. Still, I wasn't about to admit defeat. I got up, walked over to the table, grabbed the box, and shoved it into the drawer as if that would erase it from existence.

"It's nothing," I said, forcing my voice to sound casual, indifferent. *"One of my friends' things. He asked me to hold it for him, that's all."*

Her brow furrowed, her lips pressing into a thin line. She wasn't buying it. *"Stop lying to me, Dev,"* she snapped, her voice rising. *"I'm not stupid. I know you were on acid during the Goa trip, and now this? What is it this time—more drugs, more weed? Is this your genius idea for writing?"*

Her words hit me harder than I wanted to admit. For a second, I froze. But the defensive mask I'd perfected over the years kicked in quickly. *"Sarah, you have no business with this, okay?"* I shot back, my tone sharper than I intended. *"It's not your concern."*

She stepped back, letting her arms fall to her sides as she stared at me, disbelief flooding her expression. *"No business?"* she repeated, her voice low and dangerous. *"Dev Mukherjee, I'm your girlfriend. Or have you conveniently forgotten that? And while we're at it, let me remind you—you're using my credit card to fund all of this crap! And you still think it's none of my concern?"*

Her words stung more than they should have. I flinched but quickly covered it with a smirk that didn't quite reach my eyes. *"Look,"* I said, leaning against the study table like I didn't care, *"I'll pay you back, alright? As soon as I get my salary, deduct it or whatever. But you don't need to lecture me on this. I don't need that right now."*

Her laugh was bitter, sharp, like glass breaking. *"Lecture?"* she spat. *"Oh, no, Dev. I'm not here to lecture you. I'm here to tell you that you're turning into someone I don't recognize. Someone who doesn't care about anything but his so-called 'brilliance'— and apparently, drugs are part of the package now."*

I lit a cigarette, exhaling slowly, trying to regain control of the situation. *"You don't understand,"* I muttered, my voice softer now, almost pleading. *"This helps me write. It clears my head and opens up new ideas. Intoxication—it's... inspiring."*

She stared at me, her expression shifting from anger to something worse: disappointment. That was always harder to handle. *"Inspiring?"* she repeated, her voice trembling slightly. *"Do you even hear yourself, Dev? This isn't inspiration; it's destruction. You're smoking like a chimney, drinking like it's water, and now this? You promised me. One day, when you were actually happy, you promised me you'd quit all of this. But promises mean nothing to you, do they?"*

Her words hit harder than they should have. I didn't want to admit how much they hurt. Instead, I hardened my expression, masking the guilt with anger. *"Don't pin this on me, Sarah,"* I said, my voice rising. *"You don't get it, okay? I need this. I'm not asking you to understand, and frankly, I don't care if you don't. Just drop it. Please."*

She stared at me for a long moment, then finally spoke, her voice quiet but firm. *"Fine, Dev. If this is the person you've decided to be, I have nothing left to say."*

She turned and walked out of the room, the door clicking shut behind her. I leaned back in the chair, taking another drag from my cigarette, letting the smoke curl around me. The silence she left behind felt heavy and oppressive.

When she returned with the food, she didn't say anything. She placed it on the table and turned to leave again.

"Sarah," I said, trying to sound casual like nothing had happened. *"I was thinking we could have a drink together. What do you say?"*

She paused for a moment, then gave me a faint smile—one that didn't reach her eyes. *"Sure, Dev. Just the way you like it."*

Her voice was soft, almost robotic, as she turned and walked out again. For the first time that day, I felt a pang of something I couldn't name—guilt, maybe. She wasn't angry anymore. And somehow, that scared me more than anything else.

Let me be honest—Sarah and I were never one of those couples you'd write poetry about. You know, the type with dreamy Instagram captions and sunsets that somehow look brighter because *they're so in love.* No, we were far from that. Intimacy? Rare. Connection? Let's just say it was a limited-edition concept in our relationship.

Sarah was doing way too much, and I don't say this lightly. She was all in—picking up my messes, tolerating my mood swings, and, for reasons I still don't understand, staying invested in someone who didn't even pretend to match her energy.

Look, I wasn't trying to be a jerk—well, not all the time—but I wasn't exactly going out of my way to make her feel special either. Maybe it was my age, or maybe it was just me being me. Sure, I was no longer a teenager, but the recklessness? The lack of accountability? That stayed. Guess I carried it into adulthood like an old, worn-out jacket I refused to throw away.

And Sarah? She stayed too. For reasons that, honestly, still baffle me. Maybe she saw something in me that even I couldn't see. Or maybe—just maybe—she thought she could fix me. Spoiler alert: she couldn't. But that didn't stop her from trying. Oh, how she tried.

Sarah walked in, her silhouette framed by the muted glow of the late afternoon sun filtering through the curtains. She wore her usual pair of glasses, her hair lazily tied up, and carried a bottle of whiskey—the one she'd bought for me last week, still unopened. She poured a generous glass, the amber liquid catching the light, and handed it to me without a word. We shared a quiet meal of leftover home-cooked lunch, a silence punctuated by the occasional clink of forks against plates. I went back to my laptop, pretending to work, while Sarah retreated to the bed, sinking into her thoughts.

I could feel her restless energy from across the room. She lay there, still as a painting, but her silence screamed louder than words. I knew exactly what was running through her head— our argument earlier, the accusations, the disappointment. Her fingers absently traced patterns on the sheets, her face turned away from me, lost in a labyrinth of worry.

I couldn't focus. Not on the screen, not on anything. The sight of her, so consumed by the weight of us, was unbearable. I closed my laptop with a sharp snap and walked toward her. She heard my footsteps but didn't turn until I reached the bed. When she did, her eyes met mine, and in that moment, I saw everything—her frustration, her vulnerability, her exhaustion. She started to speak, but I didn't let her.

I leaned down, close enough to feel her breath hitch. My lips brushed against her earlobe, a whisper of touch before I let my tongue trace its curve. She shivered under me, her body responding before her mind could resist. My lips trailed down, slow and deliberate, to the delicate curve of her neck, where her tattoo hid—a little secret she carried like armor.

Months. It had been months since I'd touched her like this. My fingers slid up her spine, leaving a trail of goosebumps in their wake. Her breath caught as I bit down gently, then harder, drawing a moan from her lips that echoed in the small room. Her hands, once clutched against the sheets in tension, found their way to my back, her nails digging in as if to anchor herself.

The space between us disappeared. I pulled her closer, her scent—faintly floral, mixed with a trace of the afternoon heat—intoxicating. My hands slipped under the worn t-shirt she'd been wearing since last night, pushing it up and over her head. She hesitated, just for a second, before tugging at my joggers, discarding them carelessly onto the floor along with the towel around my neck.

Our lips met, soft at first, then hungry. Our tongues danced to the rhythm of shared urgency, tasting, claiming. I don't know what came over me—this wasn't just touch; it was something deeper, something darker. My hands found her hair, tangling in it, pulling hard enough to make her gasp. Her body arched beneath mine, her skin warm and flushed against me.

This wasn't just passion. This was desperation—raw and untamed as if both of us were trying to erase the mess we'd made with every kiss, every bite, every breathless moan. Whatever distance had grown between us over the months seemed to vanish at that moment, replaced by an intensity we hadn't felt in years.

And yet, in the back of my mind, I couldn't shake the thought: I'd never held her like this before. Not with this edge, this quiet violence. And the way she responded, as if she didn't care—didn't care about the argument, the hurt, the lies. All that mattered was here, now, and us. Whatever *us* meant anymore.

Love is a pretty word, isn't it? Romantic, hopeful, even poetic. But for people like me, it's nothing but an illusion—a pretty veil over something raw, messy, and often selfish. I never loved Sarah. Not in the way she needed, and certainly not in the way she deserved. What I did to her wasn't love. It was pulling her into a trap, one laced with emotional and physical vulnerability. And she let me—she always let me, no matter how much it drained her.

That afternoon, the air in Mumbai was heavy with heat, the kind that clings to your skin. But inside, as I pulled her into my arms, the room felt like it was burning. The first touch was desperate—a collision of bodies and breath as if we were two wandering souls finding refuge in each other, even when we knew it wouldn't last. The sky outside shifted as dark clouds rolled in, the kind that signals a storm as if the weather itself conspired to mirror the chaos between us.

Her nails dug into my back, sharp and demanding, as if trying to leave a mark—a claim. My hands roamed her body, fingers brushing against the curve of her thighs, gripping her hips with a roughness that wasn't gentle, but neither of us wanted to be gentle. This wasn't tenderness. This was *need*—pure and unfiltered.

The wind picked up outside, rattling the windows as I buried my face in her neck, my lips tasting her skin where it was warm and faintly salty. She arched beneath me, her breath catching in gasps that turned into moans, louder with every movement of my hands, every press of my lips. Her body trembled under my touch, her thick thighs tensing as my fingers explored, teasing and igniting every nerve.

Her breasts rose and fell with her shallow breathing, her nipples taut and begging for attention. I obliged, my mouth claiming them with a hunger that matched the storm outside. She moaned again, her voice breaking the humid stillness of the room, her hands finding me—gripping, pulling, urging. The air between us grew hotter, suffocating in its intensity as if the room itself could barely contain the passion spilling over.

When I pushed against her, her body welcomed me, wet and warm, the way a storm welcomes the first crash of thunder. Our rhythm was primal, raw, and relentless. Her voice rose to meet mine in the chaos, her moans and gasps mixing with the sound of the wind and the distant bark of street dogs. Outside, the rain finally began to fall, heavy and unrelenting, drowning the city in its relief.

We didn't stop until the storm outside mirrored the one within us, both of us spent and silent as the rain washed away the heat and tension of the afternoon.

Later, we didn't talk much. She sat on her laptop, pretending to be engrossed in work, while I lit a cigarette and returned to my writing. The silence between us wasn't uncomfortable. It was just *there*, a quiet understanding that words weren't necessary.

Mumbai, my city of chaos and beauty, had its first taste of pre-monsoon rain that evening. The roads gleamed wet under the streetlights, kids laughed as they splashed through puddles, and somewhere in the distance, an old man took a slow, measured walk through the cleaner, cooler streets. At that moment, the storm was gone, and the city breathed again.

And us? We sat in the stillness of that room, neither lovers nor strangers. Just two people caught in a cycle we couldn't escape, pretending for one brief moment that the rain could wash it all away.

✦ ✦ ✦

5

10:00 p.m.; Sunday

Mumbai

Sarah walked into the room quietly, her eyes scanning the cluttered desk I was hunched over. The air was thick with cigarette smoke, the ashtray overflowing with stubs that hadn't been cleared in a week. Without a word, she picked it up, emptied it, and placed it back on the table. Her movements were soft and deliberate like she was trying not to disturb the fragile silence that hung between us.

"*Dev,*" she said gently, her voice breaking the monotony of the evening. "*I think you should get up now and have dinner. It's been over three hours since you've been sitting there, glued to that chair, working.*" She tapped my shoulder lightly and leaned down, pressing a kiss to the back of my head. Then, without waiting for a response, she turned and walked toward the dining room.

"*Hmm... aschhi,*" I murmured, the Bengali word for coming. It slipped out almost instinctively, surprising even me with its warmth.

We hadn't been this kind to each other in months—I hadn't been this responsive, this... present. But something about the way she spoke, the quiet care in her actions, made me respond differently that night.

Dinner that night started off like any other. The silence between us wasn't unusual—It was the kind of silence you get used to in a relationship that has lost its spark. We both sat at the table, eating quietly until Sarah's phone began buzzing with notifications. At first, I didn't think much of it. She often got work messages in the evening, and I'd trained myself not to care. But this time, it was different.

The frequency of the notifications was unsettling. One after another they chimed, each one like a small electric shock to my nerves. I glanced up, trying not to make it obvious. Sarah, unfazed, got up and walked to the adjacent table where her phone was kept. She picked it up, scrolling casually, and then—she giggled.

That laugh felt like a knife twisting in my gut. I tried to ignore it, focusing on the plate in front of me, but the unease was building, creeping up my spine. I forced down a few more bites, but eventually, I couldn't take it anymore. I stood abruptly, leaving the half-eaten plate of food on the table, and walked straight to my room.

"Dev," her voice followed me. *"What's wrong? Why did you leave your dinner?"*

I didn't stop. I didn't answer. The air between us was already thick with questions I wasn't ready to confront. She trailed me into the room, her phone now clutched in her hand. Dropping it on the bed, she crossed her arms and looked at me.

"Dev, talk to me," she said, her tone gentler now. *"Why did you leave like that? Are you okay? Are you feeling sick?"*

I sat on the edge of the bed, my elbows on my knees, staring at the floor. *"Just leave it, Sarah. We don't need to talk about it."*

But she wasn't the kind of person to leave things unresolved. Her footsteps moved closer, and her voice grew firmer. *"Khana chod ke aa gaye tum. Why? What's wrong with you?"*

Her insistence was a spark to the dry tinder inside me. I snapped my head up, my voice sharp and biting. *"What's wrong with me? Really? What's wrong with you, Sarah? Who's texting you, huh? Are you cheating on me?"*

Her face froze, the color draining from it. *"What?"* she whispered, stunned. *"What are you even saying, Dev? Why would you accuse me of that?"*

She stepped closer, reaching out to touch my shoulder, but I pulled away as if her touch burned. *"Don't,"* I said coldly. *"Don't try to play innocent."*

Her confusion turned to hurt, then anger. *"Play innocent? You're being ridiculous, Dev. Where is this even coming from?"*

I stood abruptly, pacing the room. My voice rose with every step I took, my words tumbling out like a dam had broken. *"It's always the same with you, Sarah. The laughs, the little secrets. You think I don't notice? I'm not blind."*

"You're being insane!" she shouted back, her voice trembling now. *"I haven't done anything to deserve this. What's gotten into you?"*

I stopped pacing and faced her, my chest heaving. The room felt suffocating, her presence both magnetic and unbearable. *"I don't know,"* I admitted, my voice breaking. *"Maybe it's me. Maybe I've been a fool for trusting you."*

Her eyes glistened with unshed tears, but she held her ground. *"You don't trust me?"* she asked softly, her voice cracking. *"After everything, do you still think I'd betray you?"*

I turned away, unable to look at her. The weight of my words hung in the air, suffocating both of us. *"I don't know what to think anymore,"* I muttered.

She stood there for a moment, silent. Then, without another word, she walked out of the room, leaving me alone with my anger, my guilt, and the unspoken truth that we were slowly unraveling.

Dev Mukherjee—the *"perfect boyfriend,"* or so they said. Sarah's parents thought I was the jackpot, her friends couldn't stop gushing about how lucky she was, and I—well, I played along. It was easy. A few clever lines, a carefully placed smile, and a façade polished enough to convince anyone. They saw what they wanted to see: a charming, brooding writer with just enough edge to seem intriguing but never threatening. Perfect. Except, I wasn't. Not even close.

The truth? I was a disaster wrapped in layers of charm. Anger coursed through me like second nature, an inheritance from my father I swore I'd never claim but carried anyway. Sarah didn't know the depths of it—or maybe she chose not to see them until they spilled out in moments like that night. I let my frustration, my paranoia, and my bitterness fester until it erupted, aimed right at her. It wasn't love, not the kind they talk about in novels or dinner-table anecdotes. It was me, dragging someone else into the darkness I couldn't seem to outrun. And as the glass shattered on the floor, it wasn't Sarah's words that cut me the deepest—it was the quiet truth behind them. I wasn't the guy I pretended to be. I wasn't the guy she deserved.

The tension in the room felt like a coiled spring ready to snap, and when it did, it shattered every fragile emotion that had been holding us together. My words, slurred by the alcohol, were sharp and venomous, cutting through the silence with the precision of someone who knew exactly how to wound.

I staggered toward her, bottle in hand, my eyes glassy and my tone laced with mockery. "*You know, Sarah, maybe you should've been cheating on me. Would've made things easier for me, wouldn't it? At least I'd have a real reason to throw your ass out of here.*" My laugh was hollow and bitter, echoing through the dimly lit room.

Sarah clenched her fists, her voice trembling, not with fear but with frustration. "*Dev, stop. Just stop. You're drunk, and you don't know what you're saying. Let's talk about this when you're sober.*"

"*Oh, don't give me that bullshit!*" I smashed the empty whiskey bottle against the edge of the table, shards scattering across the floor like our broken relationship. "*Don't act like you're some saint, Sarah. You've been using me—using me! Just like everyone else!*"

Her patience snapped, and she fired back, her voice shaking with suppressed fury. "*Using you? Using you for what, Dev? For your talent? What talent, huh? The one book you wrote three years ago? The half-baked drafts you keep piling up while I pay your bills and cover for your tantrums? Don't talk to me about using anyone when I've been the one keeping you afloat!*"

I flung a chair across the room, and it hit the wall with a deafening crash. "*You think I need you? You think I'm nothing without you?*" I leaned in closer, my face inches from hers, and my voice lowering to a dangerous growl. "*Let me tell you something, Sarah. You're the one who's lucky to have me. Who the hell are you without me, huh? Just another washed-up editor with a failing publishing house.*"

Sarah's eyes blazed with fury. She stepped forward, unflinching despite my threatening posture. "*Who am I without you? Oh, I don't know, Dev. Maybe someone who doesn't have to clean up your mess every goddamn day. Someone who doesn't have to stay awake worrying about whether you'll spiral into another rage. Someone who doesn't have to deal with you! That's who I am."*

My hand twitched as if I might lash out, but instead, I stumbled backward, collapsing onto the bed. *"You think you're better than me, don't you?"* he muttered, his voice cracking under the weight of his own venom. *"You always have. Go ahead, Sarah. Leave. See how far you get without me."*

She laughed bitterly, tears welling in her eyes but refusing to fall. *"Leave? Oh, I'd love to, Dev. But let me remind you of one thing. This place you're so graciously offering to throw me out of? It's mine. The rent, the bills, the food—you don't even have the decency to pay for your own poison. And you know what? You're right—I wish I had cheated on you. At least then I'd have had one moment of happiness in this hellhole you've made."*

Her words hit me harder than any slap could. For a moment, the room was silent except for the sound of my ragged breathing. She turned away, grabbing her bag. *"You're not the man I fell in love with, Dev. Hell, I don't even think you ever were. You're just a selfish, broken shell, and I'm done trying to fix you."*

She walked toward the door, but before leaving, she paused. *"Get your act together, or don't. Either way, I'm done being your punching bag."* And with that, she was gone, leaving me alone in the wreckage of our life together.

The tension in the office was suffocating, and I was the source of it. Everyone could feel it, see it—hell, they probably talked about it over their morning coffee. Sarah ignored me with a precision that felt almost surgical, cutting me out of her life like I was some infection. She didn't look at me, didn't acknowledge my existence. And the whispers? Oh, they were deafening. *"Sarah Qureshi isn't Dev's puppet anymore,"* they said. They didn't even try to hide it.

And me? I was coming apart at the seams. My work—the one thing I thought I still had a handle on—was slipping through my fingers. Each column I turned in was worse than the last, a hollow shell of the writer I used to be. There were new interns too, working under Sarah, fresh-faced and eager, watching me like I was some kind of cautionary tale. And I gave them plenty to talk about—stumbling into the office drunk, pounding on Sarah's door in the middle of the night like some deranged fool.

Sarah walked through the office with her usual composed demeanor, but today, something felt different. The air was thick with uncertainty, and her mind kept drifting back to me—*where the hell had he gone?* She hadn't seen me all day, and it was unlike me to disappear without a word. She caught Prateek near the column drafts, busy looking over notes, and approached him.

"Hey... ugh, where's Dev?" Her voice carried an edge of curiosity, but it was also laced with something else—concern maybe, or frustration. She hadn't really been talking to anyone much lately, and it wasn't lost on her how the tension in the office had become palpable.

Prateek looked up, his expression unsure. *"Uh, Ma'am, I haven't seen him since this morning. He's probably around somewhere. Maybe you should ask the guards?"* He paused for a moment, glancing toward the door as if he wasn't entirely convinced either.

Sarah nodded absently. *"Okay, thanks, Prateek."* She turned to leave, but then, almost as if he had been holding back, Prateek spoke again. *"Ma'am, Sir was supposed to mentor us on the columns and hold that workshop, but he hasn't shown up for the last two days. It's... kind of strange, don't you think?"* His voice had that hesitant quality to it like he didn't want to bring it up but couldn't ignore the growing worry in the air.

Sarah stopped; her hand on the doorframe. She let out a quiet breath, trying to think of the right words. *"Right... I get it. Apologies for the delay. I'll make sure he's here tomorrow, you have my word."* She turned back with a soft smile, trying to ease the unease that had started creeping into the office. She gave him a quick pat on the shoulder as if to reassure him, though part of her wasn't so sure herself.

With that, she walked out, her steps quicker now as she moved toward the guard station, hoping to find answers, or at the very least, some sign of where I had disappeared.

The office buzzed with its own version of reality, as gossip spread like wildfire. People discussed our breakup as if it were the most public spectacle, each theory more absurd than the last. Some said I was too possessive, others thought Sarah had grown tired of my reckless behavior. Everyone had their own assumptions, their own lens through which they viewed the unraveling of what had once seemed like the perfect relationship. But if you looked closely, you'd realize something—Sarah's behavior hadn't really shifted. She still carried the weight of authority, bossing everyone around with that same unshakable confidence. She was the same as before, maybe even a little sharper, a little colder. Yet, beneath that surface, there was something else.

What no one could see was that Sarah was still searching. She dated other guys, sure, but each one was just a poor imitation of what she had lost, a failed attempt to recreate something that could never be replaced. She kept telling herself she was moving on, but deep down, she was still looking for me, still carrying the weight of what we'd shared.

Our relationship was a mess, and we both knew it. It was toxic, destructive—yet somehow, we kept coming back to each other. It was the kind of love that destroys and builds at the same time. In that strange, twisted way, we were bound to each other. Time had a funny way of playing its hand, didn't it? It was taking its revenge on both of us, slowly, relentlessly. But through it all, Sarah stood by me—through every crash, every burn. She was my anchor, even when I didn't deserve it. My writing had died a long time ago, suffocated by my own mistakes, but somehow, with her around, there was still a flicker of hope. And for a brief moment, as I reflect on everything, I wonder: Was she truly helping me, or was she just as lost as I was? The answer didn't matter as much as the question did.

6

Our generation was restless, relentless, and always rushing. We belong to the fast lane, where every decision is a sprint. Life hurtled forward for us, from the hasty chaos of morning breakfasts to the reckless leap into love, and everything in between. But back then, in the late 1990s, things felt slower—at least for me. I was born in an era shaped by the magic of Bollywood, where the Khans ruled the screens, teaching us how to dream in grand gestures and orchestrated emotions. *Dilwale Dulhania Le Jayenge, Dil To Pagal Hai, 1942: A Love Story*—those films weren't just stories; they were blueprints for romance, for life itself. And yet, while the rest of the world got swept up in these cinematic dreams, I found myself racing through the corridors of St. Mary's Public School, clueless about how real life would soon echo the reel.

It happened in the summer of '99, the first day back after the break. The corridors buzzed with students, their voices bouncing off the walls in a familiar cacophony, when I bumped into her. Quite literally. Ahaana. She was new, the kind of new that turned heads—half because of her crisp uniform and air of quiet confidence, half because she wasn't trying to impress anyone. I barely noticed her at first, distracted as usual, until I saw the sharp glance she gave me. It wasn't the look you'd expect—no dreamy, wide-eyed Bollywood heroine here. No, this was something else. Judgment. The kind of look that labeled me instantly as the so-not-serious type. And she wasn't wrong.

Later, the teacher introduced her to the class: *"Ahaana Bharadwaj. Her father's been transferred here."* Polite claps followed as she took her seat, but I barely heard the rest. All I could think about was the awkward collision in the corridor. As fate would have it, that wasn't the last time I'd run into her. By evening, I found out she was also my new neighbor. My mother and hers hit it off instantly, sharing tea and swapping pleasantries like they'd known each other forever. Meanwhile, Ahaana and I couldn't stand each other. She'd perfected the art of giving me quiet death stares whenever I got scolded in class, which, thanks to my dyslexia, happened often. Back then, no one understood it. Teachers just assumed I was lazy. And Ahaana? She made sure her mother knew all about it, which meant my mother did too. For six months, we avoided each other, talking only when forced and even then with thinly veiled politeness.

But here's the thing about collisions—they aren't always accidents. Sometimes, they're beginnings disguised as mishaps. Looking back, I didn't realize then that the storm I'd bumped into that day would become my anchor. But isn't that how it always starts in the movies? A brush of fate, a slow burn, and a story waiting to unfold.

The year was 2001, and the streets of our little town were painted with the scent of freshly washed soil and the hum of monsoon rains. It was the first day of the new session, the beginning of 3rd standard, and the air carried the smell of crisp new textbooks wrapped in brown paper covers. The school gates buzzed with the chaos of students catching up after the summer break. Parents huddled by the gates, their voices rising above the morning bustle, some scolding, others waving enthusiastic goodbyes.

For most kids, the first day of school was exhilarating—shiny shoes, bright new water bottles, and the thrill of discovering who they'd sit next to for the rest of the year. For me, it was dreadful. I wasn't one for new beginnings; I preferred the predictability of the old. My mother fussed over my uniform, her usual anxiety spilling into the way she knotted my tie too tight, wondering aloud if I'd *"cope this year."* My friends—or the two people I'd called friends—were the only solace I had, but that too was taken away when I learned I'd been shifted to a different section.

The classroom felt suffocating, its walls adorned with peeling charts of multiplication tables and an oddly smug picture of a rabbit holding a carrot. I trudged to the last bench, alone, as if the spot had been reserved for me. The other kids were already in clusters, their laughter filling the room while I wondered if this was my fate—to be alone, misunderstood, and misjudged.

That's when Ahaana walked in, a whirlwind of energy and confidence that seemed completely out of place in this dreary classroom. Her hair was tied in a hurried ponytail, a streak of blue ink on her fingers betraying her knack for writing. We had been neighbors for a year by then, though our interactions were limited to polite nods and awkward exchanges orchestrated by our mothers. She spotted me sitting alone and, with the air of someone who'd just made an executive decision, plopped down next to me.

"Why are you always sulking?" she asked, tilting her head and narrowing her eyes as if she'd cracked some mystery.

"I'm not sulking," I mumbled, avoiding her gaze, *"I just like sitting here."*

"Alone? On the last bench? Seriously?" she said, her voice tinged with mockery. *"You're like a moody character from one of those sad TV serials my mum watches."*

I didn't know whether to laugh or feel offended. Instead, I kept quiet, hoping she'd leave me alone. But Ahaana wasn't the kind to leave things alone.

"Look," she said, pulling out her notebook. *"If we're going to be desk partners, you'll have to help me with English. I'm terrible at it. In exchange, I'll let you copy my math homework."*

I blinked at her, stunned. No one had ever offered me a deal like that before. *"You're the topper,"* I said, unsure if she was being serious.

"Exactly," she replied with a grin. *"And toppers too need help sometimes."*

From that day, something shifted. She wasn't just the mischievous girl who aced exams anymore; she was the person who dragged me into conversations I didn't know I needed, who sat beside me on that last bench, making it feel a little less lonely. Ahaana wasn't like the others. She didn't see my silence as a flaw or my struggles as something to be fixed.

Ahaana was selected as the class monitor, and to be honest, I couldn't have cared less. She had already found her place among the popular kids of our batch—the ones who always seemed to run the show. It was an unwritten rule of school survival: get in good with the monitor, and you'd have a shield when trouble found you. But Ahaana, despite her sharp wit and cheerful demeanor, didn't know what lay beneath the surface of her new circle. The popular kids weren't just confident; they were bullies, and they had the rest of us walking on eggshells.

The boys' washroom was their unspoken arena. If you were called there during recess, you knew you were stepping into a lion's den, often as prey.

That day, I was the target. Rishabh, the self-proclaimed leader of their pack, summoned me. I followed, hoping it wasn't what I feared, but it always was. They surrounded me, sneering and laughing, and laid out their demand— *"We need you to step down from the cricket team,"* he said, his tone laced with mock authority. *"My friend's taking your spot."*

"No," I replied, trying to mask the fear in my voice.

The smirk on Rishabh's face twisted into something darker. *"Then you'll regret it,"* he said, motioning to his pack.

They descended on me, fists flying, laughter echoing against the tiled walls. Six boys against one—each punch felt heavier than the last. By the time they were done, my nose was bleeding, and I was barely holding myself together. Their final warning was clear: *"Keep your mouth shut, or next time, it'll be worse."*

When I returned to class, I slid into my seat, praying no one would notice. But the blood dripping from my nose betrayed me. The teacher, barely glancing in my direction, instructed the class monitor to take me to the clinic. Rohit, the other monitor, was absent, so Ahaana had to step in.

She walked up to my desk, her expression a mix of curiosity and concern. *"What happened to you?"* she asked, her voice softer than I'd expected.

"Nothing," I muttered, avoiding her eyes.

She didn't press, but as she guided me out of the classroom, I could feel her glancing at me, searching for answers I wasn't ready to give. Her silence spoke louder than her questions, and for the first time, I sensed something different in her—a flicker of care in a world that usually turned a blind eye. It was a moment I wouldn't forget, the beginning of something neither of us could have anticipated.

In the clinic, as the nurse dabbed antiseptic on my bruised face, the silence between Ahaana and me grew louder. She sat on the stool beside me, arms crossed, her eyes fixed on me as if she were solving a mystery. I stared at the floor, wishing the ground would swallow me whole.

Finally, she broke the silence. *"So... how did this happen, exactly?"* Her tone was casual but laced with curiosity. *"Let me guess—you decided to practice headbutting a pole during recess? Or was it more of a heroic dive onto concrete?"*

I groaned, trying to sound as convincing as a scared third grader could. *"No, nothing like that. I just, um, fell. You know... while practicing cricket."* I threw in a shrug for good measure as if that would sell the lie.

Ahaana tilted her head, her expression a mix of amusement and suspicion. *"Right. Practicing cricket. On a day when there's no practice?"* She raised an eyebrow, leaning closer. *"Dev, you're a terrible liar. Just tell me the truth—I promise I won't snitch to Aunty."*

I squirmed under her gaze, my resolve cracking a little. *"It's nothing, really. Just cricket stuff. And, um, why would I lie?"*

She leaned back in her chair, tapping her chin thoughtfully. *"Hmm. Yeah, sure, nothing says 'just cricket stuff' like walking into class looking like you fought a bear and lost. But fine, keep your secrets. Just so you know, I'm really good at figuring things out."*

I stayed silent, unwilling to risk her digging deeper. But something about her voice—calm, teasing, yet strangely mature—lingered in my mind. She didn't press further, and for that, I was grateful.

As we walked back to class, I could feel her glancing at me now and then, but she didn't say a word. I wanted to tell her everything: about Rishabh, the washroom, the punches, and the threats. But what could a 3rd grader like her do? She was just the class monitor. My belief in her ability to change anything was nonexistent—though, little did I know, she was already aware of the bullying.

Over the next few days, things began to shift. Other students gathered the courage to speak up about what was happening, and teachers started paying attention, though not everything was resolved. One afternoon, when we were alone in the library, I finally told Ahaana the truth.

"They made me give up my spot on the cricket team," I mumbled, staring at the floor. *"They force other kids to do their homework, bring them lunch... even mess up games so the bullies get picked for teams."*

Ahaana listened quietly, her face serious. When I finished, she sighed. *"You should have told me earlier, Dev."* Then, after a pause, she added with a small smile, *"But don't worry. I'm the class monitor, remember? Let me handle this."*

From that point on, Ahaana and I became inseparable. She still hung out with the popular kids but kept them in check, subtly steering them away from their worst behavior. My two friends became her friends too, and for the first time, I felt like I belonged.

At lunch, she'd plop her sandwich onto my desk and say, *"Here, you can have the bigger half. You look like you need it more."* And while she laughed at my jokes and teased me endlessly, there was always an unspoken understanding between us— she had my back, and I had hers.

Looking back, that was the beginning of something I couldn't quite define then. But even as kids, there was a bond growing, quiet yet unshakable, built on trust, kindness, and the shared sandwiches she never shared with anyone else.

It's strange, isn't it? How we met, how we stumbled into each other's lives, and how, as kids, we conquered challenges we didn't even realize we were facing. Back then, it all felt like some grand adventure, a fascinating stunt that life had orchestrated for me.

In this quiet town of snowfall and monasteries—a place I once thought I could never appreciate—I found a friend who changed everything. Ahaana and I began to spend nearly every moment together. Our days were filled with cricket matches that stretched till sunset, whispered stories shared under the shade of old trees, and that one diary I guarded like a treasure chest. No one was allowed to touch it, except her. She never asked about its secrets, never tried to peek between the lines. She just respected it, the way only she could.

Growing up can be tough—at least, that's what I've come to realize. Many kids I grew up with never thought about it much. Back then, the innocence of childhood blinded us to the storms waiting on the horizon. Pain, power struggles, despair, and misery—they seemed like distant tales from the grown-up world, not something that could ever touch us. But time has a way of revealing truths, doesn't it?

What I didn't understand then was how fiercely I was being shielded—from life's harshness, from the reality waiting to strike. My mother, with her quiet resilience, and Ahaana, with her unwavering presence, were my silent protectors. Together, they created a safe haven I never knew I'd been living in. And for a time, it was enough to believe that the world outside didn't matter, as long as we had cricket, stories, and a shared belief in the magic of friendship.

It was the year 2009. Bollywood was shaping dreams and aspirations with films like *Love Aaj Kal, Wake Up Sid, and*

3 Idiots. While the country debated whether they were a Rancho or a Farhan, and juggled between engineering and photography, my reality was far removed from those cinematic stories.

I had just finished my first board exams, an important milestone for most students, but in my household, it barely registered. My father's business had taken a colossal hit—losses running into lakhs. The frustration of his failure seeped into every corner of our home. My mother shielded me from the details, her silence an attempt to protect me from the storm brewing between them. But no amount of protection could hide the cracks.

He began drinking more, the alcohol eroding whatever humanity remained in him. His absences became routine—out late, intoxicated, and increasingly consumed by shady dealings. The man who once laughed at my childhood antics was now a volatile stranger. I'd often return from Ahaana's place to find my mother asleep on the couch, waiting for him—an act of futile hope.

One evening, I walked into a different kind of silence—the thick, oppressive kind that suffocates. Then, their voices broke through—a sharp argument cutting through the stillness of our small home. The words were muddled, unintelligible at first, but the tone was unmistakable. Anger. Resentment. Pain. I didn't bother to piece it together. It wasn't the first time I'd heard them fight, and it wouldn't be the last. I shrugged it off like I always did, muttering under my breath, *"Huh. Another unhappy marriage."*

But this time, there was a crack in my usual detachment. Somewhere, deep down, I knew their unhappiness wasn't just theirs. It had seeped into me, shaping the boy I was becoming.

One morning, as I walked into the kitchen, Maa handed me my breakfast hurriedly and said, *"Go to your friend's house, Dev. Don't come back until evening."*

Her voice was tense, her usual warmth replaced by a detached urgency. I paused, sensing something wasn't right. *"Why? Did something happen?"*

Before she could answer, Baba entered the room, his heavy footsteps echoing on the tiled floor. His face was stern, his brows furrowed in a way that spelled trouble.

"What have you decided?" he asked sharply, his voice cutting through the morning stillness.

Maa didn't look up. She continued stirring the tea, her movements mechanical. *"Decide ki korar ache?"* she replied flatly in Bengali. *"What's there to decide?"*

"Don't play smart with me!" Baba barked, his voice rising. *"You know what I'm talking about. Stop delaying things."*

Maa finally turned to face him, her hands gripping the counter. *"Delay? The only delay here is yours—years of delay in being a decent husband and father!"*

I stood frozen, caught in the crossfire of words that felt sharper than any slap. Baba's fists clenched, his nostrils flaring. *"Don't push me, Anu. You'll regret it,"* he hissed.

Maa's laugh was bitter, almost mocking. *"Regret? I regret everything already. Tell me, what more could you possibly take from me?"*

"Enough!" he shouted, slamming his hand on the table. I flinched, but Maa didn't move, her eyes fixed on his like steel against fire.

I tried to speak, to break the tension. *"Mum, Dad, what's going on? Why are you—"*

The tension in the air was palpable. They didn't even bother pretending I wasn't there, yet neither of them acknowledged my presence. Baba's jaw clenched, and he muttered something under his breath before storming out of the room.

I wanted to ask her, to demand answers, but the way her hands trembled as she poured the tea made me stop. *"Just go, Dev,"* she said softly, her voice carrying a weight I couldn't understand at the time.

Baba shot me a warning glare, his lips curling in disdain. *"Yeah, run along, boy. This is none of your business."*

I left, but my mind stayed back. Questions swirled endlessly. What was going on? What were they hiding from me?

That night, the answer came in the form of raised voices. I woke around 3 a.m. to the sound of Baba shouting. His words were slurred, soaked in alcohol.

"You think you're better than me? Huh? You think you can do everything on your own?"

Maa's voice, usually strong, cracked under the strain. *"I'm trying to hold this family together while you destroy it!"*

Do you even care about your son? About anyone but yourself?"

"Don't you dare drag him into this!"

A loud thud followed, and I squeezed my eyes shut, my body frozen under the weight of fear.

Maa's voice broke through the silence, soft but cutting. *"If you lay another hand on me, I swear to God, I'll leave, and this time I won't come back."*

A loud crash followed, maybe a glass, maybe something heavier. My stomach churned as I lay frozen in my bed. I knew better than to intervene.

This wasn't new. Baba's temper had always been a shadow over our lives, erupting unpredictably. When it wasn't directed at Maa, it was at me. Failed exams, poor cricket matches, or simply existing—it didn't take much for him to remind me how much of a disappointment I was.

That night, I didn't sleep. I stared at the ceiling, the muffled sounds of their argument fading into silence, wondering if this was what life was destined to be—a cycle of anger, fear, and broken pieces no one dared to pick up.

Life moved forward, as it always does. Ahaana and I started hanging out less once school reopened. Different streams, different classrooms, and just like that, we stepped into a new phase. People always say Class 11 changes things, and they're right. It's the beginning of choices—choices that shape everything that follows. Ahaana chose science, driven by her dream of medical college, a dream her parents shared. I chose humanities, though 'choice' felt too big a word for what I did.

Over time, I began to understand why Dadu believed writing was meant for me, but I didn't have Ahaana's clarity or drive. What I did have was a growing weight I couldn't quite place. She noticed it before I did—my silence, my bursts of frustration. Everyone did, except me.

By the end of the year, my parents decided to separate. I found out from Ahaana, not from them. It hit like a slap—sudden and sharp. They didn't sit me down, didn't explain. Their decision stood in front of me like a brick wall, unyielding and cold. I was left to deal with the cracks it caused in my own time.

Ahaana was there through it all, watching me crumble under the weight of it. My mind spun with questions I couldn't escape. *"Who will I stay with? What happens next? Will it ever feel normal again?"* The answers didn't come easily, but eventually, the court decided. I stayed with Maa, and I was relieved. Staying with Baba was never an option—not with his drinking, his anger, the way he turned a home into something unrecognizable.

Home. The word stopped meaning much after that. School became my refuge—its predictable rhythms, its lessons on subjects like history and economics that suddenly felt heavier, deeper, just like life. Everything else was chaos, but school stayed constant.

I rebuilt slowly. Life didn't wait for me, and I didn't have much choice but to catch up. Ahaana was still there, steady as ever, but even she couldn't fix everything. I was back to square one, trying to figure out high school, trying to figure out myself.

7

Adolescence is that awkward, ridiculous phase where your body decides to surprise you with things you never signed up for. For Ahaana and me, it was a crash course in hormonal chaos, and let me tell you, the changes were hilariously lopsided.

Ahaana was blossoming—her hair shinier, her smile brighter, and her confidence? Sky-high. She had this effortless grace about her that made heads turn, including mine, though I'd never admit it back then. Meanwhile, I was stuck in the *'what-the-hell-is-happening'* zone.

My voice started cracking like an old radio losing signal. One moment, I sounded like a normal person; the next, I was croaking like a dying frog. Ahaana found it endlessly amusing. *"Say that again, Dev,"* she'd tease, *"but maybe this time, hit the right octave?"*

And then there was the height. I shot up like a bamboo stick overnight, all limbs and zero coordination. My body was changing faster than I could keep up with—broader shoulders, a slightly sharper jawline (which Ahaana sarcastically called my 'hero face'), and let's not forget the jungle growing on my face that I had to tame every few weeks.

But for Ahaana, the changes were... different. Her curves became more prominent, and she started carrying herself with this maturity that was equal parts intimidating and intriguing. And then there was the whole menstruation thing—something I only vaguely understood through hushed classroom whispers. She once caught me staring at her after PE and said, *"Take a picture, Dev; it'll last longer."* I turned beet red while she just laughed.

The world around us didn't make things any easier. Everyone was obsessed with the stronger vs. weaker debate, as if adolescence wasn't already confusing enough. Boys were expected to bulk up, toughen up, and be ready to take on the world. Girls, meanwhile, were burdened with this weird mix of expectations—to be independent yet ladylike, strong yet delicate.

Ahaana, of course, handled it all like a pro. I, on the other hand, was just trying not to trip over my own feet. Adolescence may have been a nightmare, but looking back now, it's clear that it was also a time that shaped us in ways we never expected. And even in the middle of all the chaos, Ahaana was still the one constant—teasing, laughing, and somehow making it all seem just a little less weird.

One fine evening, with Maa off at one of her friend's parties, I found myself with an empty house and a curious mind. My friends had been going on and on about these websites that, according to them, held the key to every teenager's secret curiosity. So, after a bit of hesitation, I opened my computer, typed in the address they whispered about in hushed tones, and... whoa.

What greeted me was a labyrinth of categories, each one more baffling than the last. I had no idea the internet was so...

resourceful. This was my first brush with the side of the web no teacher, parent, or school manual ever talked about. Back then, puberty was already doing its thing—hormones firing off like Diwali rockets—making us feel things we didn't quite understand yet.

Curiosity about our own bodies? Check. Curiosity about the opposite gender? Double check. But did we have anyone to guide us through this chaos? Nope. The schools were too busy skipping over the reproduction chapter like it was cursed, leaving us to figure it out ourselves. And boy, did we try.

At the time, masturbation was a word you didn't say out loud unless you wanted to be met with awkward stares or bursts of laughter. But it was something most of us discovered in private, fumbling our way through this strange new world of growing up. For me, that evening wasn't just about curiosity; it was a moment of realization. The internet offered answers—some accurate, some downright ridiculous—to questions we were too embarrassed to ask anyone.

But here's where it got interesting: the way we started to notice girls. It wasn't just their presence anymore—it was their personalities, their smiles, and yes, the way their bodies had changed too. Among the girls in my batch, there was one who seemed to catch everyone's attention: Nandita. She had a certain charm, one that wasn't exactly *my type*, but enough to make me stop and notice. It was odd, realizing that my mind had started to wander in ways it never had before.

Looking back, my teenage years were a strange mix of confusion and discovery. We weren't just learning about math or history; we were learning about ourselves—our emotions, our bodies, and the awkward, often hilarious ways we navigated through it all. It wasn't perfect, but it was real. And that's what growing up is all about.

Nandita and I weren't exactly buddies—our worlds didn't overlap much. The only girl I spent any real time with was Ahaana, who, by the way, was just as much the talk of the boys' washroom as Nandita. Why wouldn't she be? She had grown up into someone stunning, with this air of maturity that made everyone pay attention. Suddenly, she was hanging out with the nerdy elites of her class, while boys from every corner of the school were lining up to impress her. *"Beauty with brains,"* they called her. For me, though? She was just Ahaana.

Meanwhile, I was busy with my newfound mission: figuring out a way to impress Nandita. It all happened so suddenly, fueled by my friends hyping her up like she was some unattainable trophy. With Ahaana tied up in her coaching classes and her new circle of admirers, we barely spoke anymore. So, I found myself hanging out with guys who had more muscles than common sense.

Somehow, I ended up as Nandita's unofficial tutor. Since I was doing better in school, the teachers thought it was a brilliant idea to have me help her with Economics and English literature. Nandita, who wasn't exactly known for her academic skills, didn't object—after all, her dad was on the school board, and she'd made it this far riding that wave. She didn't seem hard to impress; honestly, she needed me more than I needed her.

Most of my time was now split between cricket practice and walking Nandita through chapters she barely cared about. One day, in the middle of discussing a statistics problem, she said something completely unexpected—something I hadn't seen coming at all.

"Dev...?" *"Mm-hmm..."* I mumbled, still lost in solving the questions.

"*Don't mind me asking, but... um... do you have a girlfriend?*" Her tone was *way* too curious like she was trying to solve some great mystery.

I paused, wondering if she had lumped me in with the typical guys from our class—the ones who spent more time fantasizing about girls than actually talking to them. Nope, that wasn't me. I wasn't plotting, scheming, or even remotely planning to get into anyone's pants. I was just stuck in this weird loop of wondering why I was even drawn to Nandita, someone who was my complete opposite.

For a second, I thought about Ahaana. She'd have some painfully accurate insight about this if I dared to bring it up. But no, I was listening to the boys in my head instead, so I cleared my throat and awkwardly replied, "*Uh... no, I don't. I mean, I'm only 17, so... maybe later?*"

Nandita smirked as if she'd just cracked some big code. "*Thought so. By the way, I have news for you... something you might really want to know.*"

I perked up, intrigued. "*What is it, Nandita?*"

Her mischievous grin was the kind of thing that could make a guy's heart skip a beat or at least stumble awkwardly.

Nandita leaned in a little closer, her eyes sparkling with excitement. "*Hey, do you remember my sister, right? Aunty made you meet her at that gathering!*"

I nodded slowly, still trying to recall. "*Uh... yeah, Shruti, right?*"

"*Bingo!*" she said, grinning from ear to ear. "*So... she told me to let you know she likes you.*"

What? That escalated *real* quickly. Shruti Banerjee—a junior, sitting for her 10th boards—liked *me*? I froze, unsure whether to laugh or bury my head in the nearest textbook. Instead of reacting, I kept solving the papers, quietly plotting how fast I could run to Ahaana to share this ridiculous piece of gossip.

After cricket practice (and a minor injury), I freshened up and headed straight to Ahaana's place. It had been a month since we'd properly caught up—both drowning in new routines. Like always, she was buried in her studies, unbothered by the chaos of my day.

As I walked into her room, though, I caught her in the middle of something... odd. She was distractedly tracing her fingers over her arms, lost in thought. It felt weird—awkward even, for both of us.

We hadn't talked about things like this since high school started. Growing up meant growing apart in certain ways, especially when it came to anything remotely physical or personal. But still, this was Ahaana, and I couldn't wait to tell her about Shruti.

I leaned casually against the doorframe of Ahaana's room, arms crossed, my smirk firmly in place. She stood by the mirror, her hands trailing across her shoulders, lost in some kind of trance—or maybe just trying to make sure she still looked like herself.

Then she saw me. Her eyes widened, and she whipped around so fast I thought she'd trip. *"Dev! What the hell? Ever heard of knocking?"*

"Knocking's for strangers," I said, stepping inside shamelessly. *"You're practically family."*

She crossed her arms, glaring at me. *"I swear, you have the manners of a cricket ball. What if I was—"* She stopped, her face going redder than her favorite kurta. *"Never mind. Just knock next time, okay?"*

"Relax, Ahaana," I said, plopping onto her bed as if I owned it. "It's not like I caught you doing anything scandalous."

"You're impossible," she huffed, spinning back toward the mirror. "Anyway, what do you want? Or are you just here to be a pest?"

"Two things," I said, holding up my fingers. "First, drumroll, please—I've been nominated as the captain of the cricket team. Yes, your boy's officially a legend."

She gave me the flattest clap I'd ever seen. "Congratulations. Truly groundbreaking. Anything else?"

"Oh, don't worry. The best part's coming," I said, grinning. "It's about Nandita."

She spun around so fast that her earrings jingled. "Nandita Banerjee? What did she do this time? Wait, no, what did you do this time?"

"Hey! Don't pin this on me!" I protested. "She dropped a bomb on me during our study session. Apparently, her sister Shruti has a crush on me."

Ahaana stared at me for a long second, and then her face split into the kind of grin that only spells trouble. "Shruti? As in, her little sister who's still figuring out trigonometry? That Shruti?"

"Yeah," I muttered, rubbing the back of my neck. "I didn't even know how to react. Nandita just threw it out there, all casual, like she was offering me tea or something."

Ahaana burst out laughing. "Dev, you have to admit, this is gold. Little Shruti Banerjee has a crush on you. You can't make this stuff up."

"Yeah, hilarious," I said dryly. "Meanwhile, I'm over here just trying to figure out why I've started liking Nandita. Do you have any idea how weird that is?"

Her laughter died down, and she raised an eyebrow. *"You... like Nandita? As in, the queen of bad taste in boys?"*

"I know, I know," I said, throwing up my hands. *"It's a mystery to me too. One minute I'm helping her with stats, and the next... I don't know. She's kind of grown on me."*

She stared at me as if I'd sprouted a second head. *"Dev, are you okay? Have you been hit on the head recently? Should I call a doctor?"*

"Okay, wow," I said, rolling my eyes. *"I came here for moral support, not a stand-up routine."*

She grinned, shaking her head. *"Oh, this is too good. Dev Mukherjee falls for Nandita Banerjee while her little sister has a crush on him. I need popcorn for this."*

"You're the worst," I groaned, flopping onto her bed dramatically.

But honestly? Talking to Ahaana always made everything— no matter how weird—feel a little less confusing.

I was sprawled on Ahaana's bed, tossing one of her throw pillows up and down, pretending to be unbothered by the complete disarray of my life. She sat across the room, leaning against her study table, flipping through one of her monster-sized notebooks as if it were the most interesting thing in the world. Her focus was sharp, the soft light from her desk lamp making her look... peaceful. It irritated me how calm she always seemed.

"So... Shruti Banerjee," she said suddenly, not even glancing up.

The pillow slipped from my hand mid-toss, landing on my face. I pulled it off with a groan. *"Can we not talk about that? She's like, what? Two years younger? This feels... wrong."*

Ahaana smirked and turned a page, completely unfazed. *"Oh, come on, Dev. You love being the center of attention. A crush from Shruti is exactly the kind of chaos you secretly enjoy."*

"I do not enjoy chaos," I sat up, resting my elbows on my knees. *"And anyway, I've had enough of the Banerjee sisters for a lifetime."*

"Lifetime? Wow. Big words for someone who still can't figure out if he actually likes Nandita or just likes the idea of her."

I opened my mouth to retort but stopped. She wasn't wrong. *"Look, it's complicated, okay?"*

She finally looked up, her eyes sparkling with amusement. *"Of course it is. Life's complicated. And you? You're... Dev. The king of making simple things dramatic."*

"Wow, thank you, Dr. Freud. I'll remember that next time I need life advice."

She laughed, but it was softer than her usual laugh, tinged with something I couldn't quite place. Before I could dig into that, she added, *"Anyway, I've been spending time with someone too."*

That stopped me cold. *"Wait, what?"*

"Yeah," she said, as casually as if she were mentioning the weather. *"A guy from my coaching. His name's Aniket. He's nice."*

My brain stalled for a second, then stumbled back into motion. *"Nice? That's it? Nice, how?"*

"Smart. Funny. You know, the usual," she shrugged, twirling her pen. *"He helped me with some physics problems the other day."*

"Oh, physics problems," I said, trying for casualness but landing somewhere closer to sharp. *"How romantic. Are candlelit labs part of the coaching package now?"*

She rolled her eyes, but there was something guarded in her expression. *"You're being ridiculous."*

"Am I? I mean, it's not every day Ahaana Bharadwaj talks about a guy like this."

"Dev," she said, her voice steady now, *"why do you care?"*

The question hit harder than I expected. Why *did* I care? I couldn't answer, so I deflected instead. *"I don't. I'm just... surprised, that's all. You didn't even tell me earlier."*

She leaned back in her chair, crossing her arms. *"Maybe because we barely hang out anymore? You're too busy with cricket practice and solving the enigma that is Nandita."*

Her words stung, even though they were true. Somewhere between practices, tutoring Nandita, and my own half-baked attempts at being a teenage Casanova, we'd started to drift. I hated it, but I didn't know how to fix it.

"Fine," I said finally. *"If you're so busy with your new nice friend, I guess you don't have time for the gossip I came to share."*

Her expression softened slightly, but there was still an edge to her voice. *"You're impossible, you know that?"*

"That's why you tolerate me," I said with a weak grin.

"Barely," she smiled faintly, but it didn't quite reach her eyes.

The air between us felt heavier now, filled with things unsaid. I wanted to shake off the awkwardness, crack a joke, and make her laugh like old times. But the words wouldn't come.

"You know," she said after a moment, *"I'm happy for you, Dev. If you think Nandita is the one, then go for it. Just... don't forget to be honest with yourself."*

Her words lingered in the room long after I left, an uncomfortable reminder that something between us was shifting. And for the first time, I wasn't sure if we'd ever shift back.

The next morning, I found myself standing in front of the school noticeboard, pretending to read something. My eyes, though, were glued to a different notice altogether—Nandita, flipping through her notebook while leaning against the wall.

"Dev, staring's not gonna help," Ahaana's voice popped into my head, a mental jab from our recent chat. Maybe she was right. Maybe it was time to stop overthinking and just do something.

Before I could chicken out, I marched toward Nandita. Well, 'marched' is a strong word; I stumbled halfway when my shoe caught on the loose hem of my pants. But I recovered quickly, trying to look like I had it all figured out.

"Hey, Nandita," I called out.

She looked up, surprised. *"Dev? What's up?"*

Okay, here we go. Deep breath. Confidence. *"I was just wondering if you'd like to hang out after school today?"* I said, casually as if I hadn't rehearsed this in my head about fifty times.

She tilted her head, narrowing her eyes as if she were trying to figure out if this was a dare. *"Hang out? With me?"*

"*Yeah, with you. Unless you have plans or... you don't want to,*" I added quickly, already regretting this.

Nandita's lips curled into a smile, a hint of amusement in her eyes. "*Okay. Sure. Where are we going?*"

"*Uh...*" I blinked. I hadn't planned that far ahead. "*There's this... chai place. It's, um, nice?*"

She laughed—a soft, melodious sound that somehow put me at ease. "*Fine. After school. Don't be late.*"

That evening, as we sat at the corner chai stall, I tried to focus on the tea in front of me. But my attention kept drifting to Nandita as she talked about her latest obsession with rom-coms. She was animated, her hands moving as much as her words, and for the first time, I noticed how easy it was to laugh with her.

"*I can't believe you've never seen Notting Hill,*" she said, looking scandalized. "*You're missing out on prime cinema.*"

"*Prime cinema is Lagaan,*" I countered, grinning. "*You can't beat Aamir Khan and cricket.*"

"*Typical Dev answer,*" she teased, rolling her eyes. "*I'm going to make you watch it, you know.*"

"*Only if you don't make me sing She's Like the Wind halfway through,*" I shot back, and she laughed again.

When I got home that night, I couldn't stop replaying the day in my head. For once, I didn't feel like overthinking it. Maybe things with Nandita were going somewhere. Maybe they weren't.

But as I lay in bed, I couldn't shake the feeling that I'd crossed some invisible line—one where Ahaana had always been. Would she even care if she knew? And if she did... why hadn't she said anything when I brought up Nandita?

I closed my eyes, telling myself it didn't matter. But deep down, I knew things were about to get complicated.

8

The school farewell wasn't supposed to feel like this—heavy and final. It was meant to be about awkward poses for photos, bad jokes, and cringeworthy dance moves. But when I saw Ahaana standing by the steps outside the auditorium, everything else fell away.

She was in a simple sari, her hair falling loose around her shoulders, and she looked... different. Not because of the outfit or the evening, but because something about her felt distant, like she was already slipping away.

She caught my eye and smiled—a soft, familiar smile that made me ache for something I couldn't name.

"Finally decided to show up?" she teased as I walked up to her.

"I had to. Someone needs to make sure you don't trip in that sari," I replied, trying to keep my voice light.

She rolled her eyes, and we fell into step together, walking toward the far end of the courtyard where the crowd thinned out. The noise of the farewell dimmed behind us, leaving just the sound of the fountain and the faint rustling of leaves.

We sat on a low bench by the fountain, like we'd done a hundred times before during lunch breaks. But this time felt different.

"*Are you scared about what's next?*" I asked after a moment, breaking the silence.

Ahaana shrugged. "*A little. But it's exciting too. New places, new people... it's all part of growing up, isn't it?*"

"*Yeah,*" I said, though the thought of her being somewhere I couldn't reach felt like a weight pressing on my chest. "*It's just... weird to think about, you know? You and I, in different worlds.*"

She looked at me then, her eyes softer than usual. "*Dev, we've been a team for so long. Nothing's going to change that.*"

I wanted to believe her. I wanted to tell her how much she meant to me, how scared I was of losing her. But I couldn't. Instead, I laughed, trying to lighten the mood. "*Easy for you to say. You're the one moving on to the big leagues. I'll probably be stuck here, boring people with cricket stats.*"

She nudged me lightly with her elbow. "*You're not giving yourself enough credit. You've got big things ahead too. You just haven't seen it yet.*"

The words hung in the air between us, heavier than they should have been.

"*I don't want to lose you, Ahaana,*" I said finally, my voice barely above a whisper.

She smiled at me—a soft, bittersweet smile. "*You won't lose me, Dev. I'll always be here. Ami thakbo, mone rakhish.*"

Her words hit me like a wave, both comforting and heartbreaking. I wanted to hold onto them, to her, but something about the way she said it felt like a goodbye disguised as a promise.

The moment passed too quickly. She stood up, adjusting her sari, her movements calm and deliberate. "*It's getting late. I should go back inside before someone starts looking for me.*"

"Yeah," I said, standing too, though my feet felt heavy.

She hesitated for a moment, then reached out and squeezed my hand. *"Take care of yourself, okay?"*

"You too," I said, my voice cracking slightly.

She smiled one last time and then she was gone, disappearing into the crowd.

I stayed by the fountain, staring at the ripples in the water as her words echoed in my head. *Ami thakbo, mone rakhish.*

Even as I watched her walk away, I knew I would carry those words with me, etched into the deepest part of me. But as the night wore on and the crowd began to thin, I couldn't shake the feeling that something had changed—something I couldn't get back.

The months after school blurred into a strange, quiet monotony. Ahaana's texts, once a constant in my life, started to thin out. At first, they came daily, filled with her usual randomness— *"Dev, guess what? Worst chai ever today!"* or *"You HAVE to watch this movie, trust me."* But soon, they turned into weekly updates, then just the occasional forward. It wasn't her fault, I told myself. She was drowning in prep for her medical exams, buried under coaching classes and mock tests. But knowing that didn't make the silence sting any less.

By July, the college began. The campus was a bustling little maze of classrooms, cricket pitches, and tea stalls. Everyone seemed eager to start fresh—boys obsessed with cricket, girls raving about movies I hadn't seen, and professors determined to drain us dry with assignments. I tried to blend in, but nothing quite fit. It wasn't bad; it just wasn't familiar. And without Ahaana, it all felt off, like I was wearing someone else's shoes.

One evening, my roommates were blasting Punjabi music in our cramped dorm. I wasn't in the mood for it, so I flopped onto my bed and scrolled through old messages. I found the last real conversation Ahaana and I had. It was nearly two weeks ago.

Her: Guess what? I think I've perfected the art of staying up for 36 hours. The secret is choco chips.

Me: The secret is you're nuts.

Her: Excuse me, your future doctor is speaking.

Me: Fine, Dr. Insomniac. Call me later.

Her: Will try, Baba. Life's crazy here.

She never called.

I stared at the screen for what felt like forever before typing out a text:

"Miss your terrible chai rants. Call me sometime, doc."

I hit send, even though I knew I probably wouldn't get a reply.

Weeks passed, and I threw myself into whatever college life had to offer—cricket, late-night hostel conversations, mediocre canteen food. I even managed to score well on our first economics paper. But even when I was on the pitch smashing a six, or laughing along with my batchmates, something felt off. Like I was winning battles that didn't matter.

One day, while sitting in the campus canteen with a plate of soggy samosas, my phone buzzed. A notification from Ahaana. My stomach flipped, and for a second, I felt the old excitement return. But when I opened it, it was just a forwarded meme about doctors being superheroes. No message. Just that.

I stared at it for a long time. That's when it hit me—this was it. We were drifting apart. Not because of a fight or anything dramatic, but because life was pulling us in different directions. She was becoming someone else—someone brighter, sharper, more ambitious. And me? I wasn't sure who I was becoming yet, but it was clear we weren't walking the same road anymore.

Still, her words from that farewell night kept circling my head:

"Ami thakbo, mone rakhish."

"I'll stay, remember that."

Did I believe her? Maybe. I wanted to. But the silence between us was growing louder, and I couldn't ignore it.

That evening, I sat under a tree near the cricket field, my diary open on my lap. The words poured out before I could stop them:

"Sometimes, people drift—not because they want to, but because they must. But what stays behind are the echoes, the promises they never meant to break."

Ahaana was still here, in the quiet spaces she left behind. Not in the texts that never came or the calls that always went unanswered, but in the part of me that she had unknowingly shaped. And maybe, just maybe, that was enough.

Months passed after their separation, and my life went on. Baba's continuous attempt to convince Maa stayed on for the initial few years after their separation, but the woman had been terrified by a lot of deadly experiences from the same man she fell in love with in college.

Maa found a job at a small consultancy firm, working long hours to keep us afloat. Baba's attempts to reconnect dwindled into faint echoes over time, but his absence left a strange void in our lives. As for Ahaana, I stopped waiting for her answers. Her final words haunted me, *Ami thakbo, mone rakhish*, but her voice felt distant, almost dreamlike now. I woke one morning to the sharp jab of reality—Jessica's voice breaking through my haze: *"Get up, you idiot."*

College came with its own set of rules and rhythms. It was different, sure, but I was still the same—quiet, awkward, lost in my own world. Enrolled in English Literature, I spent my days writing and observing, never saying much. The rumors started, as they always do. Some thought I was mute, others assumed I didn't want to interact with anyone. Truthfully, I didn't care. I liked blending into the background, letting the world move around me while I buried myself in words.

Every now and then, I wrote letters to Ahaana. Maa had passed along her address in Delhi after she joined medical school, though we'd barely spoken since then. There wasn't even a proper celebration when she got into one of the best colleges in the country. I suppose that's just how time works— It moves on without waiting for anyone.

Maa and I adjusted to Baba's absence, filling the gaps with our routines. But Ahaana? I carried the weight of our silence differently. And when our parents asked if we still talked, I could never bring myself to say much. A shrug, a nod, anything to avoid admitting the truth: we had become strangers in each other's lives.

A year into college, I had managed to gather a couple of friends, scraped through awkward social interactions, and even scored decently in the end-term exams. Life was shaping up... or at least that's what I told myself. On holidays, Maa seemed hell-bent on being my personal bulletin board about Ahaana's life. For reasons only she understood, she assumed *she* was the sole gatekeeper to everything I needed to know— or maybe didn't.

On a particularly gloomy, rain-soaked December evening, I was at home, comfortably slouched in the living room, lost in Neruda's words. Maa, as usual, was buzzing about, tidying my room in ways that weren't necessary. Suddenly, she appeared beside me and said, in that tone mothers use when they're about to ruin your peace, *"Have you ever thought how wonderful you two would look together?"*

Without missing a beat, I replied, *"Me and Neruda? Ma, maybe you're onto something, but, you know, he's kind of dead."*

She gave me *that look**—a combination of disapproval and barely concealed annoyance. Maa could have written books on that look; it was her superpower. Ignoring my deflection, she pulled a chair beside me, snatched the book from my hands, and launched into her favorite topic—Ahaana.

"I heard from her mother," she began dramatically, *"that she's dating someone."*

Her pause was deliberate, designed to pierce through my calm, but I refused to bite. *"How would I know, Maa?"* I shrugged, leaning back. *"It's her life. And besides, we haven't spoken in ages. Aami ki kore janbo eshob? (How would I know these things?)"*

Her expression shifted, equal parts curious and concerned, but I powered through. *"She must be busy with college. Maybe that's why she hasn't replied to the mails or letters I sent. And Maa... if she's found someone, isn't that good? Shouldn't you be happy instead of turning this into a breaking news headline?"*

My voice betrayed me, cracking slightly as I forced the words out. Maa noticed, of course, but she let it slide, though her curiosity lingered in the air long after she'd left the room.

But her words stayed with me. *She found someone in college.* They repeated in my head, twisting and turning until they became unbearable. I told myself I wasn't jealous, that I didn't care, but the truth was murkier than I liked to admit. What was this feeling? It wasn't jealousy, was it? No... it couldn't be. Could it?

The following days were a haze of memories, mostly of *that* night—the night we had shared our silences, our vulnerabilities. The flashbacks felt like an annoying friend refusing to leave, poking at me when I least expected it.

College, meanwhile, was its own chaotic world. It was this in-between space, a liminal gap where teenage idealism battled with adult realities. You stumbled through friendships, relationships, and newfound independence, learning more from your mistakes than your victories. Some people fell in love once and for all; others fell in and out of love every two months.

I was the latter, though each fleeting crush felt hollow, incapable of filling the space Ahaana had once occupied. And Maa? She never stopped. Every phone call or visit home brought fresh updates about Ahaana—how she was thriving in medical school, how her parents were so proud of her, and how much she had changed.

For me, it had been months since I'd heard her voice, yet she lingered everywhere—in conversations, in fleeting thoughts, in the ache of unfinished sentences. Even as life moved on, there was a corner of my heart that stayed rooted in the past, stubbornly clinging to what once was.

A year into college, and I wasn't the person I thought I'd be: quiet, sure, but now I was infamous too. Infamy courtesy of Jessica, the girl who somehow found a way to make my existence her personal vendetta.

"Do you honestly think anyone would care about your play, Dev?"

Her voice rang out across the cluttered auditorium, cutting through the last of the rehearsals like a sharp knife. Jessica's eyes bore into me, cold and unwavering.

I didn't know what was worse—the venom in her tone or the smug satisfaction on her face. It had been that way from the moment we'd met in the theater club.

"You're really something, Jessica," I shot back, trying to keep my voice steady, though I could feel my pulse racing. *"Criticizing the play before it even gets started? Who does that?"*

She leaned against the wooden wall, arms crossed, looking like she owned the whole room. *"I'm just saying. This play is so... predictable. It's practically Hayavadana with a twist."*

My eyes flickered to the rest of the theater club members, who were awkwardly pretending not to listen. They'd long given up on stopping the endless back-and-forth between Jessica and me. But this? This was something new.

"What an original observation," I mocked, arching an eyebrow. *"Right, Jessica? Hayavadana—obviously."*

Her eyes narrowed. The challenge was clear. I could feel the weight of her gaze like a slap to my face.

"I don't know why you think you're so clever, Dev," she hissed. *"This isn't a critique. I'm just saying, it's boring. Just like you."*

"Stupid girl," I muttered under my breath.

And that was how it went. One shot after another. She'd take the tiniest mistake I made and twist it into some grand failure. I wasn't good enough, wasn't smart enough, wasn't *anything* enough. And no matter how hard I tried, the more I got sucked into her gravitational pull, the more I became the villain of her story.

The competition came and went, and no surprise—we didn't win. But somehow, we'd left an impression. Professor Tripathi, the head of the theater club, pulled me aside after the results were announced. *"Dev, you did better than I imagined. You've got more in you than I thought."*

I nodded, but the words barely registered. Jessica was too busy glaring at me from across the room, her lips curling into that damn smug smile that made me want to punch something.

And sure enough, when she saw the professor's praise, she couldn't resist. *"Oh, how cute, Dev. You actually think you did something."* Her laugh was a cruel melody, one that would haunt me all night.

Later, as I sat with Nitin and Bijoy—two of my few friends left in college—I asked the question that had been eating away at me for weeks.

"Does she really hate me that much?"

Nitin burst out laughing, shaking his head. *"Maybe she really does. You're not exactly easy to like."*

Bijoy added with a grin, *"Or maybe she just knows you're a total buzzard to her father. That'd piss anyone off."*

I laughed, but it wasn't funny. I didn't want to admit it, but I knew they were right. Jessica's grudge against me went deeper than anything I had done—it was a war she'd started before I even had a chance to react.

Her stories about me had spread like wildfire. *"Dev Mukherjee, the troublemaker."* The whispers followed me in the halls, in the cafeteria, and worst of all, in the theater club. Once a silent guy, now I was the one who had ruined everything.

My position as head of the club was swiftly stripped away. *"Oh, the quiet guy has balls now, huh?"* someone had muttered. *"A real man of character."*

But that was the thing. In Jessica's version of the story, I was the villain. And she, the ever-so-sweet, innocent victim.

I couldn't let it go. One afternoon, after weeks of her playing the role of the wronged angel, I ran into her outside the chai stall by the college entrance. She was sitting alone, sipping her tea, as if she hadn't just spent the last month turning my reputation into ash.

"Have I done something to you?" I asked, my voice tense, holding back the anger that had been building inside me for so long.

She looked up at me, a brief flicker of amusement in her eyes before she took another sip of her tea. *"You're a genuine problem, Dev. And I guess hating you is just... easier."*

Easier? I stared at her, confused, but my own frustration clouded my thoughts.

"You really don't get it, do you?" she continued, her tone dripping with disdain. *"I dislike your very existence in this place. Right here. Right in front of me."*

I laughed bitterly. *"As if that wasn't already obvious, Jessica. Come on, you've been making that clear for months now."*

I slammed the script of our latest play onto the table, walking away without waiting for her response.

The days after were a blur of self-loathing and regret. I'd been trying so hard to hold myself together, but Jessica's constant presence was unraveling me. And then there was the silence—the silence between Ahaana and me that stretched over months like an endless void.

Mum didn't help either. *"Dev, why don't you call her?"* she asked one evening during a phone call. *"You two used to be so close."*

But what could I say? That I didn't know why we'd drifted apart. That I missed her but didn't know how to reach out? The words stuck in my throat, unspoken.

In the mirror, I saw a stranger staring back at me. The quiet, reflective boy I'd been in school was gone, replaced by someone angrier, someone sadder. Someone I didn't recognize.

And Jessica? She was still there, an infuriating constant in my life, challenging me at every turn. I couldn't decide if I wanted to hate her forever or prove her wrong. Maybe both.

9

Holidays were mostly Maa's time to bring up Baba—news she'd picked up from neighbors, or rumors of where he'd been spotted. He hadn't given up trying to convince her to drop the divorce, and once, he'd even reached out to me at college. The man seemed willing to go to any lengths, making things more damaging than they already were. *"His issues are so complex; he needs serious help,"* I muttered, frustrated.

Maa just let out a dry chuckle, brushing my words aside with a tired flick of her hand.

"Help?" she scoffed, a hint of resignation in her voice. *"He's past all that now, Baba, especially at his age."*

I bit back a sigh, her response settling uncomfortably, a weight I couldn't ignore. But there was one thing we could agree on—neither of us wanted him anywhere near our lives.

Nitin and Bijoy came from different towns and led lives that couldn't be more different. Nitin came from money, with little interest in either sports or academics; he was here to get his degree and be done with it. Bijoy, on the other hand, had secured his place in college on a sports scholarship for cricket.

His commitment on the field had brought in a string of awards and trophies that the college proudly showcased, a testament to Bijoy's dedication.

Bijoy is the kind of guy who seems to live and breathe cricket, and it's what he's best known for around campus. Hailing from the same town as me, Bijoy wasn't from a rich family, his cricket skills were his only ticket to college. Cricket wasn't just a game to him; it was everything. While he may not take his studies or future career very seriously, he's got a fierce determination when it comes to the sport, convinced he'll make it to the Ranji Trophy someday.

Unlike Nitin, who floats through college without much attachment to either sports or academics, Bijoy has a single-minded dedication to cricket—though it's not backed by a clear plan. He's the type to shrug off worries about life or career, casually assuming cricket will somehow make everything fall into place. But his passion for the game is undeniable; his commitment on the field speaks for itself.

"Bro," Nitin would mumble, voice muffled around a mouthful of samosa, *"How do they expect us to sit through these boring lectures and study for exams? Dasgupta sir ka class toh maar daalta hai, yaar."*

"Dasgupta's class? Why do you think I sit by the back window?" I'd laugh, already picturing Mr. Dasgupta's monotone voice droning on about Victorian poetry.

Mr. Dasgupta was our History of English Literature professor—a strict, cranky old man with a permanent scowl that made him look like he disapproved of everything. His lectures were legendary for their ability to put students to sleep, and more often than not, Nitin was slumped beside me, head down and halfway to dreamland.

"But Nitin dreams of food even while Dasgupta is explaining romantic poetry," Bijoy joked one day after class.

"Food and maybe sleep," I smirked. *"He's probably planning his lunch menu during the Renaissance lecture."*

Nitin only grinned, unbothered as ever. *"Arre, poetry waale time pe toh khana aur important ho jaata hai, boss."*

His easygoing attitude made everything easier—turning exams and Dasgupta's endless lectures into things we could just laugh off. And honestly, without him and Bijoy, college life wouldn't have been half as fun—or bearable.

I dreaded Mr. Dasgupta's paper the most. His lectures always managed to go straight over my head, and he was quite a character himself. Grumpy and cranky most of the year, the old man seemed almost invisible to most students—a mere background figure.

He was a bundle of boredom wrapped in sarcasm and moody behavior, and it didn't surprise me one bit where his daughter got it from. Always buried in books, this studious, snooty girl had her own high-stakes dilemmas: *"Should I dive into Shelley's lyrical poems, explore Wordsworth's musings on nature, or maybe just read that thrilling book on criminal psychology? You know, just in case someone here needs analyzing."*

I often found it amusing to poke fun at Jessica's mind—a tangled mess of dilemmas that she seemed to control as well as a cat herding sheep. As a psychology student, she was as complex as her father and just as unreadable. Whether she was deep in a debate about poetry or lost in some obscure bit of theater, Jessica was, in every sense, difficult to please.

One gloomy afternoon, as I sat in the library reading a piece by Sylvia Plath, Jessica discovered me. She slid into the seat beside me, her gaze immediately fixed on my book. *"What's that you're reading?"* she asked.

I ignored her, pretending to be entirely absorbed, just as I often tuned out her father's lectures. But Jessica was nothing if not persistent—though maybe stubborn and relentless captured her better.

Her eyes narrowed with determination as she asked again, *"Will you at least tell me what you're reading?"*

Knowing this conversation could turn into a game of cat and mouse if I resisted, I sighed and finally looked up. *"It's Lady Lazarus. Sylvia Plath."*

She lit up. *"Oh, Lady Lazarus! Isn't that about the biblical Lazarus? And didn't it get published, um... wasn't it... a year? No, two years after she died?"*

I closed the book with a bit more force than necessary. *"Yes. Two years later. Now, Jessica, would you mind giving me a break? Between you and your father, I get more questions and lectures than any man could possibly endure."*

Her eyes widened, a mix of surprise and defiance flashing in them. *"Well, maybe if you were less... evasive, you wouldn't find it so exhausting."*

"And maybe if you were less persistent, you'd understand why I need to be evasive." I shot back, louder than intended. Heads turned, eyebrows raised, and I didn't wait for her reply. I grabbed my things, got up, and left the library without looking back.

As I headed down the hall, I caught a glimpse of her outside, sitting alone on a bench near the college garden, her face flushed with a mix of anger and embarrassment. She pulled out her criminal psychology book and stared at it as if the pages could somehow distract her from my outburst.

Nitin and Bijoy had returned early from the ground and joined me at one of the makeshift tea stalls across the street. One look at my face, and they didn't need to ask—they knew Jessica and I had clashed again. Our arguments had practically become a college tradition, infamous enough to rival any on-campus rivalry. If ever there were a gallery of great adversaries, Jessica and I would have a place of honor.

Our battles weren't confined to classrooms or libraries. It was as if we brought the drama of epic duels to every corner of college life. If ever the campus corridors could talk, they'd be groaning in complaint by now. If we'd lived in another time, we'd probably be shouting at each other in busy town squares or making a scene in crowded cafés, exchanging clever comebacks like characters in a classic play. Even in today's world, you might find us sparring in crowded canteens, in stairwells, or over stacks of dusty books, while students scatter, muttering, *"There they go again."*

"If this were a war," Bijoy smirked, tossing me a knowing look, *"you two would've emptied out the whole campus."*

"Or made it headline news," Nitin added with a grin.

I rolled my eyes, trying to brush it off, but even I had to admit—Jessica and I had a knack for making even the smallest exchange feel like the next great showdown.

But despite the tension between Jessica and me, we both seemed to relish torturing each other, with Nitin and Bijoy enjoying the front-row seats. They took sips from their tea served in a *bhar,* the traditional earthen pot beloved across Kolkata and much of Bengal. For Bengalis, tea isn't just a drink; it's a ritual, much like the Sunday classic, *pathar-mangsher-jhol*—a hearty meat curry with potatoes and steamed rice. Whether you're a local or a 'probashi' Bengali, you can count on Sunday being incomplete without it.

Similarly, *'bhar-er-cha'* has its own special place in our hearts, a bond that transcends whether it's served with milk or plain. Nitin and Bijoy savored their tea, quietly lost in thought, while I aggressively gulped down a lime soda, feeling the weight of the world pressing down on me.

Noticing my distress, Nitin broke the silence, leaning in. *"Kire bhai? Ki holo? Kichu bolbi? (Hey, brother, what's wrong? Aren't you going to say anything?)"*

I snapped, my annoyance bubbling over. *"What do you want me to say? Am I supposed to just shout over the endless chatter around me?"*

The high-pitched voices of nearby women were overwhelming, making it painfully clear that my mood had soured. For those around, my irritation must have screamed: I can't stand your presence.

I still can't wrap my head around how they took offense at my outburst. It wasn't aimed at anyone specific, but somehow, the next couple of women I saw around campus looked at me with disdain, as if I were the villain in their drama.

After being kicked out of the library, I spent the next few days on the cricket field with the boys. Nitin and Bijoy, in their usual well-meaning but chaotic way, seemed determined to set me up with someone, convinced that if I kept going the way I was, I'd be single until graduation. Not that I minded—dating sounded like just another way to add chaos to an already messy semester. It was 2012, a year that had so far only perfected the art of disappointing me.

College by itself wasn't the biggest letdown; that honor belonged to Jessica. Her father seemed to have made it his mission to see me squirm, practically salivating over the chance to catch me slipping in his class. As if one year of constant pressure hadn't been enough for him, he was sharpening his claws for the end-term papers. I still couldn't believe how ruthlessly he'd dissected my work every semester, marking my answers with the precision of a surgeon but the attitude of a critic who found my efforts insufficient at best.

Since my chances of getting a girlfriend on my own were slim, Nitin took matters into his own hands and set me up with Meenakshi. She was... well, let's just say she was the most by-the-book person I'd ever met—literally. A soft-spoken, touch-me-not kind of girl, Meenakshi was the type who carried separate notebooks for every subject, each one labeled and color-coded. She even brought a packed lunch to college daily—homemade idli-sambar, carefully wrapped, always eaten with a neatness that was almost intimidating.

Nitin found the whole situation hilarious. *"Bhai, think about it—she's like your exact opposite! You're messy, she's tidy. You can't sit through a lecture without nodding off, and she's... well, she's her."*

Bijoy laughed. *"She'll probably mark you down for poor performance before Dasgupta, Sir, even gets to it!"*

To be fair, Meenakshi was practically Mr. Dasgupta's dream student. The man treated her like a treasure, even gifting her a first edition of *The Great Gatsby* when she topped the batch that year. Meanwhile, I'd barely scraped by with 70%, and that felt like a miracle.

"Wait, he gave her The Great Gatsby?" I grumbled one afternoon as we sat by our usual tea shack. *"What kind of professor gives a love story to someone who probably sees romance as a distraction from her study schedule?"*

Nitin snickered. *"Probably thought he was inspiring her to read 'the greats', or whatever."* He made air quotes, rolling his eyes.

"Honestly, I'm just shocked she hasn't reported the three of us to the principal yet," Bijoy added, slurping his tea. *"The way she looks at us... like we're the root cause of all disorder in the universe."*

"She might not be wrong," I muttered, but I was chuckling too. Meenakshi's disdain was almost impressive as if our very existence offended her sense of order. If she'd had her way, I was sure she'd have banned all conversation and laughter from campus.

Just then, Meenakshi walked past, giving us her usual look of disapproval. I raised my hand to wave, but she only gave a curt nod in return, barely acknowledging me.

"See?" Bijoy whispered, stifling a laugh. *"She's probably off to organize her notes on how to survive our corrupting influence."*

"Or planning tomorrow's sambar recipe," Nitin smirked. *"Say what you want, but if you actually end up with her, Dev, at least you'll eat well."*

I groaned, shaking my head. *"Maybe. But only if I pass her inspection."*

Maybe, back in the time, I underestimated the woman, and what she was to transform into. While I write every bit of these events sitting beside the capricious study lamp, I discover she is busy traveling around the globe attending seminars on classic literature.

Every professor in the department swore Meenakshi was the brightest student we'd ever have in our batch. I still couldn't believe it. If I'd been in engineering, maybe she'd be a little less of an academic overlord and more of a regular person who just happened to be good at studies.

Strange comparison, right?

But Meenakshi's perfection wasn't exactly what held everyone's attention, especially not mine. That spotlight was reserved for Jessica. She had these oversized glasses with big, bold deer eyes peeking out from behind them. It was like she'd inherited every last eccentricity from her father, Professor Dasgupta. Her frames looked like they'd been around since the Stone Age—faded, chipped, and clearly long past their expiration date. I could practically see how she'd inherited her dad's infamous stinginess. *"What a weird family,"* I'd mutter to myself whenever I saw them. They'd put on this ridiculous family show during classes and even out in the corridors. Jessica would lecture him on everything from classroom decorum to basic courtesy in that dry, know-it-all tone, and Dasgupta would stand there, totally resigned, like a tree weathering a storm. The moment he left, the entire class would burst into suppressed laughter, trading looks of disbelief.

So, with all this pent-up irritation, I spilled out the library story to Nitin and Bijoy. They had been waiting for it, smirking before I even started.

Nitin leaned in with a grin. *"Bro, either the universe wants you two together, or you've got a natural talent for being a woman-repellent. Which one do you think it is?"*

Bijoy snorted. *"Forget repellent—maybe Jessica's just your type, and you're too dense to see it."*

I shot him a glare. *"Right. My type is apparently someone who could list my faults for the next five years straight."*

Nitin laughed, nudging Bijoy. *"Sounds about right. You need someone to keep you humble, after all."*

"*Spare me,*" I groaned, rolling my eyes. "*If I have to deal with both her and her father for the rest of the semester, I might actually lose it.*"

Bijoy leaned back, putting on his dramatic voice, "*Ah, the tragic tale of Dev and Jessica! The doomed lovers of the Theater Club...*"

"*Shut up, man,*" I threw a napkin at him, but he dodged, laughing harder. "*If anyone's doomed, it's her. Who willingly chooses the same college where her father works?*"

Nitin shook his head, mock-serious. "*Maybe she's trying to keep tabs on you, Dev. The daughter and the professor, one monitoring your every move.*"

I groaned again. "*You guys are insufferable. She's the one who'd be lucky to never see me again, not the other way around.*"

Bijoy grinned. "*Sure, but tell us one thing—why do you always get so worked up about her? I mean, even Meenakshi doesn't rile you up this much.*"

"*Because Meenakshi's predictable,*" I said, shrugging. "*She's like... pure, unfiltered nerd. No surprises, just stacks of notebooks and that constant glare she saves for guys like us. At least she doesn't try to dissect my taste in poetry.*"

"*Ah, yes, the lesser of two evils,*" Nitin nodded, trying to look wise. "*Let's just hope Jessica doesn't team up with Meenakshi. That might actually be the end of you.*"

The three of us laughed, the tension easing, but as much as I hated to admit it, they weren't entirely wrong. Jessica had this strange way of slipping under my skin, like a splinter you can't quite reach. But for now, I figured I'd just let it go and hope I'd survive the semester without losing my mind.

My friends only doubled down on their theories, poking fun at my helplessness. It drove me nuts how amused they were by the whole thing. The idea of Jessica being any part of my life seemed insane, and the 'issue with women' theory? That was beyond ridiculous.

Our hot-and-cold rivalry dragged on through the next two years, but I kept telling myself it had to end at some point. Yet, somewhere along the way, I started noticing things about her I hadn't before. She didn't have any real friends, and her solitary ways only made her stand out more. Early on, I'd said she'd end up alone, and honestly, I believed it. I'd think, *"Who would risk their peace over someone so prickly, so constantly on edge?"*

But over time, those words started to feel a little... hollow. She seemed increasingly isolated, and her grades even took a dip. Meanwhile, the tension between her and Professor Dasgupta only grew, and he took out that frustration on us as if we were to blame for their family melodrama. I'd sit there, clenching my teeth, thinking, *"This family circus has got to stop."*

Nitin took a long drag from the cigarette they were sharing and sighed. *"Dev, honestly, I think the Dasguptas need a holiday."*

Bijoy let out a snort. *"A holiday? You really think Professor Dasgupta's the kind of guy to spend a penny on a vacation? The man pinches pennies like it's his full-time job."*

We laughed, picturing it, but then Nitin's eyes got that mischievous glint. *"Dev, why don't you just ask Jessica what's going on with them?"*

I stared at him as if he'd grown a second head. *"Ask Jessica about her family drama. Yeah, right. We argue every other day— it doesn't make us best friends."*

"Come on, Dev," Nitin nudged, grinning. *"Just ask, casually. What's the harm?"*

"*Right, like I'd even get a straight answer,*" I scoffed. "*Jessica has a way of making anyone who asks anything feel like they're bothering her for a kidney.*"

"*Wow, Dev, you're such a caring friend,*" Bijoy teased, smirking. "*All he's saying is, show a bit of curiosity.*"

"*Fine!*" I said, rolling my eyes. "*But if she tears my head off, you two are to blame.*"

A few minutes later, I spotted Jessica in the hallway and braced myself. "*Jessica!*" I called. She turned, already looking irritated.

"*Oh, what now, Dev? Got more time to waste?*"

I took a breath. "*Relax, Jess, I'm just... asking if everything's okay with you and, uh, Professor Dasgupta?*"

She raised an eyebrow, clearly unimpressed. "*Why would you care? Last I checked, we aren't exactly close.*"

I shrugged. "*Look, it's just that he seems a bit tense lately, and well... so are you. Just thought I'd ask.*"

Her face softened for just a second, but then her usual guarded look came back. "*We're fine, if that's what you wanted to know. Anything else?*"

"*Nope. Just thought I'd be nice for a change. Clearly my mistake,*" I muttered.

She looked at me, half-smirking. "*Nice try, Dev, but leave the nice-guy act. Doesn't suit you.*" She turned and walked off, leaving me standing there, a bit confused and, oddly enough, more curious.

Back in the room, Nitin and Bijoy were waiting for me with big grins.

"So?" Nitin asked, eyes shining with excitement. *"How'd it go?"*

I dropped onto the chair, shaking my head. *"Exactly as you'd think. I asked; she dodged. And I'm starting to think you both find this way too entertaining."*

Bijoy laughed, slapping my shoulder. *"Oh, come on, admit it, Dev—you're a little hooked, aren't you?"*

"Hooked? On Jessica?" I rolled my eyes. *"That's like being hooked on sandpaper."*

"Yeah, sure," Nitin chuckled. *"Just remember: denial's the first step."*

I knew Jessica would react exactly as she did, so I'd prepared my half-hearted *concern* ahead of time, keeping my tone casual. *"I just noticed you've been looking a bit... off these past few days. We may never see eye to eye, but I thought I'd check in on you."* I patted her shoulder lightly—just enough to plant the idea in her mind, and then turned to leave. I had a strong feeling that she'd follow up.

Sure enough, the very next day, she found me at my usual haunt—the old cemetery where I'd sometimes go to read and clear my head. As I sat with my book, I felt a tap on my shoulder. *"Ugh... Dev,"* she muttered.

Internally, I grinned. *"Yes! Nitin, I knew it,"* I thought. Out loud, though, I kept my composure and just nodded. *"Yeah?"*

"Um... can I sit here?" she asked. I gave a nonchalant nod, and before I knew it, she launched into a series of apologies, tripping over her words about how she'd been irritated by me and my friends poking fun at her dad, and how she regretted snapping in the rehearsal room. It all poured out, her words a mix of frustration and something like regret.

"It's fine, Jess, really. I mean, I owe you an apology too... for, well, probably being unbearable half the time," I said, shrugging. Half of my apologies didn't mean much, but I delivered them with just the right level of sincerity. Surprisingly, she bought it.

Gestures, I thought, can be pretty convincing when used well. They could turn even the most careless apology into something genuine.

She managed a small smile. "*Thanks, Dev... And... why do I always find you here, anyway?*"

It was an easy question, one I could have answered simply. But where's the fun in that? I gave her a smirk. "*Why do you think so? Plotting ways to be a nuisance to you, of course. Gotta have my secret hideout for all the evil plans.*"

She rolled her eyes but smiled. "*That actually sounds like something you'd do.*"

"*Believe what you want,*" I said, leaning back with a grin. "*Some people think it's a quiet spot to think. I'll leave the rest up to your imagination.*"

For a moment, Jessica just sat there, looking around the cemetery with a strange, thoughtful expression. It was the first time I'd seen her let her guard down, even if just a bit. And as much as I'd planned this whole thing to goad her, I couldn't help feeling like I'd accidentally stumbled into some truth.

Jessica stood still, her voice quiet but sharp as she asked, "*Do you know what it takes for a woman to make amends with the man she's known all her life?*"

Her question caught me off guard. I blinked, a little lost. "*Uh... why are you asking me that, Jessica?*"

She shook her head, glancing down. *"Never mind. I don't know why I thought you'd understand."* She got up, wandering through the cemetery, her fingers trailing along the moss-covered headstones, her eyes tracing dates and names.

I watched her, hesitating, before calling out, *"We could talk about it if you want."* I followed her, pulling out a pack of crumpled cigarettes from my pocket. She gave the pack a glance, then turned her eyes back to the stones, ignoring me.

"Not here... not now, Dev," she muttered, almost to herself, as I lit up a cigarette.

"Oh, come on," I smirked, flicking my lighter. *"Think they'd mind?"* I gestured to the stones, chuckling.

Jessica gave me an icy stare, her voice dry. *"Why am I not surprised?"*

"Look, 'Disappointment' could be your middle name, seriously," I teased. *"Sometimes, you're like this birokto-kakima—an aunt, who is permanently annoyed with the world."*

Jessica raised an eyebrow. *"Were you always this way?"* Her tone was a mix of exasperation and intrigue as if trying to solve a puzzle that refused to fit together.

"What do you mean by this way?" I countered, studying her, half-joking, half-curious.

She shrugged, her eyes distant. *"Always so... restless? Chasing some idea of how things should be?"*

"Hey, I haven't seen you happy, like, ever. It's like you're constantly in a fight—with everything."

"Have I never looked happy to you?"

"Nope. Mostly, you look frustrated. Against every natural law that exists."

Jessica chuckled, but there was an edge to it. *"That's fair. I don't understand the laws of the world."*

I could tell we were drifting into serious waters, a strange shift from our usual banter. *"The laws of the world?"* I echoed. *"What, like society or life itself?"*

She looked away, folding her arms. *"Both, I guess. They're linked, aren't they? Life and society are tangled into some web where everyone just accepts how things are."*

I squinted, taking a drag. *"Yeah, but if you know they're connected, wouldn't it make sense to accept it?"*

She shook her head, that old irritation flashing across her face. *"That's the typical answer. And you're right—it's what everyone thinks. But it doesn't mean I have to follow along."*

"Onek ajob toh aapni," I muttered. *"You're one strange person, you know that?"*

She gave a small laugh, dismissing the conversation with a shrug, but her eyes stayed fixed on the ground. The silence between us grew heavy, so I asked, *"I've noticed you hanging around here a lot. Do cemeteries give you some kind of peace?"*

She looked up, her eyes softening. *"I wouldn't call it peace exactly. This place... it brings my mother's memory back to life."*

"Oh," I said quietly. *"I'm sorry. I didn't know..."*

"It's okay. You couldn't have known," she murmured, her voice calm, though there was something wounded in it.

After a pause, she continued. *"I've got memories wrapped up in every corner of this city. Kolkata holds so much... I used to feel at home here. Until it became a place of scars, really."*

"Scars?" I echoed, feeling strangely out of my depth.

She nodded, a shadow crossing her face. *"Memories I can't erase, things I can't forget. Some places do that, you know—they give you everything, and then they take it all back."*

I wasn't sure what to say. This girl I'd always seen as my so-called rival, my enemy, was suddenly here, laying her story bare to me as if we'd known each other forever. And in that moment, for the first time, I felt I was beginning to see Jessica, beyond the arguments, the endless irritations, and the walls she puts up.

I let the silence settle, both of us just standing there. For once, there was no need for words. As we stood there, the silence wrapped around us like a heavy fog. I couldn't help but reflect on how unexpectedly raw this conversation had become. Jessica, with her layered complexities, was no longer just the girl I loved to argue with. She was revealing pieces of herself I never thought I'd see. And there I was, standing in a cemetery, talking about scars and memories, feeling like I'd stumbled into a scene from one of those deep, angsty movies that always struck a chord somewhere inside me.

I couldn't shake the feeling that she was searching for something, even if she didn't know it. Maybe it was a semblance of peace or a connection she desperately craved, yet denied herself out of fear. It made me question my own actions, my own relentless pursuit of trivial arguments with her. Was it really just about the banter? Or was I hiding my own scars beneath a layer of sarcasm and indifference, deflecting every serious conversation because I was scared of letting anyone in?

"Is this who you really are, Jessica?" I thought to myself. *"Not just the snarky, defensive girl, but someone who feels deeply and cares enough to visit memories in a place like this?"* And then, without warning, it hit me—why was I so drawn

to this cemetery myself? I'd always told myself it was for the quiet, the solitude, but maybe that was just the easy answer. Standing there with her, I wondered if this place held something deeper for me, too. Had I been using it to bury my own unresolved feelings, to avoid the questions I'd never been brave enough to face?

Questions began to unravel in my mind like loose threads. I thought about my parents' separation and the messy fragments they left scattered in my life. Was that why I came here, to some place where everything seemed final and still, while my life back home felt so frayed? I had always brushed off my parents' split as something inevitable as if it barely affected me. But maybe I was just avoiding the grief. Maybe I didn't want to acknowledge how it made me wary of love, of commitment, of the risk of caring too much.

I watched Jessica as she traced the stones with her fingers, almost as if she were searching for something lost. Could she be doing the same thing—grappling with ghosts she'd buried away, ghosts she hadn't expected to encounter again? I wondered if she'd ever felt that same pull of a broken family, of wanting to escape the fractures left behind by the people who were supposed to stay whole for you.

And if I was here, unconsciously looking for answers about my parents, did that mean I had been missing something all along? Was this strange connection with Jessica rooted in some shared understanding, in the wounds we both carried?

The questions spiraled in my mind, filling the space between us with unspoken words. I wanted to reach out, to pull down the walls we'd both built, but fear held me back. What if I laid bare my own vulnerabilities and she didn't reciprocate? What if it changed everything?

I took a deep breath, the crisp air filling my lungs, grounding me. *"Maybe,"* I pondered, *"just maybe, this was the start of something different. Maybe it was time to stop being enemies and start being something else entirely."*

And in that moment, as we stood surrounded by memories of the past, I felt a shift within myself. It was raw, unfiltered, and strangely liberating. Perhaps I could step beyond the façade I'd worn for so long and explore the complexities of not just Jessica, but of myself too. Maybe there was room for understanding and connection after all.

With that thought, I turned to her, ready to break the silence, but unsure of how to begin. The weight of everything hung in the air, and for the first time, it felt like it mattered.

10

"**D**ev... *I know we've never quite seen eye to eye, but...*"

There was something unsettling in her calmness, a strange stillness that caught me off guard. Standing there in the middle of a cemetery, a cigarette balanced between my fingers, all those months of endless arguments suddenly felt distant, almost absurd. Jessica held out her hand, and I passed her the cigarette. She took one last drag before crushing it under her heel, the sun catching her black shoes in a warm, winter glow.

"*I don't know why, but here, in this place... our conversations don't feel like arguments anymore. I was almost certain we'd be bickering the minute I walked in. And yet... here we are.*"

I couldn't help but feel the same. Somehow, all the sharp edges between us had softened, like we'd forgotten our usual habit of clashing over every little thing. Normally, I didn't mind a difference of opinion, but something about her always set me off. And yet here we were—both of us, strangely at peace, in a place I never thought would calm us.

"*I almost want to argue with you—prove just how wrong you are about life. But for once... I have no idea where to start.*"

She laughed softly, shaking her head. "*Maybe you're just confused. Or maybe you actually agree with me, just a little.*

You're just another pawn of society, after all—accepting the rules without questioning them."

"*Maybe,*" I muttered, half-smiling. "*Never really thought about it.*" I paused, glancing away before adding, "*But...since we're here sharing a cigarette, mind if I ask you something? I promise it's not meant to offend.*"

"*Go ahead.*"

I took a breath. "*If the city holds so many good memories for you... why do you dislike it so much?*"

A tense silence settled between us, and I immediately felt a pang of regret. My words hung heavy in the air, and embarrassment gnawed at me. "*Look, forget it. That was out of line. I shouldn't have asked,*" I said quickly, trying to ease the awkwardness.

She hesitated but then shrugged. "*No, it's okay. After all, it's the first time we're actually talking instead of going at each other. Yeah, let's talk. I don't dislike the city just because...*" She trailed off, her voice growing softer. "*It's more that... I never really had any fond memories there.*"

"*Ah... so I heard you lived somewhere else before your family moved to Kolkata?*"

"*Family?*" she asked, her tone shifting just slightly. "*You mean my father, right? Mr. Dasgupta?*"

I hesitated. "*Uh... yeah, I mean, Mr. and Mrs. Dasgupta...*"

She gave a faint, bitter smile, almost lost in thought. "*We moved here when I turned two. I remember—it was 2000.*" Her gaze drifted, and she seemed far away. "*Papa... he never really talked about Maa. Every time I'd ask, he'd find some way to avoid it. Made sense, I suppose...*" Her voice trailed off like she'd said more than she meant to, and the silence that followed fell like the edges of a story left untold.

The silence between us deepened, heavy with things unsaid. As soon as she mentioned her mother, it was like a curtain lifted; so much about her guarded relationship with Mr. Dasgupta came into focus. Her gaze dropped, and I saw something raw in her eyes—a sadness that had settled there long ago. I didn't want to push, but I couldn't help myself. *"You... miss her, don't you?"*

A small, wistful smile appeared. *"I do. Though, honestly? I can barely remember her voice."*

"It must have been tough for your dad, managing everything alone."

She gave a dry chuckle, shaking her head. *"Oh, 'rough'... sure. I'm sure it was very rough—leaving a toddler with her grandparents while he stayed miles away, building his career. Can't imagine the sacrifice,"* she said, a hint of sarcasm slipping through.

Most of her childhood, I gather, had unfolded in her grandparents' quiet home in Kolkata, while her father lived across the city, almost a stranger to her. Their relationship felt distant like it was defined more by routine than closeness—a few scheduled dinners, polite conversations, both of them going through motions they knew but never questioned. It was strange seeing her, usually so fiery and guarded, now caught in the weight of memories she rarely let anyone see.

"I never really wanted my father around," she said, her voice barely above a whisper.

"What do you mean, never wanted him around?" The question slipped out before I could hold it back.

She narrowed her eyes, a flicker of irritation sparking. Without responding, she turned and walked off, her steps slow but determined, putting space between us. She stopped beneath the towering banyan tree nearby—a hulking, twisted giant, with roots that had burrowed deep over decades. Its dark branches stretched protectively over a cluster of old gravestones, casting heavy shadows that seemed to breathe in the quiet. She leaned against the rough bark, her back to me, letting the silence settle like a barrier, daring me to break it.

"Don't get any ideas, alright? Just because I've been talking to you doesn't make us friends."

She shot me a look that could have cut glass, then flicked her half-smoked cigarette to the ground, grinding it under her heel with finality. Without another glance, she turned and walked off, her footsteps echoing through the cemetery like a warning. I just stood there, caught somewhere between disbelief and intrigue. Had she really just walked away after sharing all that? Moments ago, she'd been open, vulnerable even, and now, she was gone, slipping out of sight like smoke dispersing into thin air.

I finally caught a glimpse of her turning the corner, her figure growing smaller until she vanished completely. It was infuriating and fascinating at once, the way she'd leave these fragments of herself and then disappear as if none of it had happened. There was a strange energy to her, a wildness I couldn't pin down, and the strangest sense of déjà vu. Something in her felt like a ghost of my past—a flash of fierce eyes and sarcasm, half hidden behind glasses, a presence I couldn't ignore.

The women in my life had always been fierce, bold, and impossible to forget. Jessica had already started carving herself into that list, leaving me wondering if one day she'd haunt me just the same. But that was a thought I kept close, a secret she'd never see. For now, all she'd left me with was a trail of cigarette smoke and an ache to understand.

A woman with a captivating intellect, she hides behind her glasses, though her eyes alone could craft entire sentences, expressive and unguarded. Beneath her reserved exterior lies a magnetic presence—an alluring mystery. She and her father, though poles apart on the surface, share an unspoken kinship in their disdain for the noise of the human world. Their tolerance for people is as close to zero as it could be, or perhaps even lower, as if they belong to a world apart, quietly studying others with a critical gaze.

The late autumn chill seeped into the small café, a place tucked into the corner of a quiet street, its windows fogged over as rain began to drum lightly against the glass. A few withered leaves clung to the branches outside, and the dim, golden light inside gave the place a warmth that felt distant from the brisk cold just beyond the door.

I looked at Jessica across the chessboard, the usual smirk tugging at my lips. It had been months since we'd started meeting like this, ever since she'd casually dropped a sarcastic comment about my predictable tactics after I'd mentioned playing. I'd shot back that she wouldn't last five minutes in a match against me. That was our first game. Since then, we had found ourselves tangled in these quiet battles, some unspoken force bringing us back to this table again and again, even if neither of us would admit to enjoying it.

She leaned forward, her hand hovering over her knight as she cocked an eyebrow. *"So, Dev,"* she said, her voice dripping with mock concern, *"Are you going to actually play or just sit there stalling, hoping I'll get bored and leave?"*

I folded my arms and studied the board, forcing a casual shrug. *"Wouldn't dream of boring you, Jess. Though, I do wonder if you remember that chess isn't just about looking pretty while you play."*

Jessica snorted, a quick flash of amusement in her eyes as she moved her knight with casual precision. "Is that why you're struggling? Must be hard to concentrate with all that big talk weighing you down."

"Oh, trust me," I replied, moving a pawn forward to block her next move, *"my focus is right where it needs to be. Though, I can't help but notice that you keep coming back for more. Getting attached?"*

"Attached? To what? Watching you lose?" She tilted her head, feigning an air of innocence. *"I just thought someone should help you learn humility, Dev. Clearly, I'm doing you a favor."*

I laughed, a low, genuine sound that even surprised me. Outside, the rain had picked up, creating a muted hush over the city that made their voices feel louder, more intimate somehow. My eyes drifted back to the board, but my focus kept straying to the way she tapped her fingers against her cheek when she was thinking, or the way her gaze sharpened whenever he made a move she hadn't predicted.

"Alright, since you're so confident..." I moved my rook, capturing her knight, and grinned, leaning back as if I'd just won the game. *"Care to explain how you missed that one, professor?"*

She pursed her lips, giving him a look that was equal parts amused and exasperated. *"Oh, don't celebrate just yet. Your victory lap's premature."*

Her bishop moved swiftly across the board, cornering my king. I hadn't even seen it coming, and the way her mouth curved into a triumphant smile had a strange effect on me— something that felt like frustration, but with an undercurrent of something more that I couldn't quite shake.

She glanced up, locking eyes with me, the rain-soaked world outside framing her in the window. *"Looks like I'm the one calling checkmate tonight."*

I leaned in, gaze steady, almost challenging. *"You're pretty good at this, Jess. Almost makes me wonder if there's something else you're angling for."*

She didn't look away. Her smile softened, just slightly, and for a beat, the sarcasm faded between us. *"Maybe I just like a good challenge."*

A quiet beat settled between us, and though we were still surrounded by the empty clink of cups and the low hum of conversations, I felt as though everything else had faded, leaving just the two of us and the game in front of us.

I tilted my head, studying her as if she were one of the pieces on the board. *"Well, don't think I'm going to make it easy for you."*

She raised her chin, her voice softer, almost playful. *"Wouldn't expect you to."*

We lingered in that silence for a heartbeat too long, something unspoken hanging in the air between us, an unnamed tension that neither dared acknowledge. But at that moment, I couldn't quite tell where our rivalry ended, and something else—something galvanic—might have begun.

Sitting alone in my room, my thoughts drifted back to Jessica. Funny how I could remember the exact details of her face, every stubborn line, and mocking smile, even though I'd never admit it to her. Jessica was like the color gray—not dull, no, but complicated. Layered. She was all those foggy hues mixed into one, the kind of gray that you could look at and still not see everything there was. Big, stormy eyes that could go from playful to piercing in a second. An Anglo-Indian look, with a faint olive tint to her skin that made her stand out, yet feel familiar.

Her hair was a wild, curly mess, always slightly damp from the rain that seemed to follow her around, falling over her face in a way that said she gave zero damns about trying to tame it. I'd never seen her without that untamed halo like it was some sort of symbol, a part of her armor against the world. She wore a septum piercing that suited her too well like it was crafted just for her. I couldn't imagine Jessica without it; it was the one bold thing that said *she's her own person*, and that she didn't have the time to worry about anyone else's expectations.

Then there was the tattoo—a jagged line of words curling down the side of her left forearm. I'd never got a close look at it until that night back in college. I'd almost forgotten about that moment, until now.

It was a day I'd never meant to remember this clearly. We'd just finished one of those impromptu chess matches— yet another argument between us that had somehow turned into a challenge. It was monsoon season, and by the time we left the building, the sky had opened up, drenching everything in sight. It was late, and the walk back to the dorms seemed longer than usual with the rain coming down in sheets. She hadn't complained, just cursed under her breath as she pushed wet hair out of her face, laughing that kind of laugh she did when everything was a mess, but she didn't care.

"Come on," I'd said, impulsively gesturing for her to follow me to my hostel, barely thinking about what I was saying. *"Dry off before you drown. You'll catch a cold."*

She'd given me a look, eyes narrowed. *"And you care because?"*

"Because," I shot back, trying to sound indifferent, *"I can't have my best chess rival getting sick on me. That's an easy win."*

I wasn't even sure why I said it, but she rolled her eyes and followed anyway.

In my room, she tugged off her soaked shirt with no ceremony, no hesitation, standing there in her sports bra as she rifled through my drawer for a dry t-shirt. I'd turned away, mostly to hide how flustered I suddenly felt, and that's when I noticed it—the tattoo.

I still remembered the shape of it, the dark ink curling in a messy line down her skin. The letters were small and jagged like she'd chosen them as an afterthought, but it felt... deliberate somehow like every word meant something she wasn't about to explain. I remember wondering if it was in a language I didn't know. Or maybe it was just Jessica— she'd probably enjoy the mystery, the way it kept people guessing.

"Staring?" Her voice had pulled me out of my thoughts, sharp and amused. She'd already slipped on my t-shirt, which hung loose on her frame and was grinning like she'd caught me in some embarrassing secret.

"Just wondering if you even know what that says," I'd replied, still trying to sound unaffected.

She'd tilted her head, giving me a look, and then shrugged. *"Maybe. Maybe not."* There was something playful in her voice, something that made it hard to look away.

Now, sitting here alone, I realized that moment had stuck with me for reasons I hadn't questioned at the time. Maybe it was how straightforward she was—no hesitation, no second-guessing. She was just... her. I never knew anyone who could make things that simple, even when they were complicated as hell.

And maybe that's why, all these months later, I still couldn't get her out of my head.

11

The December chill crept into the theater, making its way past cracked windows and rusted heaters, wrapping itself around the cast as we rehearsed for the annual play. Winter in Kolkata had its own quiet bite—mornings were foggy, and the evenings had a way of turning cozy spaces into close-knit worlds. Inside, the musty scent of old curtains mixed with the warmth of hot chai passed around in styrofoam cups as the theater crew scrambled to pull the production together.

I stood near the stage, waiting for my cue. I caught sight of Jessica on the opposite side, leaning against a wooden set piece. She was wrapped in a dark shawl over her costume, her hair a mess of wild curls spilling out, her big eyes fixed on the script in her hands. She looked so focused, so *there* in the moment, it was hard not to just stare.

Nitin nudged me, chuckling. *"Dev, buddy, don't drool. You're not subtle, you know."*

"Yeah, man," Bijoy added, grinning. *"You've been eyeing her like she's a seven-course meal."*

"Shut up," I muttered, but I couldn't help the smile tugging at my lips. *"Just... getting into character."*

"Right," Bijoy teased, drawing out the word. *"Good thing your character is supposed to look hopelessly in love."*

I rolled my eyes, shoving both of them playfully before making my way over to Jessica, ignoring their taunts.

As I approached, Jessica looked up, arching an eyebrow. *"Are you rehearsing how to walk, or just planning to kill time until the end of the world?"*

I casually smirked, folding my arms. *"Just making sure you know your lines. Wouldn't want you blanking on stage and making the rest of us look bad."*

"Right, because I'm the one with the problem remembering things." She tilted her head, barely hiding the amused spark in her eyes.

Another castmate called out from across the room, *"Jess, Dev, less flirting, more acting, please?"*

Jessica flashed a smile in their direction, her voice mockingly serious. *"It's called chemistry, people. Try to keep up."*

The others groaned while Nitin and Bijoy made exaggerated gagging sounds. *"Get a room!"* Bijoy called, earning laughs from everyone around them.

Unfazed, Jessica leaned closer to me, her voice dropping as if just for me. *"So, are we doing this or what?"*

There was a challenge in her gaze, playful but thrilling, the kind that made my heartbeat quicken. I held her stare, tone matching hers. *"Only if you think you can keep up."*

She stepped back into position, our banter giving way to the intensity of the scene. The play was a love story, tragic and full of tension, and now that it was our final year, the production had taken on an almost mythical importance. I couldn't tell if it was the character I was supposed to be playing or the quiet, unspoken thing that had always existed between us, but with every line, every glance, the boundary between acting and feeling blurred.

"Do you think... you could ever love me?" Jessica's voice wavered as she delivered her line, her eyes catching mine, holding them a beat too long. The question was meant for the play, yet it felt as if it lingered between us, real and raw.

I stepped closer, letting the silence stretch before I could respond with my line, my voice low, each word carefully placed. *"I think... it's too late not to."*

For a moment, I swore she held her breath. Her lips parted slightly, but she kept her composure, and I wondered if anyone else saw what was simmering beneath the surface, the almost magnetic pull keeping us there, wrapped in that quiet, electrified space between words.

The stage manager interrupted, clapping her hands. *"Okay, good! But let's work on that timing—you two keep staring as if it's a romance novel. Add some tension, people!"*

Nitin snickered from the seats, leaning back with a smirk. *"I dunno, I think we're witnessing something here. Maybe they should just go off-script and spare us all the drama."*

Jessica shot him a look, rolling her eyes. *"Keep dreaming, Nitin. Dev's not my type."*

"Oh yeah?" I shot back, grinning. *"You were just saying last week how lucky you were to have me as a scene partner."*

Jessica scoffed, folding her arms, but there was a glimmer in her eye that wasn't entirely sarcastic. "In your dreams, Dev. I said we're lucky. I didn't say anything about me needing you."

Our banter had everyone in stitches, but I noticed the way Jessica's expression softened for just a split second when the others were distracted. She gave me a quick look that was only for me, a barely-there smile that disappeared just as fast as it came.

Bijoy nudged Nitin, laughing under his breath. *"Man, this is better than the play."*

I ignored them, my eyes finding Jessica's again as the rehearsals wound down and people began to pack up. She tossed her shawl around her shoulders and gave me one last look as she headed toward the door, her smile playful, her eyes lingering.

"Are you coming, or are you just going to stand there?" she asked, her voice echoing through the nearly empty room.

I just shook my head, smiling as I followed her out into the cold winter night.

The night air was crisp, cutting through the usual Kolkata haze with a sharpness that made everything feel a little more alive. I walked alongside Jessica, our steps in sync, the city quiet and wide open in a way it rarely was. We'd fallen into a comfortable silence since we left the theater, both of us wrapped in our own thoughts, maybe too aware of each other's presence to break the moment with words.

Finally, I cleared my throat, sneaking a glance her way. *"So, tell me—when you're off to... wherever it is you're planning to go after all this, who are you going to torture with your so-called acting skills?"*

Jessica smirked, pulling her shawl tighter around herself. *"Torture? Is that what you call it? Because from where I stand, I'm the one carrying the whole show."*

"Right," I replied with a laugh. *"You mean the scene where you almost tripped on the props? I'm shocked they haven't rewritten that part just for you."*

She elbowed me, grinning despite herself. *"You're never going to let that go, are you?"*

We rounded a corner and spotted a small tea stall, tucked under the glow of a streetlamp, a single light in the otherwise dark street. The vendor waved us over, and we exchanged a glance before heading toward it. We ordered a cup of chai, letting the steam curl into the cold air, drawing warmth into our hands.

"So," I began, voice soft, *"you've got some grand plan, don't you? After college? Going to take over the world or something?"*

Jessica took a sip of her tea, her gaze distant. *"I thought I did. But it's funny how you think you have things sorted, and then you end up... somewhere else entirely."* She paused, then continued, her voice steadier. *"I'm leaving for London soon."*

I raised an eyebrow, trying to hide the flicker of surprise. *"You're really doing it? For theater?"*

"Yeah," she looked down as if the words she was about to say were as unexpected for her as they were for me. *"I'm leaving everything else behind. Psychology, all of it. My father... Well, he doesn't understand. Or... doesn't want to. I think I'm throwing away all these years for a pipe dream."*

I wanted to say something reassuring but sensed there was more she needed to get out, a heaviness she rarely showed. She took a breath, her fingers tightening around the cup.

"Ever since my mum passed, my dad and I... we just don't talk like we used to. It's like we're strangers in the same house." Her voice softened, almost to a whisper. *"I used to think he'd come around, that he'd see this is what I want to do for myself. But now I know... he just doesn't want me to go."*

I remembered a conversation we'd once shared at South Park Street Cemetery, her words quiet and vulnerable against the weight of the past. She'd opened up to me back then about her mum, the loss that had changed her world and left her and her father drifting further apart. And now, here we were again, with her on the verge of a whole new path, and the unresolved weight of that conversation lingered between them.

I wanted to reach out to close the space between us somehow, but I held back, simply letting the words hang between them. *"So... why London? Why not stay here, maybe try the theater scene?"*

She shrugged, a spark of defiance in her eyes. *"Because this is my choice. Not his, not anyone else's. It's something I have to do. I think... I owe it to myself."*

There was a quiet strength in her words, one I admired, even as the thought of her leaving gnawed at me.

"Guess that means you'll have to find someone else to push you, huh?" she said, her voice softer now, breaking into my thoughts.

I chuckled, keeping it light. *"Or maybe you'll have to stick around so I don't fall into mediocrity."*

She looked up at me, that familiar teasing glint in her eyes, but something softer, too. *"Oh, so the guy who's going to be a writer one day suddenly needs motivation?"*

I felt my pulse quicken. She was the only one who knew about this dream of mine, something I'd always kept close, too close to share with anyone else. *"I'm not going to be a writer. Just... trying to get better. It's not really my 'big move' like yours."*

Her gaze lingered, and for a moment, it was just us in the little aura spilling from the tea stall, and the quiet street around us. *"I think you'd be good at it,"* she said, her voice almost a murmur. *"In fact, I think you're afraid you might be."*

I felt the words land, the truth in them sharp but not unkind. *"Maybe I am,"* I admitted, barely louder than a whisper.

A rickshaw puller haggling with a passerby broke the silence, and Jessica looked away, giving a quick laugh, as if to brush off the weight of everything we hadn't said.

"Come on," she said, her voice playful, but her cheeks flushed, maybe from the cold, or maybe something else. *"Let's get moving before you turn all poetic on me about the night sky or whatever writers like you do."*

I laughed, feeling the warmth of the tea and the chilly night air all at once, my heartbeat unsteady. *"Too late. I'm already coming up with your exit monologue."*

She rolled her eyes, but her smile was soft, that hidden look lingering on her lips. As we walked back into the night, I couldn't shake the feeling that we'd just stepped closer to something real—something we couldn't quite put into words, yet couldn't stop wanting all the same.

A Lazy Afternoon in the College Field

It was one of those rare winter afternoons when practice wrapped up early, and the three of us—I, Nitin, and Bijoy— collapsed on the grass, talking idly. The air was chilly, with that earthy scent that seemed to cling to every inch of the Kolkata campus.

Nitin nudged me with a mischievous grin. *"So, Dev, you never told us—what was the deal with that Nandita girl back in school?"*

"Oh, you mean the one who used to follow him around the entire year like a lovesick puppy?" Bijoy chimed in, raising an

eyebrow. *"Always hanging by his side whenever he wasn't too busy being hopeless over... What was her name again? Ah, right. Ahaana."*

I rolled my eyes, lying back against the grass. *"You guys have too much free time to remember my middle school drama."*

"Oh, come on," Nitin teased. *"You were practically famous for it. There you were, clueless as ever, while Nandita trailed after you, trying to get your attention. But nope, all you saw was Ahaana, who didn't even know you existed half the time because she was too busy with that science guy. What a tragic love triangle."*

Bijoy laughed, adding, *"And don't even get me started on the epic 'Notebook Scandal.' Didn't Nandita once write Dev + Nandita on your notebook cover?"*

"Don't remind me," I groaned, but couldn't help grinning. *"It was in the middle of history class. I turned to find the notebook, and there it was, written in huge letters."*

"And what did you do? You tried to scratch it out, right?" Nitin was practically in stitches.

"Like a madman!" Bijoy laughed. *"Probably had no clue Nandita was right there, watching him butcher her masterpiece. Imagine her heart-shattering in slow motion."*

I chuckled, my head shaking. *"It's not my fault she had terrible timing. Besides, Ahaana was the only one I saw back then. Nothing anyone did could change that."*

"Ah, Ahaana," Nitin sighed theatrically as if reminiscing over an old crush. *"The girl who could bring down empires with her half-smile. And there she was, dating that science guy. Poor Dev, tragically heartbroken before he even had a chance."*

I threw a piece of grass at them both, laughing. *"Keep talking. Remind me why I still hang out with you two."*

"Oh, we're all you've got, man." Bijoy slapped my back, grinning. *"And who else would drag up every embarrassing memory you've tried to forget? What else are friends for?"*

Nitin sighed dramatically, rolling onto his back. *"At least you had someone to pine over. What about us? All I've ever gotten is I think we're better as friends on repeat. It's like the universe conspired against me."*

Bijoy chuckled. *"What did you expect, Nitin? Your idea of flirting is asking a girl if she wants to watch you bowl in cricket practice. That's not exactly charming."*

"Hey, some girls find sports attractive!" Nitin protested, crossing his arms. *"It's just that they seem to prefer guys who can actually hold a conversation, unlike me. Maybe I should try texting instead of talking."*

"Yeah, because texting has done wonders for your love life," Bijoy snickered. *"Remember the girl you texted your entire cricket strategy to? She ghosted you faster than I've ever seen."*

Nitin groaned, hiding his face in his hands. *"Can't a guy just live in peace? Meanwhile, Bijoy, your plan to become a cricket coach is working out great, right? I mean, how many girls do you think are lining up for the guy who wears cricket pads everywhere?"*

Bijoy shot him a mock glare. *"Hey, I have plans! I'll coach the state team, and when I do, I'll be swimming in admirers. It's just a waiting game, really."*

I rolled my eyes as I felt the warmth of their banter settle around me. These two—their ridiculous humor, hopeless dating lives, and endless cricket dreams—had grounded him in ways he couldn't fully put into words.

They lay back in companionable silence, letting the laughter fade as they watched the sky. For a few moments,

Dev let himself soak it in—the easy banter, the teasing, and the sense that no matter what the future held, he'd always have memories like this to ground him.

Bijoy leaned back, looking over at Nitin with a raised eyebrow. *"So, Nitin, what's the big plan after college? Joining the textile empire, then?"*

Nitin gave a wry smile, his usual carefree sarcasm in full swing. *"Arre haan, bas yeh English ka degree khatam karo, then straight to my uncle's business. All this Shakespeare, Milton—it's fun and all, but you think it's gonna help me sell fabric in Bihar?"* He chuckled, his words rolling out in his unique Hindustani-Bengali accent, each sentence a playful blend of the two worlds he straddled.

Nitin had a rugged look about him, wiry and sharp-featured with messy curls that seemed to defy any attempt at control. Tall but lean, he carried himself with a mix of cocky confidence and laid-back charm. He dressed casually—rolled-up sleeves, frayed jeans—and somehow always looked like he'd just come from a cricket game. His accent was a reflection of his roots, his Hindi fused with the occasional Bengali word and a thick, earthy tone that made every conversation feel like a scene from a Mumbai masala film.

"Imagine me," he continued, *"standing at a bazaar stall, convincing these bidi-smoking babus to buy cotton, explaining supply and demand in English! Half my relatives think my degree is just a fancy pass to sit in my uncle's office. Not that I mind, but it's hilarious they're right."*

Nitin leaned back, gesturing wildly. *"Arre yaar, you two won't understand. Picture this—I walk into my uncle's office, and all his guys, these proper paan-chewing types, are looking at me like, Yeh kaun hai jo humare textile ka raja banega? And here*

I am, with an English degree in one hand, trying to explain the benefits of polyester blend in my best Queen's English."

I chuckled, *"Yeah, and then they'll throw you out on the street. Yeh English babu nahi chalega yahan, they'll say."*

"Exactly!" Nitin pointed, laughing. *"Arre, these guys will say, Yeh shirt aur jeans waala aa gaya factory sambhalne. They don't care about Conrad, Keats, none of that. All they wanna know is how I'm gonna help them sell fabrics from Patna to Patiala."*

Bijoy couldn't resist chiming in. *"So why even bother with this degree? You could have just skipped all this and gone straight to the empire."*

Nitin shrugged, putting on a mock-serious face. "Kya karoon? Maa wanted me to be 'educated,' to have degree ka izzat, as if that's going to change my luck with girls here." He winked, adding with a grin, "Though, maybe when I'm rolling in textile cash, I'll be more popular. Tab toh tum dono mujhe bhool hi jaoge."

I snorted. *"More popular? With your Hindi-Bengali accent convincing everyone you're some big-shot businessman?"*

"Arre haan, you laugh now, Dev, but when I'm importing silks and linens, you'll be the first one asking for a discount," Nitin shot back, his face splitting into a grin. *"Mere kapde me toh tumhara likhne ka obsession bhi chamak uthega."*

The three friends strolled over to the chai stand just outside campus, where the clatter of clay cups and sizzling pans welcomed them like an old ritual. The warm, spicy aroma of chai filled the air as they leaned against the counter, cups in hand.

Nitin took a slow sip, looking over to me and Bijoy with a raised eyebrow. *"So you two go way back, huh? I still can't* believe you played on the same cricket team in school and didn't even talk to each other. What were you, rivals or just clueless?"

Bijoy chuckled, shrugging. *"Rivals? Nah, we weren't even that interesting. Just batchmates. Dev was always quiet, keeping to himself, and I was busy bowling my heart out, hoping someone would notice."*

I smirked, nudging him. *"Don't play modest. You were basically a celebrity with your bowling. Remember that one match where you took four wickets? Everyone thought you'd make it to the under-16 state team."*

"Yeah, except I didn't," Bijoy laughed, shrugging it off. *"But I'll admit, cricket gave me a reason to show up to school. I wasn't exactly the academic type."*

Nitin gave a dramatic sigh, shaking his head. *"And look at you now. All that practice, and what's it gotten you? A spot on our underpaid, underappreciated college team, and a coaching dream you aren't even sure about."*

Bijoy rolled his eyes but couldn't hold back a laugh. *"As if you're in a better place, Mr. Textile Mogul. You can't even pick between Browning and shalwar-kameez."*

"Touché, touché." Nitin raised his chai cup in mock surrender, grinning. *"At least you two have history. I didn't even know Dev existed until college. And here I thought I was the only tortured soul who hated exams."*

I laughed, glancing at Bijoy. *"Yeah, well, school didn't exactly set us up to be best friends. It was mostly cricket, then home. We barely even talked back then."*

"But somehow," Bijoy added, smirking, *"we both ended up here, with you as our third-wheel idiot."*

"Oi!" Nitin huffed, clutching his chest in mock offense. *"I'm the star of this friend group, and don't you forget it. Someday, when*

I'm rich off textile money, you'll both be begging me to sponsor your obscure cricket dreams and Dev's writing aspirations."

"*Writing?*" I scoffed, rolling my eyes. "*Please, as if I'm some tortured artist scribbling life's secrets in a dusty journal.*"

But Nitin wasn't convinced. He narrowed his eyes, smirking. "*Sure, sure. Then what's that notebook you're always guarding like a family heirloom? You think we don't see you scribbling away at night?*"

I shrugged, trying to play it off. "*Just notes, random stuff... nothing important.*"

"*Right,*" Bijoy chimed in, grinning. "*Random notes you'd rather die than let us read. I bet there's a whole saga in there, waiting to be published. You already act like a poet half the time— brooding, mysterious, thinking we haven't noticed. Just admit it already; you've got the writer bug.*"

I tried to brush it off with a laugh but could tell by the look on Nitin's face that his friend knew more than he let on. Three of us stood there, sharing a look that spoke more than any words could. We weren't just classmates or teammates anymore; somehow, between the jokes and jabs, we'd become the people who knew each other's dreams and fears, even if we didn't always say it out loud.

Nitin lifted his chai cup again, eyes gleaming with humor. "*To us—the cricketer, the mogul, and the writer. May our futures be as bright as this burning hot chai.*"

They all laughed, clinking their cups together, each secretly hoping that somehow, despite the uncertainty, they'd all find their place in the world.

12

"*London? You're serious?*"

The words slipped out of me before I could filter the shock from my voice. But there was no time for restraint; Jessica had just dropped the news casually, in that carefree, half-smiling way of hers, as though she were commenting on the weather. But I knew her better—there was a nervousness in the way her hand clenched around her coffee cup, as if maybe even she was still trying to believe it.

The semester was slipping through our fingers, each day swallowed up in a rush of projects, farewells, and last-minute plans. Winter cast a final chill over campus, and graduation was approaching faster than I'd ever imagined. Everything felt like a frenzied blur of goodbyes and last experiences, but somehow, Jessica had taken me by surprise.

Nitin and Bijoy were right there with us, and from the stunned silence, I knew they were just as taken aback as I was. The three of us exchanged glances, the weight of her words slowly settling in. Bijoy raised an eyebrow, half-laughing, trying to mask his surprise with the usual humor. "*London, huh? So, what? You'll just be sipping tea, wearing fancy hats, and forgetting all about us, right?*"

Jessica rolled her eyes but laughed, her fingers tapping against her cup. *"It's theater, not tea parties. And yes, Bijoy, I'll send you a postcard if you promise to stop bothering me on Facebook."*

Nitin leaned in, nudging her shoulder. *"And your dad's cool with all this? Mr. Dasgupta just happily waving goodbye to his daughter running off to the arts?"*

Jessica paused, her expression flickering, but she covered it with a shrug. *"Not exactly. But this isn't about him. This... this is something I need to do for me."*

There was a finality in her voice that hit me in a way I wasn't prepared for. Everyone knew Jessica was ambitious, that she wasn't bound to stay in one place for long. But London... that was real, that was final.

The conversation drifted after that, dissolving into the usual banter as Bijoy and Nitin steered us back to safer ground, throwing around jokes about how we'd all end up unemployed artists if we didn't play our cards right. But all the while, I kept glancing at her, that part of me struggling to grasp that, in just a few months, she'd be gone. We all would.

The sky started to dim, casting long shadows across campus as we lingered on the quad, reluctant to let the day end. The others eventually peeled away, Nitin and Bijoy heading off to join some of the guys for an impromptu game of cricket. Jessica and I were left standing alone, our steps slowing as we neared the old tucked-away courtyard on the east side of campus, where the ivy-covered walls felt like they were holding our secrets, the chill air thick with the smell of damp stone. She sat down on one of the stone benches, pulling her coat tight around her—the place where so many of our late-night talks had happened over the years.

The air thickened with the scent of damp earth and winter's fading chill. We sank onto the stone steps, side by side, the weight of our unfinished conversation hanging between us.

I broke the silence first, though my voice came out softer than I intended. *"You're really doing this. London."*

She looked at me, her face trying to catch the last traces of sunlight, but there was something bittersweet in her smile. *"I have to. Staying here... it would be safe, comfortable even. But this is my shot. If I don't take it now, I'll spend my whole life wondering."*

I nodded, but the words tangled in my chest. I wanted to say something, anything to let her know how much it mattered that she was here with me. But that felt selfish, like asking a bird to stay grounded just because you enjoy watching it fly.

Jessica sighed, her voice dropping, as if she could sense the hesitation in me. *"Dev, it's not goodbye forever. We'll still... we'll still have this. Here."* She placed a hand lightly over her heart, her eyes searching mine.

Something inside me gave way, the careful distance I'd tried to keep from her slipping through my fingers. I reached out, brushing a stray curl away from her face, letting my hand linger longer than I probably should have. Her breath hitched, just barely, and in that moment, with her so close, I felt the weight of everything I hadn't said, hadn't dared to say.

"Then don't forget us," I murmured, my voice barely more than a whisper. *"Don't forget this."*

She held my gaze, her fingers lightly curling over mine. *"Dev,"* she whispered, her voice laced with something raw, something that made me ache. *"I couldn't even if I tried."*

We sat there as the campus lights flickered on, illuminating us in a soft glow. And though neither of us moved, I knew that this—these few precious moments—were as close as we would get to saying everything we couldn't put into words.

In hindsight, Jessica's acceptance into that London theater program hit me harder than I'd let on. I told myself I was proud, that this was her moment, her chance to live the dream she'd hinted at between all the psychology classes and restless college nights. But underneath the congratulations and the jokes, there was this gnawing ache, a sinking feeling I couldn't shake. Jessica wasn't just leaving for a course; she was leaving us, leaving everything we'd built here. Part of me wanted to say something, to ask her to stay or to admit what her absence would actually mean. But another part—the part that always held back, always tried to play it cool—kept me silent. She was going to London, and I'd just have to learn to be proud of her from a distance, knowing that the girl who'd shared pieces of herself with me would soon be a world away.

The Annual Play – A Last Act Together

The night before Christmas, the college auditorium was alive with last-minute preparations. Our play, the final one for our college careers, had an electric energy to it as if everyone knew this was the end of something unforgettable. Exams were over, holidays were just around the corner, and soon enough, all of us would be going our separate ways.

I paced backstage, trying to settle my nerves. I'd played cricket in front of a packed crowd more times than I could count, but the stage felt different. Maybe it was because tonight, I wasn't just another player. Tonight, I was sharing the spotlight with her.

Jessica brushed past me, adjusting her costume, her presence familiar and grounding. Even in the chaos, she looked effortlessly calm, her eyes sharp with focus. She didn't say anything at first, just gave me a small nod, a signal that we were in this together.

"Hope you don't forget your lines, Dasgupta," I muttered, trying to mask my own nerves.

She scoffed, smirking as she adjusted her collar. *"Please. I've only been carrying this play on my shoulders all semester. Try to keep up."*

Our friends—Nitin, Bijoy, and the rest—were all front and center, eagerly waiting to heckle us from the audience. The plan was to go out afterward for a farewell celebration, but this moment, right here, felt like our true goodbye.

The play began, and everything flowed, each scene more intense than the last. Our characters were locked in an emotional arc that strangely mirrored our own. My character's lines, once just memorized words, felt real like I was saying things to her I'd never have the guts to say otherwise.

In our last scene, Jessica's character had to confess her hidden feelings to me. Her voice dropped to a whisper, raw and vulnerable, the whole room fell silent.

"There are truths I could never speak, ones you'll carry unknowingly in the quiet spaces between us." She murmured, her eyes meeting mine in a way that felt like a secret just for us.

Her hand reached toward me, just as rehearsed, but this time it lingered longer. I felt the warmth of her fingers brush mine, and for a heartbeat, the whole stage faded away, leaving just the two of us. Her gaze, intense and searching, had an edge of something real, something that wasn't just part of the script.

When the play ended, the crowd erupted in applause, but we barely heard it. The rest of the cast took their bows, but

Jessica and I stayed close, stealing glances, our breathing still in sync. For that brief moment under the hot stage lights, with the audience cheering, we were the only two people in the world.

Backstage afterward, Nitin and Bijoy cornered me, grinning like idiots.

"So, what's next, Dev? Off to Bollywood together?" Nitin teased, nudging me in the ribs.

Bijoy laughed. *"Maybe she'll call you from London when she's famous. Or forget all about you."*

I forced a laugh, brushing it off, but Jessica caught my eye from across the room. She walked over, mock-smirking at our friends as if daring them to say more, and looked directly at me.

"Walk me out?" she asked quietly.

I nodded, leaving the others behind as we stepped out into the chilly December air, where the campus was blanketed in a soft winter quiet. We walked along the familiar path near the old library, neither of us speaking at first, both of us knowing that words were unnecessary.

After a while, she broke the silence. *"London's a big leap, you know?"*

I shrugged, struggling to keep my voice light. *"Yeah, but you've never been one to stay still. It suits you."*

She let out a soft laugh, but there was an edge to it. *"I'll miss all this... the college, the people. You."*

The last word hung between us, heavy and raw. She looked down, fidgeting with a loose thread on her sleeve. *"We'll still keep in touch, right? Facebook messages, maybe a call now and then?"*

I swallowed, my throat tight. *"Of course. You can't get rid of me that easily, Jess."*

She smiled, but it was a sad smile, the kind that hinted at things left unsaid. Her hand brushed mine, her fingers cold and tentative, yet familiar. We stood there, our breaths clouding the air, the weight of the moment settling over us like the softest snowfall.

Just before she turned to go, she whispered, *"Goodnight, Dev,"* her voice soft but lingering, leaving something unfinished in the air between us. The way she looked at me, eyes steady and unguarded, felt like a question I couldn't answer yet—a promise waiting on the edge of tomorrow.

As she walked away, the campus lights softened her silhouette, casting a glow that made her seem almost unreal, a part of this place and yet already beyond it. I watched her disappear into the winter quiet, an ache settling somewhere deep, the kind that only grows as time edges closer to goodbye.

And I stood there alone, knowing we'd have one more moment together before everything changed, a final act waiting for us, as if the curtain hadn't yet fully fallen on whatever this was, whatever it might still be.

The college farewell was in full swing: laughter and music filled the old, decorated hall, friends posing for last photos under the fading yellow lights. But soon, Jessica and I slipped away, unnoticed, ducking through the back gate and out into the cold night, leaving the chaos behind us. We found a quiet spot by an empty terrace on campus, a place we'd sometimes escape to between classes. That night, though, it felt different, almost too quiet, charged with the weight of everything left unsaid.

Jessica pulled out a flask, a little smile playing on her lips as she handed it to me. *"Couldn't leave without a proper send-off, right?"*

I chuckled, taking it from her. *"Trust you to keep things interesting."* The burn of the alcohol spread warmth through my chest, grounding me in that moment, just the two of us, passing the flask back and forth. The hum of campus life faded into the background as we sat shoulder to shoulder, gazing out at the faint city lights.

"Bet you're relieved," she teased, her voice quiet, her guard dropped in a way that felt rare. *"Free to leave Kolkata, start fresh in Mumbai—new city, new faces, no strings."* She kept it playful, but I noticed the faint tremor beneath her words.

I leaned back, smirking. *"Says the one bound for London with stars in her eyes. If anyone's got big plans, it's you."*

Jessica rolled her eyes and nudged my shoulder. *"It's not that simple. London... It feels like jumping into the unknown. A lot to give up."*

I studied her face, the way her eyes drifted to the sky as she spoke. *"Maybe that's what it takes. You've always wanted this."*

She nodded, almost whispering. *"Yeah, I do. But... not everything I want is there."*

Her words settled between us, heavier than I'd expected, and for a moment, I just looked at her. She seemed so different, almost vulnerable, and as she looked away, her hand brushed against mine—just a quick, fleeting touch, but enough to make me pause. Her fingers lingered a second too long before she pulled back, cheeks slightly flushed.

We sat there in silence, not really seeing anything except each other, the world around us fading out until it felt like it was just us in that shared quiet. And before I even registered what was happening, we were leaning toward each other, closing the distance that had always lingered between us. I reached up, brushing a strand of hair from her face, my fingertips grazing her cheek, and for that breath, everything we'd held back slipped free.

Our lips met halfway, hesitant at first, then deepening into a slow, gentle kiss. It was unplanned, unguarded, a release of every unspoken feeling wrapped up in one quiet moment. Her warmth met mine, her breath mingling with mine, and I felt that pull as if we were unraveling all the restraint we'd ever practiced.

When we finally pulled back, both a little stunned, she let out a soft laugh, though I could hear the ache in it.

"Well... that's one way to say goodbye," she murmured, trying to sound light, but her voice wavered.

I laughed, rubbing the back of my neck, though my chest tightened at the thought of leaving her. *"Guess so,"* I managed, but something in me wished she'd say more.

Instead, she reached into her bag, pulling out a book I hadn't noticed her carrying all night. It was a worn first edition of one of my favorite authors, something I'd mentioned in passing years ago. She handed it to me with a quiet smile.

"Here," she said, her voice almost a whisper. *"I thought you might want some company in Mumbai."*

I stared at the book, stunned, then looked back up at her. *"Jess, this... you didn't have to."*

"I wanted to." She looked away, smiling softly. *"You've always been the dreamer, Dev. Thought you could use a reminder."*

She didn't tell me about the letter she'd tucked between the pages, the one she'd rewritten a dozen times. I wouldn't find it until later, those raw, unspoken words finally laid bare. But in that moment, she leaned back, her face serene, as if she'd given me something precious that she'd held onto for far too long. I didn't open the book then. Instead, we sat there in the quiet, our unspoken story tucked between pages I'd discover later when she was already miles away.

New Year's Eve arrived, bringing with it an air of inevitable goodbyes. Jessica's flight was in a few hours, and the three of us—Nitin, Bijoy, and I—had gathered on campus for one last send-off. There were laughs and jokes, the usual, each one of us hiding what it really meant to see her go.

"London will never be the same again after you, Jess," Bijoy said with a grin, raising an imaginary toast.

Jessica rolled her eyes. *"Stop, Bijoy. I'll be back to haunt you guys soon enough."*

Nitin smirked, nudging me. *"Not so sure about this guy here though,"* His voice softened, and he shot me a look that held more weight than he'd usually dare. *"He might even miss you."*

We all laughed, but I could feel the tension tightening around us. After a while, Nitin and Bijoy made excuses to leave, clapping me on the shoulder and giving Jessica a final wave. And then, it was just the two of us, standing in the quiet emptiness of the campus.

"You know, it still doesn't feel real," I said, looking down at my shoes. *"That you're leaving."*

She laughed lightly, but I could hear the ache beneath it. *"It doesn't feel real to me either."* She paused, catching my gaze, a sad smile hovering at the edges of her lips. *"Promise you'll keep in touch? At least a text now and then?"*

I nodded, managing a faint smile. *"Promise. And hey... London's just a few hours away, right?"*

"Sure," she whispered, her voice barely audible. *"Just a few hours."*

We stood there, the silence stretching between us, neither of us ready to break the spell. Finally, as the clock struck midnight, I took a breath, reaching for words that seemed just out of reach.

"Jess, I... if things had been different... if I had the words to say it..." She looked up, her eyes shining with something I couldn't name, and nodded as if she understood. She gave my hand one last squeeze, her fingers lingering just a second longer than usual before slipping away.

Then, with a small, knowing smile, she whispered, *"Goodbye, Dev."* And just like that, she turned and walked toward the waiting taxi, her silhouette fading into the night as the city lights glimmered in the distance.

13

Mumbai in 2015 was nothing short of a sensory overload. The moment I stepped out of the station, it hit me like a scene from one of those old Bollywood movies—Shah Rukh's *Dilwale Dulhania Le Jayenge*, perhaps, but grittier, faster-paced, and far from any picturesque European backdrop. Here, it was the hum of the local trains, the scent of masala in the air, the unapologetic chaos of crowds pushing through narrow lanes under flickering street lights.

For all the noise and rush, there was a magnetic quality about this city, a feeling I could only describe as... alive. That part struck me. Every street seemed like it had its own story, its own voice. This was the year when *Tamasha* was stirring hearts, and in a way, I felt like Ranbir's character—trying to make sense of my own story, blending in, but always feeling slightly apart, like I was watching it all from behind a camera lens.

The office was nothing like I'd imagined—a dingy building tucked away from the glamour of Marine Drive, more fitting for an indie film set than any glitzy rom-com. I was part of a small publishing house, assigned to a team where everyone had a dream novel tucked into their desk drawer, though they'd never admit it. It was strange, this world where words were currency, each draft fought over as if it might change the world.

Writing, for me, felt like catching whispers in a crowd and piecing them together to form a picture no one else had quite seen before. And yet, every time I tried to explain it, I felt... tongue-tied. I'd scribbled words down in notebooks for years, but to say *I'm a writer* felt heavy. It's as if declaring it out loud would make it real, and there was a part of me that wasn't ready to confront it just yet.

Settling into my new life in Mumbai was like learning a new language. The city breathed differently, with a rhythm I could barely keep up with. The days at the publishing house were long—endless hours of editing manuscripts, wrestling with clunky paragraphs, coaxing stories into shape. It felt like I was seeing words from the inside out, the small stitches that held them together. There was a thrill to it, knowing each page could be a stepping stone to something bigger, even if right now I was just one pair of hands in a massive, unseen machine.

Evenings, though, were mine. I'd walk the narrow lanes of Bandra or Dadar, seek out small cafés hidden between old bookshops, and find the city's secret places where writers and artists gathered. Mumbai had its own current of people who lived in words, who recited poems to strangers over chai and argued about Neruda in dimly lit rooms. Here, finally, I felt I could belong, blending into this strange, beautiful mosaic.

But even with all this, Jessica still slipped into my thoughts. Sometimes, I'd catch myself on Facebook, fingers hovering over her profile. I'd scroll, wondering if she was already swept up in London's whirlwind. I'd imagine her in some rehearsal space, completely absorbed, looking as fierce and focused as I'd seen her during our college play. I'd convince myself she was too busy to think of Kolkata, to think of us—of me. And maybe, I told myself, that was how it should be.

One night, as I was sorting through manuscripts, my supervisor handed me a new draft—a story by an emerging writer, one that needed heavy edits. I skimmed the first few lines, and something stopped me. The story was about a character leaving his hometown, chasing dreams in a city where he didn't belong. I didn't know why, but it resonated. I read it again, slowly this time, tracing every word, letting each line sink in. It felt too close like the writer had somehow gotten into my head, lifted bits of my own life, and placed them here.

Over the next few weeks, I worked on this story late into the nights, almost obsessively. I rewrote passages, reworked dialog, and poured myself into every small revision. Somewhere in the process, I started to understand something about writing. It wasn't just about capturing life—it was about translating everything left unsaid, putting feelings into words that would never find voice otherwise. It was a way to hold onto things, to keep people close, even when they were miles away.

And somewhere in those quiet hours, I began scribbling in a notebook of my own. It felt different this time. I wasn't just pouring out thoughts in a journal—I was creating something. This was for me, not hidden away or guarded, but something I could finally own. And for the first time, I felt ready to put my own story down, line by line, as if somehow, in all of this, I was finding my way back to myself.

That weekend, after I'd finally gotten a few days to myself, I decided to sort through the pile of books I'd hauled from home. They'd been sitting in the corner of my new place, stacked haphazardly, still dusty from the train ride. I'd shoved them aside when I'd first arrived, caught up in the whirlwind of new beginnings. Now, with some time on my hands, I started pulling them out, one by one, arranging them on the small, creaky shelf by the window.

When my fingers brushed against a familiar, worn cover, I froze. Jessica's gift. The first edition, the one she'd handed me that night in Kolkata. I hadn't opened it since I'd left; in some strange way, I'd almost been afraid to. I turned it over, feeling the slight texture of the cover, the corners soft from use. As I flipped through the pages, a small piece of paper fell out, fluttering to the floor.

It was her handwriting. The letter.

Dev,

This isn't a goodbye, not really. I don't think I could ever say goodbye to you, even if I wanted to. You've been... I don't even know how to put it into words. This steady, quiet presence, the person who saw me when no one else was looking. And I think that's what scares me most about leaving. The idea of not having you there, in the little ways I've gotten used to—the way you finish my sentences, how you somehow know exactly what I'm thinking just by looking at me.

You've always understood me, even when I didn't understand myself. It's like we've existed in this strange space all our own, and it never needed explaining or fixing. Part of me wonders if I'll ever find that again, this... thing we've had, whatever you'd call it.

I'm not just chasing some dream, Dev. London is where I'm supposed to find out who I am and who I want to be, but every part of me aches to think about doing it without you. And the truth is, if I ever had the choice—if there was even a sliver of a chance—I'd want to live that dream with you. With your quiet confidence, your ridiculous stubbornness, your way of listening to every word I say as if it means something.

When I lost my mum, I told myself that opening up wasn't worth it, that feeling too much was dangerous. But then there was you, with your smirk and those eyes that could look right through every wall I put up. You've made me feel like it's okay to be who I am, messy and complicated and unfinished.

Maybe I never said the words because I was afraid they'd come with consequences I couldn't control. But here they are now, written down, too late for me to take back. If you're reading this, I hope it means you're somewhere far away, living the life you always dreamed of. And if you ever think back on us, I hope you remember this, Dev—I loved you. Completely and quietly, in a way that I thought would keep us safe. I loved you, even if we never called it that.

Take care of my heart, Dev. You've been holding it all along.

Yours,

Jess

I closed my eyes, her words still ringing in my mind, bringing her vividly back to me as if she were right there, standing beside me again. I didn't know what to do with the flood of emotions crashing over me. Part of me wanted to laugh, to cry, to call her right then and there, but I knew that wasn't what she wanted. She'd left her words for me to keep, just as I had left things unsaid.

I folded the letter and placed it back between the pages, carefully, as though sealing something fragile. There, among my other books, it would stay. And maybe one day, I'd find the right words, the way she had, to answer the parts of me she'd left behind. Alone in this vast, foreign city, the silence felt unbearable, so I did the only thing that made sense—I called Nitin.

The phone rang for what felt like forever before Nitin's voice finally cut in, groggy and annoyed. *"Bro, it's late. This better be good."*

I hesitated, my voice unsteady. *"Sorry, man. I just... I found this letter from Jessica."*

He paused, and I could sense the shift in his tone immediately. *"Jess? You mean, that Jess?"*

"Yeah." I took a shaky breath, not sure how to explain what I was feeling. *"I don't know, Nit... She wrote things I—I think I felt the same way but never managed to say. And now she's gone, you know? It's too late."*

There was a short silence on his end before he sighed. *"Hang on, let me add Bijoy."*

A few moments later, Bijoy's sleepy voice joined the line, and without much explanation, I began reading pieces of the letter aloud. My voice barely held steady, but I knew they were listening, even though we were miles apart.

When I stopped, Bijoy's voice was the first to break the silence. *"She's in London now, right? You know, Dev, sometimes people drift apart because they need to find parts of themselves that don't fit in the places they started. That doesn't mean they forget who they left behind."*

Nitin, softer than usual, added, *"Jess was... different. But you were different with her, too, Dev. Maybe you needed each other back then, just to get to where you are now."*

I let out a long sigh, watching the faint glow of the city lights outside my window. *"It's just this... empty feeling. Like she's still here but also not. Like I'll never get the chance to say what I should have said."*

"Maybe you don't have to," Bijoy murmured. *"You loved her, Dev. And maybe she knew that, even without the words. Maybe that's enough."*

Their words settled in, offering an odd sense of comfort, even as the ache lingered. I could hear Nitin trying to lighten the mood. *"You know, Jess always said you were too much of a dreamer. You're in Mumbai now, buddy—maybe it's time to live some of those dreams instead of just talking about them."*

I managed a small laugh. *"Yeah, maybe,"* and with that, I felt a warmth I hadn't felt in days, knowing that even though they weren't here, I wasn't entirely alone.

We drifted into lighter talk after that, laughing at old stories until the night softened everything. By the time I finally said goodbye, I felt ready to tuck Jessica's memory somewhere safe without letting it weigh me down. I looked at the letter one last time before slipping it back between the pages of the book. With a quiet smile, I whispered, *"Goodbye, Jess,"* and shut the book, somehow feeling lighter, ready to face tomorrow.

After that night, I buried myself in the chaos of Mumbai. Work at the publishing house was fast-paced and demanding— barely a second to pause, just the way I needed it to be. Every morning started with a crowded train ride, crammed shoulder to shoulder with people who, like me, were all chasing something. The city seemed to never rest; it pulsed with a strange energy that was both exhilarating and exhausting.

The work itself was relentless but rewarding. I spent hours buried in manuscripts, editing paragraphs, and sifting through stories. Some were brilliant, others barely passable, but every now and then, I'd find a gem—a line or a character that would jump off the page and make the grind worth it. Mumbai had a way of making me feel like a small part of something vast as if each day had its own rhythm that I was slowly learning to keep up with.

I started to discover pockets of the city that became my escape: a quiet bookstore tucked away in Fort, the food stalls by Juhu Beach, and the small coffee shop near my rented flat that served the best masala chai. These little places became my own, grounding me amidst the whirlwind of deadlines and night shifts. Sometimes, I'd find myself on Marine Drive after a long day, staring at the sea and letting the noise of the waves drown out everything else. The city stretched out in front of me, filled with lights and possibilities, and even though it was overwhelming, I felt strangely at home.

The new responsibilities at work also brought a sharper focus to my own writing. For the first time, I started to understand how stories were shaped, and how the smallest edits could shift a character or even an entire plot. I'd always been a reader, but now I was getting a glimpse of the craft that turned words into something more. Late at night, I'd come home, open my own notebook, and scribble ideas down, fueled by a sense of purpose I hadn't felt in years.

And, inevitably, days started to stack up, then weeks. The memory of Kolkata, of Jess and the life I'd left behind, began to fade into something quieter, softer. I could still feel the ache now and then, a lingering thought in the back of my mind, but Mumbai had a way of keeping me too occupied to dwell on it. Here, everything was new—new places, new people, new challenges. It was as though life was nudging me forward, leaving little space for looking back.

In those crowded trains, the late-night edits, and the endless hum of Mumbai, I was beginning to find my footing again. The city might have been wild, even ruthless, but somewhere within its frenzy, I was learning what it meant to live and to let go.

Four months had passed since that literary festival, and in all that time, Sarah's black card had remained buried in the depths of my wallet, tucked away between old receipts and forgotten notes. I'd thought about calling her countless times, each time convincing myself it wasn't the right moment, or that I was too busy. But as the days blurred into weeks and the noise of Mumbai became the soundtrack to my life, I found myself thinking of her more often than I cared to admit.

One evening, after another long day at the publishing house—sifting through manuscripts, editing copy, and trying to make my mark in an industry that felt as fast and unpredictable as the city itself—I decided, on a whim, to pull out the card.

My apartment was quiet, the city's usual hum of horns and chatter seeping in through the window. I stared at the black card for a moment longer than I intended. It felt like a symbol of something I couldn't quite grasp. I had no clear idea of why I had hesitated for so long, but tonight, something shifted. I wasn't sure if it was the weight of the city itself, the unspoken loneliness of it all, or just a curiosity to reconnect with someone who, in that brief exchange at the festival, had felt like a spark in a place that had otherwise felt like a blur.

With a deep breath, I dialed her number.

It rang for a few moments before she picked up, her voice clear and familiar. *"Hello?"*

I hesitated, my heart quickening at the sudden rush of memories. *"Hey, Sarah. It's Dev. From the lit fest."*

There was a beat of silence, and then her voice, softer but warm, reached me. *"Dev? Wow, I wasn't expecting to hear from you. How's Mumbai treating you?"*

"Busy as ever," I said with a slight chuckle, trying to sound casual, though I could feel my pulse quickening. *"Getting used to it, though."*

"I think that's the key," she laughed. *"It's like the city makes you keep up or get left behind."*

I smiled, leaning back against the couch. The conversation was easy like it had been back at the festival, the way we had slipped into talking about books, life, and everything in between. But then she shifted the tone, making me realize this call wasn't just a casual catch-up.

"You know," she began, her voice taking on a more thoughtful quality, *"my father runs a publishing house here in Mumbai. I've been meaning to reach out to you about some opportunities. It might be a good chance for you to get involved in the industry beyond what you're doing now."*

The words struck me, and I sat up straighter, suddenly alert. *"Your father runs a publishing house?"*

"Yeah, he's been in the business for years," she explained. *"And I think you'd fit in well here, especially with your experience at the intern level. Maybe we could meet and discuss it more? I can introduce you to some people."*

I was quiet for a moment, trying to absorb what she was saying. A part of me was caught off guard by the offer, the suddenness of it. Another part, though, couldn't ignore how perfectly this seemed to align with everything I'd been working toward. A chance to break into the publishing world for real, to find my place in it, to carve out a future that didn't feel like a distant dream anymore.

"Are you serious?" I finally asked, my voice betraying the surprise and excitement building in me.

She laughed lightly. *"Of course, I'm serious. I wouldn't offer if I didn't think it could help. Besides, I like the way you think about writing. There's a lot to discuss."*

"Yeah, I think we definitely need to meet," I said, the words tumbling out before I had a chance to filter them. *"I'd love to hear more."*

We settled on a time to meet—soon. And as I hung up the phone, I felt a strange mix of anticipation and uncertainty. Maybe Sarah wasn't just a fleeting part of this city's puzzle. Maybe this was the start of something. Something that might lead me to more than just a job, but to a future I hadn't yet been able to imagine.

As I stared out at the city skyline and the buzzing of the streets below, I wondered how much had changed since I first arrived in Mumbai. And how much, perhaps, was still to come.

The day I met Sarah again felt like the turning point I'd been waiting for, even though I didn't realize it at the time. We met at a small café in South Mumbai, the kind of place where the windows were fogged up with the humidity of the city, and the air smelled of freshly brewed coffee and rain. It was quiet enough for a conversation, but bustling enough to remind me that Mumbai was always moving, always alive.

She was already there when I arrived, sitting by the window with a book in hand. There was something different about her now—more confident, more poised. When she looked up and smiled, it wasn't just a greeting. It was a welcome, a promise of something more, though I couldn't quite place what.

"*Dev,*" she said, her voice smooth, and she stood up, taking a step closer. "*You made it. I thought I was going to be talking to myself today.*"

I smiled, my eyes narrowing slightly as I took in the way she looked. She was wearing a black dress that clung to her in all the right places, her hair falling softly around her shoulders. There was an undeniable charm about her now—something that wasn't there before. It wasn't just the city, though I could tell she'd adapted to it well. She had a new energy, a kind of self-assuredness that I couldn't ignore.

"*Wouldn't dream of leaving you hanging,*" I said, taking the seat across from her, a smirk tugging at my lips. I wasn't used to this version of me—more confident, more certain—but I liked it. I liked it a lot.

She raised an eyebrow, her lips curling into a playful smile. "*Good. So, tell me about your writing. Have a story in mind? Or is it just a hobby for now?*"

The question caught me off guard, but only for a second. I leaned back in my chair, tapping my fingers on the table. "*I think it's more than just a hobby now. I've been... working on something.*"

She leaned in slightly, her eyes twinkling with curiosity. "*Something, huh? You're not just teasing me with this something, are you? What's it about?*"

I could feel the shift in the air. Her gaze lingered just a little too long, and I found myself enjoying the tension more than I should have. "*It's personal. About... the things we don't always say. The stories we keep buried.*"

Her lips parted slightly as if she wanted to say something, but then she let it go. "*Sounds intriguing. But you're still being mysterious, I see. You know, you're making it hard for me to figure you out.*"

I chuckled, leaning forward, the air between us thickening with something that could have been more. *"I don't make it easy, do I?"*

"No," she said, her voice lower now. *"But that's kind of what I like about you."*

I had to stop myself from smiling too much. I knew I should have felt a little more cautious, but there was something in the way she spoke that made me want to press further. This was new, this back-and-forth. I wasn't used to this feeling, this subtle challenge.

I could feel her eyes on me, studying me, waiting for me to open up. But the truth was, I didn't want to just give it away. There was a part of me that wasn't ready to let go of the walls I'd built around myself, even with her.

"I've been thinking a lot lately," I said, my voice taking on a more serious tone. *"About what I want. What I really want. And I don't think it's just about writing anymore. It's about... building something. Making my mark. You know?"*

She tilted her head, her expression softening, but there was something sharp in her gaze now. *"What do you mean?"*

"I mean," I paused, leaning in just a little closer, *"I'm done waiting around for things to fall into place. I'm going to make it happen. And if that means stepping on a few people along the way... so be it."*

She stared at me for a long moment, her lips pressing into a thin line. *"You don't mean that,"* she said softly.

I met her gaze without flinching. *"Maybe I do."*

The words hung in the air between us, heavy with something that neither of us was fully ready to confront. But it was the truth. I was no longer the same person who had first arrived in Mumbai, uncertain and wide-eyed. The city had a way of changing you, shaping you into something you didn't always recognize. And maybe, just maybe, I was starting to like who I was becoming.

Sarah didn't say anything for a few moments, and I could see the wheels turning in her head. Finally, she spoke, her voice tinged with something I couldn't quite place. *"You're going to be a force to reckon with, aren't you?"*

I grinned, leaning back in my chair, allowing myself to revel in the truth of it. *"That's the plan."*

She met my gaze with an intensity that made my chest tighten, her fingers idly tracing the rim of her coffee cup. *"Well, in that case, Dev... I'd love to see what you're really capable of."*

And just like that, the conversation shifted. What had started as a casual meeting began to feel like something else— something more charged, more dangerous. The lines between us blurred, and for a moment, I allowed myself to entertain the thought that maybe Sarah wasn't just someone who could help me with opportunities.

Maybe she was part of the new path I was forging. Or maybe she was just another distraction in a city that thrived on them.

Either way, I wasn't ready to let go of the moment. Not yet.

"I'm serious about this book, Sarah," I said, my voice steady. *"And I'm not stopping until I get it out there. So, if you're really offering a way in, I'll take it."*

"I'm serious too," she replied, her smile both teasing and earnest. *"But you'll have to prove you're worth it."*

I grinned, the hunger for success, for validation, for something that could finally be mine, burning a little brighter now. *"I don't think proving anything is going to be the problem,"* I said, my voice low, as the city pulsed around us, waiting for whatever came next.

14

The next few weeks were a blur. I dove headfirst into my writing, the energy between Sarah and me lingering in the back of my mind like an unresolved chord. She kept in touch, always pushing me to write more, to take my ideas further, and to think beyond what I thought I could do. At the same time, I could feel her presence getting closer—not just professionally, but personally. She wasn't shy about her feelings. And I was starting to realize that I wasn't entirely indifferent.

But then, something shifted.

The publishing house Sarah's father ran had connections, doors to open, and opportunities I'd only dreamed of before. It wasn't long before I was sitting in a room filled with people who knew exactly what they were talking about when it came to books when it came to publishing. Sarah was there too, always close by, offering quiet encouragement. But as much as the world around me seemed to be falling into place, I felt myself getting restless. There was a hunger, a need to prove something—more to myself than to anyone else.

I worked harder than ever on my manuscript, constantly rewriting and refining it, unsure if I was making any real progress. The pressure from Sarah and the publishing house was immense, but it wasn't what weighed on me. It was a subtle shift within myself. The more time I spent in the publishing world, the more I felt detached from the person I used to be—the quiet, unsure guy who had spent his time romanticizing words and stories.

Now, I was a person who wanted success, validation, and recognition. Writing had become a tool, not just a passion, and I couldn't shake the feeling that I was playing a game I hadn't quite learned the rules of yet.

One evening, after another tense meeting with Mr. Qureshi's team, I found myself standing on the balcony of my apartment, staring out at the city that had swallowed me whole. The lights of Mumbai stretched out before me, a sprawling ocean of possibilities and I felt so small, so insignificant in the face of it all.

A notification flashed on my phone. It was from Sarah.

"I've got news about the book deal. Call me when you can."

I stared at it for a moment, a strange sensation creeping up my spine. Was this it? Was this the moment that would define everything I'd been working for?

I dialed her number, my heart racing as the phone rang in my ear.

"Hey, Dev," she said, her voice warm, but there was something a little distant in it. *"I've got good news. The team wants to move forward with your manuscript. They're offering a contract."*

I paused, feeling the weight of the moment settle over me. This was everything I'd wanted: the validation, the recognition. But somehow, it didn't feel as satisfying as I thought it would.

"That's... amazing," I said, trying to keep my voice steady. *"Really amazing. Thank you for pushing for me."*

There was a brief silence on the other end. *"You're welcome. But I think you know that you did this on your own, right? I just pointed the way."*

I leaned against the railing, watching the city below. The words seemed hollow, almost empty. Was I really doing this on my own? Or had I become a puppet in this whole process, being pushed and pulled by everyone's expectations?

"I know," I replied, but it didn't feel like the whole truth. *"I guess... I guess I'm just trying to figure out what this all means for me."*

She didn't respond right away, and when she did, her voice was softer, almost like she was trying to read between the lines. *"It means you're closer to your dream, Dev. You're getting exactly what you wanted."*

I didn't respond immediately. The truth was, I didn't know if that was true anymore. Did I want this book deal because it was part of my dream? Or had I gotten so caught up in the game that I forgot why I started writing in the first place?

"Yeah," I said finally, my voice barely above a whisper. *"I guess I am."*

We talked for a little while longer, but my thoughts kept drifting. The validation was there, but something felt off. I was no longer the person who wrote for the joy of it, who had dreamed of telling stories that mattered. Now, it was about numbers, contracts, and the next big thing.

When the call ended, I didn't feel elated. I didn't feel like I'd just won a victory. I felt... disconnected. It wasn't what I expected. I wasn't sure if it was the city, or Sarah, or the success itself, but I could feel myself changing, and not in the way I'd imagined.

And that's when I knew: I wasn't just going to write a book. I was going to make a career out of it, whether I liked it or not. Because in this city, where every dream felt like a battle, there was no room for anything less than full commitment to the grind.

I glanced at my reflection in the glass door, the faint outline of my tired face staring back at me. I had crossed a line, and I wasn't sure if I could ever go back.

The hunger inside me had only grown. But whether it would destroy me or drive me to something greater, I wasn't sure.

The months passed by in a blur. My book was finally ready—polished, edited, and ready to be sent into the world. The publishing house that had been guiding me, Sarah's father's company, was pushing everything forward, but it was Sarah who had been the real driving force. She'd been with me every step of the way, always just a message or a phone call away, making sure everything was on track.

And in that time, something had shifted between us. The professional banter had turned into something else. Late nights in the office turned into dinners, and dinners turned into something more.

It was subtle at first, just the occasional lingering touch or a look that lasted a little too long. But soon, we were spending weekends together. Sometimes we'd talk shop, but mostly, it was just us—two people navigating a city that felt like it was swallowing us whole. It wasn't perfect. It wasn't simple. But it felt... right.

One evening, after a particularly stressful meeting with her father's team, we found ourselves in a quiet bar in Bandra, a rare moment of downtime. Sarah had her hair down, no longer the boss lady, but the girl who laughed at my bad jokes and let her guard slip just enough to make everything feel real.

"You know," she said, leaning in, her fingers lightly tracing the rim of her glass, *"I'm proud of you. Your book is going to be huge."*

"Thanks," I replied, taking a sip of my own drink. I couldn't help but notice how different she seemed when she wasn't in her work mode. There was a softness to her—something I hadn't seen before. *"It feels... surreal, you know?"*

She smiled, her eyes warm. *"You deserve it. But I have to admit... I didn't expect you to become such a success so quickly. Didn't think you'd be so... driven."*

Her words were soft but pointed, and I couldn't help but notice the hint of something in her voice. She didn't mean it as an insult, but it made me feel something shift inside me— like maybe I was becoming someone else, someone she didn't fully understand anymore.

"Yeah, well," I chuckled, *"you get used to it after a while. The city does that to you. Makes you want to keep moving forward, you know?"*

She looked at me then, her gaze shifting from playful to something else. Something more serious. *"It's easy to get lost here, Dev. In all the noise. Just... don't forget who you were before."*

I wasn't sure what she meant by that, but I didn't ask. I wasn't sure I wanted to know. The truth was, I felt like I was changing, and maybe that was just part of the process.

A few weeks later, my book was out. The launch party was everything I'd imagined it would be: bright lights, flashing cameras, and people congratulating me and asking about my next project. Sarah was there by my side, but her role was different now. She wasn't just the boss. She was my partner, my support in the sea of faces that were trying to get my attention.

I hadn't seen her like this before—confident, but also... softer on the edges. When she spoke to me, it wasn't the business-savvy Sarah I'd come to know. It was Sarah who wanted to know about my day, about what I was thinking, about what I really wanted from all of this.

"Do you think we made the right choice?" she asked me quietly as we stood away from the crowd, looking out over the party. *"Do you think this book is everything you thought it would be?"*

I glanced at her, the weight of her question settling over me. *"I think it's just the beginning,"* I said, my voice low. *"But I wouldn't have gotten here without you, Sarah. You pushed me when I didn't want to be pushed."*

Her smile was soft but genuine, her eyes holding something unspoken between us. *"I'm glad I did."*

Later that night, after the party had died down and most of the guests had left, we found ourselves alone in a quiet corner of the venue. She leaned in, her breath warm against my ear, her hand resting lightly on my arm.

"You know, you don't have to keep proving yourself to me, Dev," she whispered, her voice a little softer, a little more vulnerable than I was used to hearing it. *"I see the person you're becoming, and I think I'm... I think I'm okay with it."*

It was a strange moment—like a crack had appeared in the carefully constructed walls we'd both built. But I didn't answer right away. Instead, I just took her hand in mine and let the silence speak for us.

Somewhere in the distance, the city was still alive, still moving forward. And so was I. The world was changing, and so was I, but I was learning how to live in it, how to survive it, and how to let it shape me. The hunger inside me had only grown. And now, with Sarah by my side, I was ready to see where it would take me next.

I was riding high as if the world had finally started bowing to me. My book was a success, I was being invited to more events, and my name was starting to get recognition. Mumbai was becoming my playground, and I had every intention of making it mine. And Sarah? She was always around—close, supportive—but I was starting to feel like I didn't need her approval anymore. I was the man now, and that fact was beginning to settle comfortably into my bones.

One evening, after a long, taxing day of meetings and calls, I found myself at Sarah's place. I knew she'd be there, alone, as usual. I hadn't called ahead, but it didn't matter. I walked in as if it were my own, tossing my jacket on the couch, ignoring the look she shot me from across the room.

"You're late," she said, half-accusing, half-amused.

"Am I?" I smirked, already walking toward her. *"I've got more important things on my mind now than keeping track of time."*

She raised an eyebrow, setting down the glass of wine she'd been holding. Her eyes were softer tonight, but there was a nervous energy behind them. It was always there when I was close. She knew something was different about me now, and I could see it in the way she reacted to my every move.

"I was just thinking of how successful you've become," she said, her tone casual, but there was something else there. Something unspoken, like she was trying to assess the man standing in front of her.

"Successful?" I chuckled, stepping closer until I was inches from her, the air between us thick. *"It's not just success, Sarah. It's power. And I'm starting to realize how much I like it."*

Her gaze flickered with something unreadable, a spark of hesitation, but I didn't care. I wasn't the same guy anymore. I wasn't going to wait for her signals or her permission.

"Don't look at me like that," I said, my voice low, almost dangerous. *"You know exactly what's happening between us."*

She shifted, her hands finding their way to my chest, her fingers trembling slightly. There was a pull in her eyes, a temptation I could see but not fully understand. It was the same conflict that ran through her every time I touched her, every time I kissed her.

"I never asked for this, Dev," she whispered, but the words were weak as if she knew they had no power at that moment.

"You didn't have to," I said, brushing her hair out of her face, leaning down so close our lips nearly touched. *"I've never asked for anything before. But now? I'll take it."*

Her breath hitched, her body responding to me without thought. I felt her pulse racing under my hand as I cupped her face, forcing her to look up at me.

"I'm not the boy you knew anymore," I said, my voice turning dark, demanding. *"I don't need to ask for your approval, Sarah. I don't need anything from you except what I want."*

She swallowed, her chest rising and falling with every breath. I could feel the tension between us—the way she was still trying to hold on to some semblance of control, but I could see it in her eyes: she was losing it. And I wasn't going to let her get it back.

Without another word, I kissed her again—harder, fiercer this time. I could feel her resistance, but I wasn't interested in stopping. My hands moved to her waist, pulling her closer, pressing her against me. She gasped, but it wasn't enough.

I kissed her neck, my lips brushing against her skin as I moved lower, my hands slipping under the fabric of her dress, feeling the heat of her body against mine. She let out a soft moan, and I couldn't help but smirk.

"You wanted me, Sarah. I can see it in your eyes. You're just afraid to admit it."

She tensed in my arms, but this time, she didn't push me away. Instead, her hands found their way to my shoulders, pulling me closer and urging me on. I was in control, and she was allowing me to be. I wasn't the same naive, uncertain guy who waited for permission. I was the man now—the man who took what he wanted.

My lips met hers again, deepening the kiss as if to prove a point. My fingers trailed down her spine, feeling the curve of her body under the dress, my mind lost in the rush of power, in the way she surrendered to me, even if just for this moment.

I pulled away slightly, my lips brushing against her ear. *"You're mine now. No questions. No hesitation."*

She shivered at my words, her breath ragged, but she didn't pull away. Her lips parted as if she wanted to say something, but nothing came out. I could see the confusion and desire battling in her eyes.

And I didn't care. I was past that. I wasn't going to second-guess myself anymore.

I kissed her again, this time more urgently, as if I couldn't get enough of her. My hands were everywhere—on her waist, her back, tracing the line of her dress. She moaned softly, her body responding, but there was something else there, something deeper, more raw.

This wasn't about love, not for me. This was about taking control, about owning this moment, about having her in ways I hadn't before. I was no longer that unsure person. I had become something else—something colder, something more dangerous. And I wasn't going back.

When we finally broke apart, both of us breathless, I looked down at her, my chest rising and falling with every breath. She was still trying to figure me out, her hands clutching at my shirt as if she wanted to say something, but she couldn't.

"Don't worry, Sarah," I said, my voice dripping with the arrogance I now wore like a second skin. *"You'll get used to me taking what I want."*

Her eyes flickered with a mixture of longing and something darker—something that scared her, but she wasn't leaving. She was still here, still close, still looking at me like I was the only thing that mattered.

And maybe, at that moment, I was.

March 2021

Somehow, in the middle of all the upheaval, I found myself reconnecting with Ahaana.

It started with a few messages—casual, the way we'd always picked up right where we'd left off. She was back home to be close to her parents, and I was here, too, unexpectedly grounded. One evening, on impulse, I texted her: *"Feel like going for a walk? Masks and social distancing, of course."*

Within minutes, she replied, *"Meet you outside in five. And you'd better have your mask on!"*

True to her word, she appeared at the corner of the street, mask on, hair tied back, looking every bit the doctor she had become. We strolled down quiet lanes, the whole town in lockdown, our voices the only sound cutting through the silence.

"So, how's it been?" I asked.

She sighed, a weight in her voice. *"Honestly? It's exhausting. Long hours, seeing the same patients come in and out. Sometimes we can help, but... sometimes..."* Her words trailed off, and I could see the toll it had taken on her. She looked out into the distance. *"It's weird. You'd think I'd get used to it, but every time I lose a patient, it feels like I'm losing them for the first time. I don't know how to explain it."*

I nodded, feeling an ache for her. *"I don't think anyone gets used to that."*

She gave a small smile. *"You know, they say you shouldn't take work home. But these days, I can't leave it anywhere else."* Her phone buzzed with an alert, and she checked it, shaking her head. *"Another emergency shift tomorrow. It's never-ending."*

I managed a small laugh. *"Remember when the only emergencies we had were cramming for exams?"*

She laughed too, her eyes lighting up. *"Or sneaking out to watch movies when we were supposed to be studying."* She glanced at me, her eyes softening, and for a moment, it felt like we were back in those simpler times.

"Maybe that's why this feels... okay," she said, almost to herself. *"Being back here with you. It's like this small piece of normal that I can hold onto."*

We didn't have much left to say after that. But the silence between us didn't feel empty. It was like we'd both come back to something we'd left behind, something that had been waiting patiently for us. The next day and the next, we'd meet at the same time, the same place. Sometimes, she'd talk about her patients, about her colleagues at the hospital who had become like family to her. Other times, she'd go silent, just walking next to me as if she needed that closeness without needing to fill it with words.

And for the first time in a long while, I didn't feel the need to escape.

The hours had dragged on as I sat at my desk, the quiet of the room wrapping around me like a heavy blanket. My pen moved mechanically across the paper, the words coming slowly but steadily. It felt good, though, to let my thoughts spill onto the page. I wasn't sure what I was trying to say, but the act of writing had become a sort of ritual for me now. I needed it.

The day had been another blur of routine—Ahaana gone most of the time, back to her shifts at the hospital. She'd left earlier with her usual quick kiss on the cheek, but there was nothing more to say than the standard goodbyes. It was like the weight of the world had shifted in some strange way. Things were quieter now and more settled, but I still found myself lost in thought sometimes. My mind wandered back to Sarah.

I'd spent countless nights trying to figure out where things had gone wrong with her. I couldn't pinpoint the exact moment, but I knew something had shifted between us. There was no clear answer, no grand revelation. I just knew that the connection we once had had faded, leaving behind only bits and pieces I could never quite put together.

I scratched the pen against the paper, lost in the rhythm of my thoughts, when my phone buzzed on the desk, breaking the stillness. I glanced at the screen, a small smile tugging at my lips when I saw the name.

Nitin.

I swiped the screen, pressing the phone to my ear. *"What's up, man?"*

"Bro!" Nitin's voice came through, full of energy, as if he'd been waiting to call me for hours. *"I'm alive, don't worry. You? Still stuck in your deep thoughts phase?"*

I couldn't help but laugh. *"Yeah, something like that. Just trying to make sense of... well, life."*

"Ah, that classic writer's thing, huh?" he teased. *"I knew it! So, tell me, is it a love story or some dramatic life crisis? Or are you just trying to fix the world in a single paragraph?"*

I leaned back in my chair, the corners of my mouth twitching into a grin. *"I'm not sure yet, Nitin. Honestly, I'm just writing whatever comes to me. It's like the story's already there— I'm just putting it down."*

"Dude, you're definitely deep in it," Nitin chuckled. *"Well, since you're all busy being the next great Indian writer, what have you been up to otherwise? Still too cool for a drink?"*

I let out a breath, leaning back further into the chair. *"Actually... Maybe I do need a drink. Haven't had a night out in ages."*

"Ha! Knew it!" he laughed. *"You need a break, bro. I've got some free time this weekend. Are you good?"*

"Yeah, sounds good," I said, feeling a weight lift off my shoulders. *"Let's do it."*

His tone shifted, more serious now. *"Just don't go writing about me, all right? I've got enough drama in my life as it is."*

I smiled. *"I'll try, man. No promises."*

As the call ended, I sat there for a moment, staring at the screen. There was something about that conversation—a simple thing, really—but it had pulled me out of the fog I'd been drowning in. Nitin had always been good at that, at making things feel a little less heavy, a little more... normal. It was like a breath of fresh air, even if it was just for a moment.

I wasn't sure what had gone wrong with Sarah, or what was coming next for Ahaana and me. But right then, at that moment, I didn't need to have it all figured out. I had the words in front of me. I had the people around me who cared. For the first time in a long while, I didn't feel the weight of the world pressing down on me so hard. And that was enough.

The phone call with Nitin had lifted something off my chest, even if just for a little while. I found myself staring out of the window, the sky turning a dull orange as the evening set in. The last few months had felt like a haze—isolated, quiet, but somehow... filled with space to breathe. Yet, as the evening stretched on, the familiar weight of old memories began to seep back in.

Sarah.

Her name echoed in my mind as if the past was somehow waiting to be unpacked. I hadn't thought about her much lately, but there was something about the call with Nitin that made me question whether I'd ever really understood the reason behind our breakup. It had never made sense to me. She'd said things—words that felt so true at the moment—and then they hadn't. Was it something I missed? Was I blind to the signs?

I rubbed my temples, frustrated with myself for letting things stay so unresolved. Maybe that was just my pattern, running from the uncomfortable parts, never really facing them.

But then again, it wasn't all on me.

I stared down at my phone, my thumb hovering over Sarah's contact. I hadn't reached out since... well, since everything ended. I didn't know if I was ready to talk to her. But maybe I was ready to understand it a little more.

Before I could hit send, my phone buzzed again. This time it was a message from Ahaana.

Hey, are you still up?

I smiled at the simplicity of it. No formalities. No pretenses. Just her.

Yeah, still here.

Good. I was thinking of getting dinner. I'll grab something on my way back from the hospital.

I leaned back in my chair, trying to focus on the present. I needed to stop overthinking everything. My fingers hovered over my keyboard, the blank page in front of me a reminder of what I needed to focus on. Writing. The one thing that gave me peace. Ahaana would be home soon, and maybe it was time to just enjoy the moment without dragging the past into it.

Ahaana walked in a little later that evening, the smell of hospital antiseptic still clinging to her white coat. She tossed her bag on the chair and sighed, the exhaustion in her voice palpable.

"I thought I'd never make it out of there," she said, kicking off her shoes. *"They've been throwing me into everything lately,*

from emergency surgeries to dealing with irritable patients. I feel like I'm losing my touch with the basics."

I couldn't help but smile. *"You're probably just overthinking it. You're good at what you do."*

She raised an eyebrow, a playful smirk tugging at her lips. *"Easy for you to say. What do you know about the ins and outs of saving lives?"*

"More than I'd like to admit," I said, looking back at the screen. *"My own life's been an emergency room of its own, just... without the surgeries."*

She laughed lightly and walked over to the table where I had set up dinner. She didn't even ask, just grabbed a plate and started serving herself. As usual, her ability to make herself at home in any space I was in had never failed to amuse me.

"You've been doing a lot of thinking lately, huh?" she said, her voice softer now, as she took a seat across from me.

I paused, the weight of her observation hanging in the air. *"Maybe. Just... stuff from the past, I guess. It's strange how things resurface when you least expect them."*

Ahaana looked at me, her eyes thoughtful. *"You've been carrying a lot, Dev. I can see it. Whatever happened before, it doesn't have to haunt you."*

I shrugged, trying to make light of it. *"It's not about haunting. More like... unfinished business. But I'm learning to live with it."*

She leaned back, watching me closely. *"You know, I'm here for that unfinished business, right? You don't have to handle it alone. You can talk to me about whatever you want."*

Her words, simple as they were, hit deeper than I expected. The weight in my chest seemed to ease, just a little. There was something about her steadiness—how she never seemed to judge or rush things—that made everything feel safer.

"I know," I said, voice low. *"It's just... I don't know how to explain some things. Like Sarah. I mean, we never really talked about what happened between us. I've got my theories, but... I never really got the full picture."*

Ahaana didn't say anything at first. She just watched me, her face soft. After a long moment, she finally spoke.

"People change, Dev. Sometimes, relationships do, too. But not everything has to make sense right away. You'll get there."

I nodded, though I still wasn't sure if I fully believed it. There was a comfort in her words, though, and for a moment, I allowed myself to feel like I might just figure things out. But for now, it was enough to be here with her.

We ate in silence for a while, the sound of our silverware clinking softly in the background. It wasn't uncomfortable, just... familiar. Even though a part of me was still holding on to past questions, another part felt lighter. I was starting to realize that some answers might not come right away—and that was okay. What mattered was the present, and in this moment, I was content.

15

It was a quiet Sunday afternoon, the kind where time seemed to stretch into nothingness. The world outside had slowed down, locked behind its own barricades of uncertainty. The town felt smaller, the hum of life muffled by the invisible weight of the pandemic. I sat by the window, the pale light of late afternoon filtering through the half-open blinds, casting long shadows across the room. The air was thick with a stillness that pressed against the glass, just like the words in my mind—waiting to be written but never quite forming.

The keys of my laptop clicked under my fingers, the sound rhythmic but hollow. I had been trying to write for hours, but every time I reached for the right words, they slipped through my fingers, like water. Instead, I found myself staring out of the window, watching the occasional person walk by, their faces half-hidden behind masks.

Ahaana's voice, loud enough to reach me through the open window, carried across the small distance between our houses. She was moving about, getting ready for yet another shift at the hospital. Even in these strange times, she was always on the move. I knew she had a demanding schedule, but there was something about the way she carried herself— always calm, always in control—that made me feel, well, small in comparison.

I leaned back in my chair, stretched my legs out in front of me, and let out a long sigh. My mind wandered back to Sarah.

It had been months since we last spoke, but her presence still lingered. The way we had ended things—those late-night arguments, the silences that stretched longer than they should have—sometimes felt like a dream as if they had never really happened. We had been so different, but I had loved her in a way that made it hard to let go, even when I knew we weren't right for each other. My thoughts about her were complicated, a jumbled mess of what-ifs and why-did't-we's.

But I didn't think about it for long. I couldn't. Not now.

I looked at the clock on my desk—4:45 pm. Ahaana had mentioned she'd be heading out soon, and sure enough, I could hear her footsteps approaching. I wasn't sure what exactly had shifted between us. It wasn't some grand declaration of feelings, nor some slow-burn romance. It was simply that, somehow, over these last few weeks, we'd both started filling the empty spaces that had once been occupied by the people we used to be. There was no need to put a label on it, not yet. But when I looked at her, I saw someone who wasn't just a memory from my past, but someone who was becoming more real in my present.

"Dev," Ahaana's voice called out from the hallway, the sound of her knock on the door followed immediately.

I glanced up, and for a moment, my thoughts scattered. She was standing there, her white coat on, and a stethoscope around her neck. Ahaana, the doctor, was always ready to step into the role she was born for, even when the world was falling apart.

"Are you sure you don't want to take a break? You've been at this all day," she asked, motioning toward the laptop.

I shook my head, running a hand through my hair. *"I just can't seem to get anything right today. It's like the words are stuck somewhere."*

She smiled knowingly, stepping into the room. *"It happens. You know, you've been in the same spot for hours. Maybe you need a change of scenery or a change of place."*

I smiled back, despite the tension in my chest. *"Easy for you to say. You're out there saving lives every day."*

She shrugged, a flicker of humility in her eyes. *"It's just a job, Dev. And it's just life. We all have our own battles to fight. You're fighting yours right now. Just... don't give up on it."*

I met her gaze, the quiet assurance in her voice grounding me. *"I won't,"* I replied, the weight of her words settling in.

I watched her for a moment longer as she grabbed her bag, the urgency in her movements a reminder of the world outside. *"I should get going,"* she said, her voice softer now. *"You should take a break too. When I get back, maybe we can do something—watch a movie, talk. Just... take your mind off things for a while."*

"Sounds good," I said, nodding. *"I'll be here, hopefully making some progress."*

She gave me a wink before she turned to leave. *"I know you will."*

As the door clicked shut behind her, I sat there for a long moment, the quiet of the room wrapping around me like a blanket. The feeling was familiar, yet different now. I wasn't alone, not in the same way I had been before. Ahaana was out there, doing her part in a world that was unraveling, but she always came back. And in that small, unspoken way, she was grounding me. She was here, in this moment, and I knew that I wasn't the only one finding comfort in the spaces we shared.

I looked down at the laptop again, but this time the words came easier. I began typing—slowly at first, then faster, as if something inside me had clicked. It wasn't perfect, but it was a start. And that was all I needed.

By the time Ahaana returned later that evening, I was lost in my own thoughts again, but this time, there was something more: a flicker of hope. Maybe, just maybe, I was starting to find my way back to myself. And maybe, just maybe, Ahaana and I were starting to find something more between us too.

It was late one evening when I first realized things had shifted between us. The town had quieted down as it always did by this hour, but there was a stillness in the air that wasn't just about the night. I was sitting on the small balcony of my apartment, the chilly breeze tugging at my shirt as I tried to focus on the words that weren't coming.

My phone buzzed.

Ahaana: What's up? Are you okay?

I smiled at the screen, the familiar text from her bringing something warm inside me. We had been talking like this for days now—casual, easy, but always a little more than what it used to be. She wasn't just a part of my past anymore. She had found her way back into my present and, in doing so, into the spaces of my mind, I hadn't known I was leaving open for her.

I typed back:

Me: Just thinking. About... things.

A minute passed. Then another text popped up:

Ahaana: Want to talk about it?

I stared at her message, a part of me unsure. We hadn't really gotten into the deeper stuff yet—not in the way I had with Sarah, not in the way I thought I could. But something in the simplicity of her message made me feel like I could.

I hesitated before replying:

Me: Yeah... Maybe. Just not sure where to start.

A few dots appeared, signaling she was typing. Then:

Ahaana: Start with whatever's on your mind. I'm not going anywhere.

The way she said that made me pause. There was no rush, no expectations. It wasn't like the past, where I felt like I had to be something specific, say the right things, or follow the script. With her, everything felt different. Easier, somehow. Like I could breathe.

I set my phone down and took a moment before responding. The cool night air seemed to quieten my mind for a second.

Me: It's just... I was thinking about Sarah. About how things ended.

Her reply was swift but not urgent:

Ahaana: You're still thinking about her?

It wasn't accusatory, more like an observation.

Me: I guess. I don't really know what happened, you know? It just ended. She stopped... replying, and I never really understood why.

I leaned back in my chair, my fingers absently running over the armrest as I waited for her reply. The sound of the world around me faded; the distance between me and her shortening in the space of a few words.

Her message came after a long pause:

Ahaana: Sometimes we think we understand something, but we're not looking at it the right way. Maybe you didn't get closure with Sarah because you weren't supposed to.

I read her words over and over, the simple truth of them struck me in ways I hadn't expected. She didn't try to explain Sarah's actions, didn't offer me a version of the past I could cling to. She just... accepted it. It was a quiet kind of wisdom, and it left me feeling lighter like a weight I hadn't even known was there had been lifted.

I looked down at my phone, but it was her words that stayed with me.

Me: I never thought of it that way.

There was a long pause this time. The kind that made me wonder if I'd said too much. But then, a new message popped up:

Ahaana: You don't have to understand everything, Dev. Sometimes the answers come later.

And there it was. The simplicity of it. No frills, no dramatics—just her way of saying that it was okay not to have everything figured out. Maybe it wasn't about Sarah at all. Maybe it was about me, figuring out how to move forward without the need for all the answers. And in that moment, I realized I had been holding on to something that wasn't mine to keep anymore.

I couldn't tell her everything I was feeling, but somehow I didn't have to. Just having her there—always so steady, so simple in her support—was enough.

Me: Thanks, Ahaana. Really.

She didn't reply right away, but I didn't need her to. I knew, somehow, that she understood.

As I sat there, the town stretching out beyond me, the noise of the world seemed a little softer, a little more bearable. I could see her—her laugh, her eyes, her presence filling the spaces that had once felt empty. Ahaana had come back into my life, but not in the way I expected. She was quietly changing everything, piece by piece, without rushing me. Just like the night air, she filled the gaps with something gentler.

It wasn't love, not yet, not in the way we both knew it once was. But it was the beginning of something else—a kind of peace, a kind of knowing that maybe, just maybe, we were both ready for something new.

And I was finally ready to embrace that.

Days passed, but something about the space between Ahaana and me felt different now. There was an ease in the air when we spoke, an unspoken understanding that didn't need explanation. I hadn't realized how much I'd missed her until I felt it—the comfort of her presence in the small, everyday moments.

It wasn't like before, when we were kids—when everything was uncomplicated and simple. But it didn't need to be complicated, either. It felt like I was slowly uncovering parts of her again, little things I hadn't known I'd forgotten. The way she'd push her hair behind her ear when she was thinking, or how she never seemed to get tired of reminding me to drink water, even though I'd always pretend I'd forgotten. The way she smiled, almost imperceptibly, when she was about to make a sarcastic remark, and how it made me want to stay quiet just to see how long she could hold it in before bursting into laughter.

We were walking one evening, just down the lane that separated our houses, when the silence between us started to feel comfortable. It wasn't like we were walking side by side every day—it was more like we were slowly stitching together moments that had once been lost. The streetlights cast soft shadows on the pavement, and the night felt too calm for the chaos outside.

"Have you ever thought about what we were, back then?" I asked, my voice barely above a whisper, though I knew she heard me.

She glanced at me, her eyes flickering with something I couldn't quite place. She'd always had that effect on me—the ability to make the simplest questions feel significant. *"What do you mean? Like... school times?"* She sounded cautious, but not uncomfortable. That was one thing I noticed. With her, there was always an openness, an understanding that we could say anything and still be okay.

"Yeah," I said, kicking a loose pebble out of my way. *"Back then... when everything was so simple. When you didn't have the weight of everything on your shoulders, and I didn't have to worry about writing words that mattered."*

She nodded slowly as if she were processing something deep. *"I think... We were just kids, right? We didn't know how to hold onto things, but we knew how to feel them."*

That was true. Back then, we were too young to understand what we had and too reckless to keep it. But now, it felt like we were older, wiser in some ways, but still holding onto the parts of each other we hadn't been ready to let go of.

"*I missed this,*" I said, and the words sounded too simple, too light. But they were the truth. I had missed this—the ease, the quiet moments, the feeling that even when we didn't speak, we still understood each other.

She looked at me for a moment, her expression thoughtful, then her lips curved into a quiet smile. It wasn't the kind of smile that asked for attention; it was the kind that simply acknowledged something unspoken between us. "*Yeah,*" she said softly, her voice steady but warm. "*Me too.*"

Looking back, I can see the small ways it all started to shift. It was so subtle, almost imperceptible at first, like watching the sunrise inch by inch. One moment, we were just neighbors— old friends catching up over tea or evening walks; the next, I was noticing things about her that hadn't crossed my mind before.

One evening, she laughed at something I said, and I found myself watching her in a way that made me feel like a stranger to my own thoughts. The way her eyes crinkled when she laughed, the way she'd absently twirl a strand of hair around her finger—these were details I'd never noticed before, or maybe I had, but never with the kind of focus I feel now.

It happened slowly. I began waiting for her text each evening, some little message about her day or a meme she thought I'd like. I'd catch myself looking out of the window around the time she'd take her tea outside. And sometimes, when she was telling me a story, I'd find myself leaning in as if her voice alone had some pull over me.

I remember one night in particular. We'd been sitting outside under the porch light, just the two of us, while the rest of the world felt quiet. She was telling me about her shift, a long day, but she somehow made it sound like an adventure, her eyes lighting up with each twist in the story. I don't even remember the details; I was too busy thinking about how completely and utterly myself I felt around her.

It was nothing dramatic—just a touch on her arm as she laughed, but in that moment, I felt this quiet certainty, like a piece of a puzzle slotting into place. I could feel the weight of it settle somewhere in my chest, warm and unhurried.

That night, as I lay in bed, I couldn't shake the thought of her. Not in a loud or overwhelming way, but something subtler, like a hum at the back of my mind. It wasn't just her laugh or the way she knew exactly what to say when I had a tough day. It was the feeling of being understood like I didn't need to be anything but myself.

And from there, it was as if my life had slipped into a quiet kind of orbit around her. No confessions, no declarations—just a growing comfort in knowing she was there, in those small shared moments that needed no words.

I had started to feel almost at ease around Ahaana again, finding myself laughing at her stories, exchanging the kind of inside jokes only two people who've known each other forever could understand. But then, just as things felt perfectly aligned, she mentioned a colleague—a name I hadn't heard before. Her eyes lit up as she described how they'd worked late one night, brainstorming over the details of some cases.

I felt something twist inside me. I wasn't prepared for the quiet, unfamiliar stab of jealousy. She spoke of him with a sort of warmth, a familiarity that didn't sit well with me. I laughed it off at first, trying to brush the feeling away as if it were nothing more than a misplaced thought. But even as I joked, I knew there was something underneath—a certain edge to my voice that betrayed me.

"You two seem close," I said, keeping my tone as casual as I could manage. *"Spending a lot of late nights together?"*

She glanced at me, sensing the undertone. There was a pause, almost as if she were considering her answer more carefully than usual. *"He's just... a friend,"* she said, her gaze holding mine a bit longer than necessary. There was something in her expression, something I couldn't quite place. Understanding? Or maybe caution?

The silence that followed stretched just a little too long. I found myself staring at the floor, my mind racing with questions I didn't dare ask. What was wrong with me? Since when did I care so much about who she spent time with?

Ahaana shifted slightly, her eyes drifting as if studying me from a new perspective. I wanted to explain it away, to shrug off the feeling and pretend I was unaffected. But even I couldn't deny it—the simple truth that, somehow, Ahaana had come to matter more than I'd let myself admit.

The weight of my own thoughts lingered in the air like an unspoken truth. I could feel Ahaana's eyes on me, almost as if she were waiting for me to say something, to break the silence that had settled between us. But all I could do was focus on my breathing, the subtle fluttering in my chest that I didn't quite know how to explain.

Finally, Ahaana spoke, her voice soft but direct. *"Is something bothering you, Dev?"*

Her question was like a gentle nudge, pulling me out of the haze I'd slipped into. I should have laughed it off, should have brushed it aside. But there was something about her that made me want to be honest, even when I didn't fully understand what I was feeling.

"I don't know," I said, my voice barely above a whisper. *"It's just... I guess it's nothing. I just don't like the idea of you being around other people—close to them, I guess."*

Ahaana's brow furrowed, her lips pressing into a thin line as she processed my words. *"You mean, you don't like the idea of me working with someone else? Or... being friends with them?"* she asked, her voice tinged with uncertainty as if she were testing the waters.

I felt a jolt of realization, but it didn't hit me like a light bulb. Instead, it was slow, creeping, as I realized just how possessive my words had sounded. And yet, I couldn't deny it. That gnawing feeling in my chest was real.

"Yeah," I muttered, looking away. *"Maybe it's stupid, I don't know. I just... it's hard for me to see you with someone else. Even if it's just work or friendship."*

Ahaana was quiet for a long moment. The room felt too small, the space between us growing wider despite her sitting right across from me. Finally, she spoke, her voice calm and measured. *"Dev, I'm not yours to control. We're friends, and I've told you before—my life doesn't revolve around anyone else. But you need to understand something."*

Her words made me flinch, though I didn't show it. I had to bite back the urge to explain myself, to justify my feelings. But Ahaana was right. She wasn't anyone's possession—not mine, not anyone's.

"*I just...*" I trailed off, unsure how to say what I needed to. "*I don't know how to do this—being so close to you. It messes with my head sometimes.*"

She nodded, her expression softening. "*I get it, Dev. It's complicated. But we're not in a relationship, and I'm not going to stop having a life outside of this, outside of us.*" Her words weren't harsh, but they were firm.

I nodded slowly, but inside, I felt something shift. Her words stung, but they also grounded me. It was a reminder I needed but didn't want to hear. And maybe that was the problem. I wasn't ready for something as simple as letting her have her own life without it affecting me.

For a long time, neither of us spoke. The air between us had thickened, and I couldn't shake the feeling of unease that had settled in my chest. But, eventually, Ahaana broke the silence.

"*Look, Dev,*" she said, her voice softer now, more understanding. "*We're friends, okay? And I care about you. But I also care about the people in my life, and I'm not going to apologize for that. If you're feeling like this, maybe you need to think about why.*"

Her words hit harder than I expected. She was right. This wasn't just about her and her colleagues. It was about something deeper—something I hadn't fully understood until now.

I leaned back, staring at the ceiling, my mind a whirlwind. Could I even admit to myself what was really going on here? Maybe I was too attached to her? That this wasn't just friendship for me anymore?

Ahaana was waiting for me to say something—anything— but I didn't know how to explain what I was feeling. All I knew was that I didn't want to lose her, even if that meant stepping back from everything I'd thought I understood about our relationship.

The rest of the evening passed quietly, the distance between us palpable but unspoken. I couldn't shake the weight of my own thoughts, but I knew one thing for sure: I was going to have to face these feelings—whether I was ready or not.

16 August 2021

The end of summer inched closer, and the days had that lingering stillness, like time itself was holding its breath. Ahaana and I had been seeing each other more often, her presence becoming a steady part of my weeks, like a familiar scent that settled into the fabric of my life. I was sprawled across the couch, waiting for a message from her, the only bright spot in an otherwise muted season, when Ma's voice drifted in from the kitchen. There was a heaviness in her tone I hadn't heard in years.

"Dev, I spoke to someone... about your father." She paused, measuring her words, as though they'd been stewing in her mind for days. *"He's... he's tested positive for Covid."*

My shoulders tensed. A sharp pang hit me, then faded into something hollow. I almost shrugged, trying to brush it off, though the news clung to the air like smoke. *"After all these years, you're still worrying about him?"*

Ma stepped into the room, wiping her hands on a dish towel, her gaze heavy yet searching. *"He may have been... difficult, but he's still your father, Dev."*

"Difficult?" A bitter laugh escaped me. *"Ma, he was cruel. I remember every time you tried to cover the bruises, how he'd come home and look at us like we were... in his way."*

She didn't flinch, though her eyes grew sadder, their weariness seeping through. *"People change, Dev. And maybe he hasn't, maybe he has. But when you've shared a life with someone, even if it was flawed, it's hard to... just cut it off completely."*

My throat tightened. *"So now you want me to care?"*

Her eyes shifted, softening as she looked away. *"I'm not asking you to care. I just thought you should know."*

The silence that followed felt like a shadow, deep and stretching over years of resentment and memories I'd buried long ago. I wanted to end the conversation, to shake off the weight of it, but her words clung to me, haunting their quiet truth. My mind flashed back to all those tense moments growing up, the twisted dynamic that had shaped us. I'd spent years trying to erase him, to be anything but what he'd been. Yet, now that he was struggling—at the edge of life, or perhaps change—something unsettled stirred within me.

It was one of those nights where silence wraps around you like a thick blanket, and the air feels heavy with things left unsaid. The house was still; only the quiet hum of the ceiling fan stirred the darkness. I lay on my bed, staring up at the shadows that drifted across the ceiling, the faint light from the street casting soft, fractured patterns. Nights like these bring out things you think you've buried—the kind of thoughts that only surface when it's just you and the quiet.

I don't know why I'm telling you this. Maybe it's because, for once, it feels like someone should hear it, or maybe it's that kind of night when everything that's been hiding just demands to be seen. I've learned over time that we carry fragments of our past, pieces we think we can tuck away and forget. But somehow, they find their way back, usually in the quiet, asking to be acknowledged.

It was on a night like this, lying there in the shadows, that my phone buzzed on the nightstand. Ahaana's name glowed on the screen. Seeing her name filled me with an odd mix of relief and something else—something that felt like I'd been holding my breath without knowing it.

I picked up, my voice low as I answered. *"Hey."*

"Did I wake you?" she asked, her tone soft, carrying the warmth of familiarity but tinged with exhaustion. I could tell her day had been long.

"No, I wasn't asleep," I replied, letting out a small sigh. *"Couldn't sleep if I tried."* I paused, then added, *"You just got back?"*

"Yeah, another endless shift," she said with a tired laugh that warmed something in me. *"Some nights, I wonder if I should just move my bed to the hospital. It would save me the commute."*

The faint laughter faded, leaving us in silence. The kind of silence that wasn't empty but seemed to have its own rhythm. She didn't rush to fill it, just waited, her quiet presence steady on the other end. And somehow, in that stillness, I found myself saying something I hadn't planned to share.

"Ma told me about my father tonight," I began, the bitterness slipping out in a way I hadn't intended. *"Apparently, he's... sick. Covid, or something like that."*

She didn't say anything right away. Just a soft breath that reminded me she was there, listening.

"Oh... Dev, I'm sorry," she said finally, her voice gentle, as if she sensed that simple words wouldn't be enough.

"Yeah," I muttered, the bitterness threading through my voice. *"After all this time, I don't know why she even cares. It's been years. She doesn't owe him anything."*

Ahaana stayed quiet, letting me continue. It was as if she understood that the words had been waiting, bottled up and brimming to escape.

"She used to hide everything," I said, surprised by how raw it all felt. *"The bruises, the shouting, all of it. She'd tell me things were fine. I could never understand why she didn't just... walk away. And now she's worried about him?"*

"I don't think she's asking you to feel anything specific," Ahaana replied, her voice soft but certain. *"Maybe she just wants to let herself feel whatever's left. It doesn't mean she's forgotten or forgiven. Maybe it's just her way of letting go."*

I lay there, her words sinking in, mingling with the memories. There was a strange comfort in her voice, in her steady, unwavering presence.

"It's strange," I said quietly, almost as if I were talking to myself. *"Part of me wants to hate him. Maybe I should. But... I don't know. There's just this... mess. And I don't know what to do with it."*

"That's okay, Dev," she said, her voice like a balm. *"You don't have to know. Sometimes, feeling lost in it is part of figuring it out."*

Her words grounded me. I found myself gripping the phone tighter, as though her voice alone could tether me. *"Thanks for listening,"* I murmured, surprised at how much I meant it.

"Any time," she replied softly. *"And Dev... you don't have to carry it alone."*

We drifted into a silence, a silence that felt less lonely, her breathing a steady rhythm on the other end. And for the first time in a long time, it felt okay to just be. In that moment, with her voice grounding me in the stillness of the night, I felt something loosen in my chest. The shadows on the ceiling softened, and somehow, I felt a little less alone.

There are certain hours of the morning that feel like they've been abandoned by the world, haunting and hollow, like something that never should have existed. It was 4:14 a.m. when I heard her—a sound that barely made it through the haze of sleep, like a broken whisper, then the soft push of my door creaking open.

When I opened my eyes, Ma was standing there, her hand covering her mouth as though holding in something too heavy, too sharp to let out. The light spilling in from the hallway hit her face, hollowed and gray like she'd been drained of all but the pain. At that moment, I knew.

She stepped forward, her hand trembling as she lowered it, and I could see she was on the edge of shattering. *"Dev..."* Her voice was hoarse, stretched thin by the weight of words she could barely say aloud. She took a breath that seemed to drain her even more. *"He... your father... he didn't make it."*

The words crashed over me, leaving a strange, hollow ache in their wake as if I'd swallowed something I couldn't quite digest. I didn't know what to say or how to react. There was no gasp, no tears, just... silence.

Ma let out a broken sound, her shoulders slumping forward as though she'd been hit by a wave. She held onto the edge of my bed to steady herself, her face crumbling as the grief finally spilled out of her, unstoppable and raw. *"He's gone,"* she whispered, her voice dissolving into sobs. *"Just like that, he's... he's gone."*

I watched her, feeling a gnawing ache in my chest, yet somehow nothing felt real. The memories of my father—the man who'd left so many scars on us both—clashed with the image of Ma now, drowning in sorrow I couldn't fully grasp. I wanted to hold her, comfort her, but I felt paralyzed by something I couldn't name.

Ma dropped down, her knees hitting the floor, her fingers gripping the side of the bed as though it was the only thing keeping her from collapsing entirely. She clutched her chest, the grief twisting through her as if it were alive. *"I... I don't know how to be alone after all these years, Dev. I didn't think... I didn't think it would hurt this much..."*

I knelt beside her, feeling helpless, unsure what to do with this gaping chasm between us. My own heart felt heavy, but it wasn't grief—not like hers. It was more like a hollow space, an emptiness that echoed every time I tried to reach for something real, something to feel. I should have hated him for everything he put us through, but I couldn't even summon that. He was gone, and all I had left was a bitter, uneasy calm.

She looked up at me, her eyes red and glassy, pleading for something I didn't know how to give. *"Dev... I know he wasn't... he wasn't easy, but... we had years together. And no matter how much he hurt us, I thought—"* Her voice broke, and she pressed her hand to her mouth again, trying to stifle the sobs that wracked her body.

For a moment, I hated myself for not feeling more, for not being able to join her in the grief that was tearing her apart. I wanted to share her pain, to be the son who could hold her through this, but all I felt was this strange, hollow ache that felt as empty as the early morning air around us.

I reached out, placing my hand over hers, a small gesture, but it was all I could manage. She squeezed it tightly, as though drawing strength from me. *"I just... I don't know how to do this without him, Dev."* Her voice was a faint whisper now, lost in the quiet of that terrible hour.

We stayed there, side by side on the floor, as the dawn crept closer, her sobs fading into the silence. And as I held her hand, I could feel the weight of everything that had gone unsaid, the things we'd both buried for years. Now, they were floating in the air around us—grief, regret, anger, and something that felt like release but wasn't quite.

In the end, it was just silence that filled the room, a quiet that sank into my bones, a reminder that we'd both lost something different that night. For her, a husband. For me, the chance to understand what it was to have a father at all.

I don't think I've ever felt this weight before—this sinking feeling that clings to you like tar, hardening in your chest with every breath.

I never expected it to hit me like this. His death, I mean. All those years of anger, resentment, frustration, and in the blink of an eye, all those emotions suddenly crumbled into nothing. Gone. As if they were never really there at all. What was I holding on to? His cruelty? His absence? For years, I had built up this wall of bitterness, letting it define who I was, and now... now it was just gone. The wall had been shattered by the news of his death. But what was left in its place?

The hollow ache inside me wasn't anger. It wasn't even regret. It was an emptiness I couldn't explain. I sat there beside Ma, trying to comfort her, but in that moment, I realized... I didn't know how to comfort myself. I couldn't even make sense of my own feelings. The pain, it was there, but it was tangled with something else.

I thought about my father, and all I could see were flashes of that angry man who used to come home late, drunk, his face twisted with resentment. I thought about the way he'd look at Ma like she was just a piece of furniture in the corner of his life. How he'd disappear for days, leaving us to wonder if he was even alive. How he'd storm into the house like the world owed him something, making us feel smaller with every word.

But then... there was this strange, quiet sorrow. For a man who never showed any emotion, for a man who'd broken everything he touched, how was it possible that his death would leave me feeling... lost?

I should have felt free. I should have felt this weight lifting off me. But instead, I was left with nothing. No closure. No answers. Just this lingering ache, like a void that wasn't there before. And for the first time in a long while, I wondered if that emptiness wasn't just about him, but about me too.

Maybe I'd spent too long blaming him for everything—the way he'd shaped me, the way I'd turned into someone I wasn't proud of. Maybe it wasn't just him. Maybe I had been running from something I couldn't even name. His death wasn't the end of something; it was the beginning of me facing all those things I'd buried deep inside myself.

I glanced at Ma, her grief consuming her in a way I couldn't even begin to understand. She was mourning a man who had once been her partner, and in some strange way, I envied that. She had memories of him that I never would. There was no way to reconcile who he was to her and who he was to me. To her, he was still the man she married, the father of her child. But to me, he was a ghost, an absence I'd learned to live with, and now, with his death, he left me with only more questions.

How had it all gotten so tangled? I wasn't ready for this. I didn't know how to process it, how to deal with this emptiness gnawing at me.

I couldn't go back to the way things were. I couldn't look at Ma the same way again, knowing what we had lost. But I couldn't move forward either. How do you move forward when the past is still bleeding into the present; when it feels like you're carrying a weight that never belonged to you?

I wanted to call Ahaana. I wanted her here, to hear her voice, to have her tell me that everything would be okay, but I wasn't sure I even deserved her comfort right now. I wasn't sure I deserved anyone's comfort.

This wasn't a loss I had prepared for. It wasn't the kind of grief I thought I'd feel. But here I was, sitting on the floor of my room, wrapped in the kind of sorrow I hadn't known existed.

For the first time in a long while, I realized I was just... lost. And I didn't know how to find my way out.

Two days. Two days of silence, of my mind reeling from the suddenness of it all, unable to make sense of the loss. I couldn't feel anything—couldn't allow myself to. The house felt emptier without my mother's voice, a coldness hanging in the air that settled deep in my bones. I stayed in the same spot for hours, barely eating, barely thinking, just existing in the numb space where nothing seemed real. The world outside had continued, but inside, I was frozen.

And then she came.

The door creaked open softly, the sound too delicate for the heaviness in my chest. I didn't expect anyone. The silence in the house felt final like nothing could pierce it. But there she was, standing in the doorway like she belonged there, like she always had. Ahaana.

She looked different. Her face was pale from lack of sleep, the worry etched deep around her eyes. It didn't take much to know she'd heard. Her parents had probably called, and the news had spread like wildfire. But still, she came. Not a word yet, just standing there, as if waiting for permission to step into the storm that had become my life.

I couldn't move. I couldn't find my voice. I just stared at her, my breath catching in my throat. It was as if seeing her there broke something inside me, something I hadn't realized I'd been holding back all this time.

"Ahaana," I managed to croak. The word came out thick as if it were caught somewhere between relief and guilt. I didn't want to show her this broken version of myself. I didn't want her to see me so raw, so stripped bare of everything I thought I was.

She didn't speak right away. She didn't need to. She just crossed the threshold and came closer, the weight of her presence soothing something inside me. She wasn't rushing to fill the silence and wasn't pushing me to talk. She was just there. And in that moment, it was everything I didn't know I needed.

"I'm so sorry, Dev," she whispered, sitting down beside me on the bed, but keeping some space between us, as if she wasn't sure how close she could come to the broken parts of me. *"I heard from my parents... I should've been here sooner. I just—"* Her voice faltered, and I saw the vulnerability in her eyes. *"I didn't know how to..."*

I let her words trail off. I didn't need the explanation. I knew. I knew she hadn't been here, not for a reason, but because sometimes, there were no words, no right time. She wasn't like everyone else, showing up with sympathy or empty comfort. She came with understanding. And that was something I hadn't realized I was desperate for.

"I didn't think it would hit me this way," I whispered, the rawness of the grief creeping up in my voice. *"I thought I'd be okay, that I wouldn't care. But now that he's gone, I feel... hollow."* I shook my head, the words stumbling out of me. *"I don't know what to do with all this space. All this emptiness."*

She didn't say anything, but she shifted closer, her hand tentatively reaching out to mine. It was such a simple thing, but it felt like a lifeline. I didn't pull away. I couldn't. The warmth of her fingers in mine was a small comfort, but it was enough. It felt like a permission slip to feel something I hadn't allowed myself to feel—pain.

"You don't have to figure it all out now," she said softly, her voice like a balm. *"Grief doesn't have a timeline. It doesn't have rules. And it doesn't mean you have to understand it right away."*

Her words hung in the air, a truth that settled deep within me. For so long, I'd buried everything—my anger, my regret, my abandonment. I thought I could live without confronting it, without acknowledging it. But now, in the silence of this room, I realized I couldn't escape it.

"I've spent so long hating him, pretending it didn't matter," I continued, my voice breaking slightly. *"I told myself I didn't care, that it was his fault, that he deserved everything that happened. But now... now that he's gone, I don't know what I feel. I don't know who I'm supposed to be without all that anger."*

Ahaana didn't speak. She didn't need to. She just sat there, her hand in mine, her presence like a steadying force. I wanted to pull away. I wanted to close off, to shut down, to keep the walls I'd built around myself intact. But the warmth of her hand in mine—the way she was just here, without judgment, without expectation—made me feel things I wasn't ready to confront.

"*I'm scared, Ahaana,*" I whispered, the words spilling out before I could stop them. "*I'm scared of feeling this much. I don't know how to do this.*"

Her thumb gently brushed over the back of my hand, a soft, reassuring gesture. "*You don't have to do it alone,*" she said, her voice low but certain. "*You never have to do it alone.*"

She sat with me in the stillness for what felt like hours, saying nothing, but offering everything. In the quiet, I realized that maybe, just maybe, I wasn't as lost as I thought. Maybe, with her by my side, I could start to rebuild the parts of me that had been shattered for so long.

16

The chill of mid-November had settled in, seeping through the walls and wrapping the room in that familiar, quiet cold that only winter knows. I'd been holed up in my room for hours, my notebooks scattered around, the half-light from the table lamp casting shadows across the pages. My fingers were stained with ink, and my mind was burning—thoughts spilling out faster than my hand could capture them. The grief I'd tried to ignore had turned into a relentless drive, like a haunting rhythm that wouldn't let go until I'd exhausted every word.

I was startled when Ahaana knocked softly and came in, wrapped in a thick scarf, her cheeks tinged pink from the cold outside. She looked at me with that quiet concern I was beginning to see more often. Without a word, she sank onto the rug beside me, eyes scanning the chaotic mess of paper and half-drunk coffee cups that had overtaken my room. But I didn't look up. My eyes were locked on the lines I'd scrawled at some ungodly hour, words that came in a haze of grief, exhaustion, and that relentless, unexplainable ache.

I took a breath, letting the silence settle before I began to read:

I wonder if love and ruin are two sides of the same coin, if all we ever inherit from those who shaped us is the debris of their own broken worlds. My father—he was a hurricane, a force that tore through every room he walked into, leaving cracks that no amount of years could fill.

They say I look like him, that I carry his shadow in the angles of my face, in the way I stand, like something unfinished. But God, if I could strip away that likeness if I could peel it from my bones, I would. Because I am not him. I am not his rage, his hollow promises, his cruel laughter echoing in the walls.

Yet here I am, writing these lines with hands that shake like his did when he'd reach for another drink, with eyes that hold the same restless hunger, the kind that no amount of love or art could ever quiet. Maybe in some twisted way, I did inherit him—a darkness that I both resent and can't seem to let go of. But I will make art of it, turn this pain into verses that bleed, that begs to be seen if only to remind myself that I am not just a shadow, that I can be something more.

The words faded into the room, leaving a hollow, reverberating quiet. I couldn't look at Ahaana, afraid that speaking these lines had exposed too much as if each syllable had peeled away a layer of armor I didn't know I still wore.

But then her voice, soft yet unwavering, broke through the quiet. *"Dev,"* she murmured, her gaze steady, deep. *"Do you ever wonder if... maybe you're not just transforming it? Maybe you're feeding it, letting it become a part of you in ways you don't even realize?"*

A shiver ran through me, not from the cold, but from the truth her words pried open. I wanted to protest, to tell her she was wrong. But instead, I found myself staring down at the page, at the jagged ink of my own words, wondering if maybe, just maybe, she was right.

The room felt small, closing in on us as if the weight of everything unsaid, the wounds that lingered beneath words and glances, had found a way to bridge the silence. I sat there, my chest tight, feeling the reality of it all in a way I hadn't before—a mixture of love, longing, and the kind of ache that makes an artist out of a man, even as it breaks him piece by piece.

It was late—another night where I'd been staring at words, letting them coil around me like a vice. The room was a mess of drafts, half-burned cigarettes, and notes scattered like fallen leaves. I was too deep into the piece to notice much else until I felt her presence in the doorway.

Ahaana stood there, soft in her sweater, arms crossed lightly, her face etched with a familiar worry. She didn't interrupt; she just watched me, her gaze holding an unspoken question that I couldn't shake: How far are you willing to go with this, Dev?

Finally, she took a quiet step inside, her voice breaking the silence in that careful, considerate way she always had. *"Have you eaten?"*

I glanced at her, the pang of guilt flaring up, but I brushed it off just as quickly as I'd done every night this week. *"Not yet. I'm close to finishing this piece."*

Ahaana sighed, barely audible, but I heard it. She came closer, reached for one of the scattered drafts, and began to read. She absorbed each line in silence, her expression shifting, softening, hardening. I could feel a kind of tension in her, something she'd been holding back, something I wasn't sure I wanted to face.

After what felt like an eternity, she spoke, her steady voice forced me to listen. *"Dev, I know you need this—writing, I mean. It's part of you; I get that. But... sometimes, it feels like you're letting it take over. Like you're disappearing into it."*

I shook my head, unwilling to let her words dig too deep. *"You don't understand, Ahaana. This—this is the only thing that makes sense to me right now. If I don't pour it all out, if I don't let this pain fuel something, then what was it all for?"*

She looked at me then, sadness mingling with a quiet resolve. *"Maybe... maybe it's not about the art right now, Dev. Maybe it's about just being here, being present, with people who care about you."* She hesitated, as if weighing each word, then added, so softly it almost didn't reach me, *"With me."*

A silence settled between us, thick and unyielding. I looked down at the pages scattered on my lap, feeling the weight of her words pull at something fragile within me. I knew, somewhere deep down, that she was right. But I was caught in this spiral, convinced that this pain was the only thing keeping my art alive.

After she left, her words lingered, echoing in the empty spaces she'd left behind. *Was I really losing myself to this?*

18th November 2022

It was late, nearing 3 a.m., the kind of quiet where every sound feels too loud. I was sprawled on the floor, my head against the edge of the couch, an empty glass of whiskey at my side and the taste still sharp in my mouth. Cigarette stubs lay scattered around me, the faint smoke clinging to the dim light in the room. I stared up at the ceiling, lost in the haze of another night where sleep refused to come.

Then, a gentle knock, almost a whisper against the silence. Ahaana. She slipped inside, moving softly across the room until she was by my side, her expression caught between worry and exhaustion. She knelt beside me without a word, lifting my head and settling it in her lap. Her hand found its way to my shoulder, tracing gentle circles, grounding me in a way that only she could.

For a long time, we just stayed like that, surrounded by the quiet. I closed my eyes, letting myself sink into her touch. She didn't ask questions, didn't scold or pry. Her presence was steady and patient, and in that silence, it felt like we were speaking in a language only we understood.

After a while, I found myself mumbling, more to the room than to her, *"Do you ever feel like you're chasing something... something you can't even name?"*

She didn't answer right away. Her gaze was soft, searching my face as if trying to find the right words. *"Sometimes,"* she said, her voice gentle. *"But maybe the chase is where we find ourselves."*

I opened my eyes, looking up at her. There was something raw in her face, a softness that both calmed and unsettled me. *"And what if I can't find it?"* I murmured, barely audible.

Ahaana's hand pressed against my chest, right above my heart, her fingers resting there as if feeling for something deeper. *"Then I'll help you look for it. Wherever it is."*

Her words settled into the silence, becoming part of the room, an unspoken promise that weighed on me in a way I couldn't shake. She was like the anchor in the storm I'd thrown myself into, the one person who could pull me back when everything else felt like it was falling away.

I felt my breath hitch, a tightness in my throat I couldn't swallow down. She looked at me, a quiet sadness in her eyes, and leaned down until her forehead brushed against mine. My eyes slipped shut, and for that one moment, I let myself surrender, feeling her warmth, letting myself be seen in a way I'd almost forgotten how to be.

"You know... your mum's worried about you," she whispered softly, her voice laced with the kind of concern that both

comforted and pricked at my guilt. *"She and I... we talked about this. She's scared you're getting lost in all of this."*

We stayed there, her hand in mine, our breaths mingling in the quiet. I couldn't say the words that lingered in my mind; I didn't know how to say them. But as her fingers tightened around mine, I realized that maybe, this was as close as I could come to saying it back. This was my way of holding onto her, even if I didn't know how to admit it yet.

And in that fragile silence, wrapped in the soft warmth of her presence, I felt that she might have already understood.

January, 2022

It was late afternoon, the kind of gray January day that felt like the town was holding its breath. The past few weeks had been fast, the turn of the new year nothing but a distant memory in the fog of drafts, empty bottles of alcohol, and too many nights spent staring at a blank screen. I had written my soul into those pages, and yet, something always felt incomplete, as though I was chasing something elusive.

My phone rang, the sudden interruption almost jarring against the quiet of the room. It was an unknown number. Normally, I would have ignored it, but something made me pick up. I pressed the phone to my ear.

"Hello? Is this Dev Mukherjee?"

The voice was calm and professional, and I could sense that they were accustomed to speaking with creatives like me. I sat up straighter, instinctively bracing for what came next. *"Yes, this is Dev. Who's this?"*

"I'm Rachel from 'Velvet Press'," she continued. *"We've been following your work for a while now, and we'd like to discuss the possibility of publishing your latest piece. Do you have a moment?"*

I froze. The words took a few seconds to sink in, and when they did, they felt almost surreal. *A publisher? Interested in my work?*

My heart pounded. I glanced at the mess on my desk, the scribbled notes, the scattered drafts, and all the late nights that had led up to this moment. It felt like everything I'd been working for, every ounce of pain I had poured into my writing, was suddenly worth something. My fingers gripped the edge of the desk as I tried to steady myself.

"Yeah, sure. I... I'd love to discuss it," I managed, my voice rougher than I wanted it to be.

Rachel explained the details, asking about the manuscript and offering to connect me with the right people in the editorial team. Her words seemed to melt together, but I was too focused on the thudding in my chest to fully absorb them. It wasn't just an offer—it was validation.

It was everything I'd hoped for, yet in some strange way, it felt distant. The excitement I thought I'd feel wasn't there. Instead, there was a heaviness in my gut, as though this was the turning point, again. The moment that could either push me forward into something greater—or pull me away from everything I had built in my personal life.

When the call ended, I sat there, staring at the blank screen in front of me. The room was quiet again, save for the hum of the refrigerator in the distance. I had a choice now. An opportunity. Something to pour my energy into, something to replace the hollow ache I'd been feeling.

But as I sat there, I couldn't shake the feeling that I was losing myself. What I had wanted so badly was finally here—and it had come at the cost of everything else.

✦ ✦ ✦

"You're really here." The words slipped out before I could catch them. I'd barely registered her figure standing at the door, one hand carrying a bag of takeout, the other smoothing her hair as she stepped in. She looked exhausted from her hospital shift, but there was this quiet warmth, a kind of solace she carried with her.

She set the bag on the table, a faint smile curving her lips. *"Your mum said she'd be gone tonight, so I thought I'd bring you something to eat."*

For a moment, I just stared at her. There was something so grounding about her presence that night, something that had been missing in the whirlwind of drafts and emails with the publisher. When she turned to me, I saw it—the understanding in her eyes, and something else I couldn't quite place.

We talked quietly for a while, just small things, about work, about the publishing house's interest in my novel. But there was this pull between us, a silence that wasn't uncomfortable but filled with something far more intense. She caught my gaze, her eyes softening in a way that spoke volumes.

"It's all happening, Ahaana," I whispered, the exhaustion in my voice barely hidden. I didn't know if I was trying to convince her or myself.

Her eyes flickered with pride, mixed with something else. Concern, perhaps. *"I'm happy for you, Dev. But... just take care of yourself, please. Your mum's been worried, and we all—"*

I cut her off with a faint, hollow laugh. *"I know. But this... this is everything."*

She just sighed, a small shake of her head, before she reached over, her hand grazing my shoulder in that grounding way she did. Something shifted in the air, a kind of unspoken understanding settling between us. The tension of days and weeks of missed moments lingered there, hanging heavily. I could see it in her eyes, the way her breathing slowed, her gaze softer yet weighted.

And in that moment, I felt an urgency—like every word left unspoken between us had transformed into something visceral. I closed the space between us, my fingers trailing over her arm, gentle at first, then possessive, hungry. Her breath caught as my hand slid to her waist, pulling her closer, feeling the warmth of her skin beneath my fingertips.

I pressed my lips to hers, and she melted into me, a sigh escaping her. I could feel her pulse beneath my hand, quickening with mine, her body responsive to every touch, every move, yet there was something in her that seemed to hesitate, just for a second. But as I deepened the kiss, her hands clutched at my shoulders, pulling me in with an intensity that mirrored my own.

Our movements became more urgent, more frenzied as if we both knew that words weren't enough—that this was the only way we could bridge the gap between us. She allowed me to guide her toward the couch, her hands sliding up my chest, fingers tangling in my hair as I lowered her down, covering her with my body. I could feel her heartbeat against mine, the rawness, the quiet desperation of it.

Her breath hitched as I traced the line of her jaw with my lips, moving down to her collarbone, leaving a trail of kisses that felt both possessive and fragile. Her hands roamed over me, finding every scar, every line. There was no need for gentleness anymore, no pretense—just the aching need to consume and be consumed.

But there was something different in her gaze, a kind of curiosity mixed with a quiet fear. She held me close, yet I could feel her noticing—the way my grip tightened on her hips, the roughness in the way I pulled her to me, my fingers pressing into her skin as if she were the only real thing I could cling to in a world that felt increasingly unreal.

She moved beneath me, her breath shallow and quick, and as our bodies met in that space, there was an intensity in my touch that bordered on obsession. I wanted to hold her, to keep her here with me, to possess her in a way that felt absolute. Every touch, every kiss was a silent plea—a wordless confession of the need that threatened to devour me whole.

In the quiet aftermath, as we lay tangled together, her fingers traced lazy circles on my shoulder, her breathing finally steady. She looked at me with a softness I didn't deserve, her gaze lingering on my face, studying the parts of me I rarely let anyone see. But in her eyes, there was something else—a shadow of concern, as if she was starting to understand just how deeply my need ran, and the darkness that came with it.

And as her fingers brushed over my face, her gaze caught mine, and I could see the question lingering there—the one she hadn't yet dared to ask: *Is this the only way you know how to love?*

The morning after was quieter. The chaos of the night before had dissipated, replaced by a strange calmness in the air. Ahaana had the day off, and she made her way to my house early in the morning, her hospital scrubs replaced by a cozy sweater and jeans. There was something warm about her, something that felt like home, especially after everything that had happened. She moved around the house, humming softly to herself, pulling the blinds open to let the light filter in. The brightness of the day felt oddly soothing.

"Do you want coffee?" she asked, looking over at me as I sat slouched on the couch, still tangled in blankets in the aftermath of the night.

"Not yet," I muttered, my voice still hoarse, *"I think I need to wake up first."*

She gave me a smile, that quiet, knowing smile that always made me feel seen. *"Okay,"* she said with a grin, and before I could stop her, she was already moving toward the bathroom. *"I have an idea. You're looking like you've been through hell."*

I blinked at her, confused, but soon realized she had something planned.

Before I could react, Ahaana returned with a razor and shaving cream in hand. *"I'm shaving your beard today."*

I raised an eyebrow, half-laughing at the absurdity. *"You're serious?"*

"Yes," she said firmly, the glint in her eyes showing she wasn't going to let me off the hook. *"You've been letting your beard grow wild for weeks now. It's time."*

I could feel my cheeks flush slightly, but I didn't resist. There was something in her eyes that made it hard to say no, a warmth that softened the hardness of the world around us. And besides, I couldn't remember the last time I'd done something this simple, something that felt so... normal.

I sat up, wiped the sleep from my eyes, and leaned back against the couch as she knelt in front of me. She applied the shaving cream carefully, her fingers gentle but sure, spreading it across my face. I closed my eyes, letting the moment stretch on, her touch grounding me in a way I hadn't realized I needed.

The sound of the razor moving along my skin was oddly soothing, a quiet rhythm that made me feel like time was slowing down, giving me a moment of peace. Ahaana's concentration was intense as she worked, her focus on me in a way that made the world outside feel far away.

As she shaved off the last remnants of my beard, she smiled up at me. *"There,"* she said with a soft laugh, *"Much better."*

I ran my hand over my now smooth face, surprised by how good it felt. *"You missed your calling as a barber,"* I joked, and she laughed in return, her eyes lighting up with that easy affection she always gave me.

She reached up to tuck a stray piece of hair behind my ear and, for a moment, we just sat there, the world outside suspended in time. There was no tension, no weight of unspoken words between us—just a quiet, simple connection. She leaned in to kiss my forehead, soft and lingering, before standing up to grab the breakfast she'd brought with her.

"Come on," she said, holding out a plate of eggs and toast. *"You need to eat. And after that, we're watching a movie. No writing today. No work. Just us."*

I nodded, a smile creeping onto my face. There was something so peaceful about this—about her, about the feeling of being taken care of, of being seen in the way only someone who truly cared for you could see. We ate together, sitting side by side, talking about everything and nothing. It felt so effortless, so... right.

And for once, I wasn't thinking about the next draft, or my art, or my past. I was just here, with her. With Ahaana.

Ahaana sat next to me on the couch, the plate of food between us forgotten as I leaned back, stretching my arms above my head. She picked up a pillow and tucked it behind my back, adjusting it until I was comfortable. I caught her gaze, her soft smile making my chest tighten. She always knew how to make me feel like everything would be okay, even when I couldn't see it myself.

"Thank you for this," I murmured, my voice hoarse from the late nights of writing and the weight of everything on my mind. *"I didn't even realize how much I needed a day like this."*

Ahaana tucked her legs under her, curling up beside me, and I pulled the blanket over both of us. She leaned her head against my shoulder, her hair soft against my skin. I let out a breath, trying to relax, but the warmth of her closeness was making everything inside me feel like it was shifting, slowly, gently.

"You don't have to thank me," she said, her voice muffled slightly by the fabric of my shirt. *"I like doing things for you. I like being here."* She shifted closer, her fingers lightly tracing circles on my arm. *"It's been a while since we had a morning like this."*

I nodded, looking down at her, my hand instinctively moving to rest on her knee. I wasn't used to these moments of calm—these soft, real moments of intimacy—but I didn't want to let go of them. Not now, not ever.

She raised her head to look at me, her gaze warm and steady. *"What are you thinking about?"* she asked quietly, her voice low, as if she didn't want to disturb the fragile peace between us.

I sighed, rubbing my hand over my face. *"Just... everything. The writing. The publishing house. The future."* I paused, feeling the weight of my own words. *"But it's not all bad, you know? Not with you here."*

She smiled, the kind of smile that made my heart twist. *"Good. Because that's all I really care about right now—being here for you, in all of this. Whatever it looks like."*

We sat in silence for a while, just letting the moment stretch on. The only sound was the soft rhythm of our breathing and the occasional creak of the old wooden floor. She shifted again, this time curling into me, her head tucked under my chin as she placed a kiss on my chest. Her lips were warm and soft. As she pulled back, her eyes met mine, filled with something I couldn't quite name.

Before I could say anything, she kissed me again, her lips tentative at first, as though she was waiting for permission. I pulled her closer, letting the kiss deepen, my hands sliding down her back to pull her more firmly against me. She sighed against my lips, her body pressing into mine, and it felt like everything else—the noise of the world, the pressure of my art, even the future itself—just disappeared. There was only us, here, together in this quiet, stolen moment.

Her hands slid up to cup my face, and I kissed her with a tenderness I didn't realize I had inside me. She responded, her lips soft and sure, her body leaning into mine as though she couldn't get close enough. My heart raced, the pull between us undeniable, raw.

In the midst of the kiss, I realized something—something that hit me like a quiet wave. The way she touched me, the way she made me feel seen, it was different from everything else I had ever known. It wasn't just passion; it was care, an unspoken promise that she would always be here, even in my darkest, most broken moments.

She pulled away slightly, her forehead resting against mine, and I could feel her heartbeat echoing in sync with mine. There was a softness in her touch now, a gentle reassurance. *"I know you're carrying a lot, Dev. I know it's not always easy for you... for us. But we're here, okay?"*

Her words lingered in the air, heavy with meaning. I wanted to say something back, something that matched the way I was feeling, but all I could manage was a quiet, *"Yeah. We're here."*

Ahaana gave me a soft, affectionate smile and snuggled closer, wrapping her arms around me as she rested her head against my chest. Her fingers traced random patterns on my skin, slow and steady, and I let myself be lost in the simple, beautiful moment. We didn't need words to explain what we were doing.

This—intimacy, connection—was enough.

As Ahaana's head rested against me, I couldn't help but think about the difference between her and Sarah. With Ahaana, there was no need to figure it out, no guessing game. It just *was*. Easy, steady, like we'd always fit together. But with Sarah, I always felt like I was chasing something I couldn't quite reach—trying to decode what was never clear.

Ahaana was the calm, the certainty. Sarah had been the fire, the confusion. And maybe that's why it had never made sense.

July 2022

The summer heat hung heavy, pressing against the windows as I sat at my desk, hands trembling over the keyboard. There were days when the words came easily—uncontrollable, raw, like a flood. And then there were days when I felt like I was suffocating, trapped in this loop of writing that didn't feel like it belonged to me anymore. It wasn't me writing anymore. It was the pain. It was the fear. It was the demons that wouldn't leave me alone.

I took another drag from the cigarette, watching the smoke curl into the dim light. Every time I looked at the screen, it felt like the words were mocking me. They wanted pain. They wanted chaos. My fingers hovered over the keys, but I couldn't move them. I couldn't bring myself to write without feeling like I was betraying something.

The sound of the door opening broke my thoughts. Ahaana. She was back. I didn't know why she kept coming back, honestly. But she did.

She dropped the bag of takeout on the table, her eyes scanning the room. They lingered on the desk, the half-empty bottle of whiskey on the side, the cigarettes. She didn't say anything, but I could feel the disappointment hanging in the air, thick like fog. I knew she hated seeing me like this.

"Did you eat today?" she asked, a bit too softly. The question seemed like an accusation, even though I knew it wasn't.

"Yeah," I mumbled, looking away. *"I ate."*

Her hand found mine on the desk, her fingers curling around mine as if she were trying to pull me back. She didn't say anything else, just sat beside me, not touching me, but close enough to make me feel the weight of her concern.

I couldn't look at her. I was too far gone. The words on the screen were still taunting me. But this time, it wasn't just the writing. It was everything. The more I thought about it, the more I realized it wasn't just my art that was slipping away—it was us. I was losing her.

And she wasn't saying anything, but she could feel it too. I could see it in the way her lips pressed together, the way her fingers twitched against the edge of the table as if she was holding herself back.

"Ahaana..." My voice broke, and I hated myself for it. *"I... I can't keep doing this."*

She didn't ask what I meant. She didn't need to. Her gaze flickered to the empty glass next to me, then back at me, and I saw it—the hesitation in her eyes. The realization that I wasn't just struggling with my art, I was struggling with us.

"You're pushing me away," she said softly. Her voice wasn't accusing, just tired. Like she had said it a thousand times already.

I pulled my hand away and stood up quickly, knocking the chair back. *"I'm not pushing you away. You just don't understand. You don't understand what I need."*

"What do you need, Dev?" Her voice wasn't soft anymore. It was sharp, but it didn't scare me. *"You need to stop running from everything. You need to stop using your writing to destroy yourself. And stop making me the one who has to watch it happen."*

I looked at her, my heart pounding in my chest. *"I don't know how to stop. Do you think I can just stop?"*

She stood up now too, her eyes searching mine, but I couldn't look at her. The pain in her eyes was too much, and I didn't want to face it. I was the one who had created it, after all.

"You can't keep doing this," she whispered. *"This isn't just about your writing. This is about you. About us."*

I laughed bitterly, walking away from her. I couldn't stay in that moment any longer. The weight of her words was suffocating, and I needed space. I needed to breathe, but I didn't know how.

"I don't know how to be the person you want me to be," I said, my voice rough. *"And I can't stop writing. Not when it's the only thing that makes sense anymore."*

"Then maybe..." She stopped herself, her voice trembling. *"Maybe I'm not the right person for you."*

That hit me harder than anything she had said. I spun around, my chest tight with something I couldn't name. *"What did you just say?"*

Her lips trembled, but she didn't look away. *"Maybe we're not what we thought we were. Maybe this... this isn't enough anymore."*

The room felt like it was closing in on me. I couldn't breathe. *"Are you leaving me?"* My voice was raw, almost a scream, but she didn't flinch.

"I'm not leaving, Dev," she said softly. *"But I don't know how much more I can take."*

And then, before I even realized what I was doing, I was moving toward her, pressing my mouth to hers. It was desperate, needy—my hands grabbing at her, pulling her closer as if I could consume her and make this pain stop. She didn't pull away, but I could feel her hesitation in the way she responded, the way she kissed me as if she was trying to hold back like she knew this wasn't just about us anymore. It was about everything that was wrong between us.

I kissed her harder, trying to drown out the fear, the panic, the realization that I had no control anymore.

And then, in the middle of it all, I felt her pull back, just slightly. Her hands were on my chest, pushing me away gently, but I didn't let go. Not yet.

"I can't... keep doing this," she whispered. *"This isn't love anymore, Dev. This is something else. Something darker."*

The words hit me like a slap. My chest tightened, my heart pounding so hard I thought it might stop.

And I knew.

I had lost her.

And in that moment, I realized that this—*us*—was always going to be a fight. Not just between me and her, but between what I wanted and what I needed. Between art and love. And no matter how much I loved her, the art was always going to come first.

17

September 2022

"You really don't get it, do you?"

Her voice cut through the heavy silence like a shard of glass, sharp and raw. I could see the pain in her eyes, etched deep, and it tore through me in a way that nothing else ever had. I opened my mouth to say something, to defend myself, to hold on to her just a little longer—but the words wouldn't come. They stuck in my throat, a silent admission of all the things I'd done wrong.

Ahaana took a shaky breath, looking away, her hands trembling as she tried to keep it together. *"Dev, you're killing me,"* she whispered, barely louder than a breath. *"Loving you feels like... like I'm suffocating like I'm losing myself piece by piece, and I can't... I can't keep doing this."*

I tried to reach for her, to close the space between us, but she stepped back, and the hurt in her eyes was like a knife twisting in my chest. I hated that look, that guarded distance that had settled between us, and then I realized how far gone we really were.

"Ahaana," I choked out, my voice a broken whisper. *"Please, you know I need you."*

She laughed, but it was hollow, bitter, filled with a pain I could barely comprehend. *"Need me?"* she repeated, almost mocking. *"You don't need me, Dev. You need something to fill this... this void inside you. And I've been trying to do that, trying to be everything for you, but it's never enough, is it?"*

Her words hit me like blows, each one a painful truth I had been too blind to see. I could feel the anger rising, but it was more than that. It was desperation, a last attempt to hold on to the only thing that had ever made me feel whole.

"Ahaana, don't," I whispered, reaching for her hand, but she pulled away, her eyes glistening with unshed tears.

"I have to," she said, her voice trembling, but her gaze was unwavering. *"Dev, I can't keep losing myself in you. I love you, God, I do. But I can't keep drowning just to keep you afloat."*

She took a deep breath, looking down, her voice barely a whisper. *"You don't see what you're doing to me. You don't see the way you twist everything, the way you pull me in and push me away. I can't breathe anymore, Dev."*

I wanted to shout, to scream, to tell her that she was wrong, that she was overreacting. But deep down, I knew she wasn't. I knew that I had taken and taken, never giving her the space she needed, never understanding that love wasn't meant to feel like this, like a storm that tore everything apart.

"I can change," I said desperately, my voice a hollow promise I wasn't sure I could keep. *"I can—"*

"No, Dev," She cut me off, her gaze sharp and filled with a finality that made my stomach drop. *"I've been waiting for you to change. I've been waiting for you to see me, to really see me, but you're so wrapped up in your own pain that you don't even notice how much you're hurting me."*

Her words were a slap in the face, a brutal reminder of everything I had refused to acknowledge.

"I thought..." Her voice cracked, and she wiped a tear from her cheek, looking away. *"I thought love would be enough. That I could hold on to you, that I could fix whatever was broken inside you. But I can't, Dev. I'm breaking, too."*

I couldn't breathe. The reality of her words settled over me like a crushing weight, and I felt the walls closing in, the panic clawing at my chest. I had never felt more helpless, more terrified.

"Ahaana, please," I whispered, my voice cracking, but she just shook her head.

"I've already made up my mind," she said softly, her voice trembling, but there was a strength in her gaze that told me she was serious. *"I got a job offer in Bangalore. I wasn't going to take it, but..."* She swallowed, her voice thick with emotion. *"Maybe it's time I put myself first."*

The words echoed in my head, a cruel reminder that she was leaving, that I was losing her, and there was nothing I could do to stop it. I reached for her, desperate, pleading, but she stepped back, her gaze filled with a sad determination.

"Dev," she whispered, her voice soft, almost tender, and it broke something deep inside me. *"I love you, but I can't keep sacrificing myself for you. I can't keep waiting for you to be okay. I need to be okay, too."*

She looked at me one last time, her gaze lingering, filled with a sorrow that tore me apart. Then, without another word, she turned and walked away, leaving me standing there, alone in the empty room that felt like it was caving in around me.

I sank to the floor, the weight of it all pressing down on me, crushing me. My chest felt hollow, my heart a raw, open wound that refused to heal. I wanted to scream, to rage, to beg her to come back, but I knew it was too late. She was gone, and it was my fault.

For weeks, I drifted through life in a haze, burying myself in work, drowning in the silence that her absence left behind. Maa tried to reach out, tried to understand, but I pushed her away, too. I didn't want anyone. I didn't want anything but the numbness that kept the pain at bay.

Then, a couple of months later, my mother called, her voice cautious, as if she was afraid of breaking the fragile silence between us.

"She's moved, you know?" she said, her voice soft, hesitant. *"To Bangalore. I thought... I thought you knew."*

I felt my chest tighten, the words hitting me like a punch to the gut. I hadn't known. I hadn't let myself think about where she was or what she was doing. I had spent every day trying to forget, trying to drown out the memory of her leaving, the way she had looked at me with that quiet resignation that still haunted me.

And there, lying on the table like a reminder of everything we had been and everything I'd lost, was her stethoscope, left behind in a rush on one of those nights she'd come to check on me. It lay there, cold, a piece of her world intruding on mine, her pulse that had once intertwined with mine, a symbol of her steady heart in the chaos of us.

I picked it up, feeling its weight, her heartbeat against mine, lingering in the absence. And in that quiet moment, I realized it was all I had left—just a faint echo of her, of us. A heartbeat I could no longer reach.

I felt like an unfinished painting, strokes of color fading into the canvas, leaving nothing but emptiness behind.

Her absence wrapped around me like a shroud, every breath heavy, every thought hollow.

The world kept spinning, but I stood still—lost in the void she left.

Mumbai, 2028

I was living an author's dream. In the years since my first book, I've written five more, each one a bestseller, my words capturing the hearts of thousands across the country. I was no stranger to fan meets and book signings now, and yet, standing there in a small, packed bookstore in Bandra, I felt a quiet reverence. This wasn't just a crowd, after all—these were people who saw pieces of themselves in my stories, who'd carried my words into their own lives.

The evening had been full of laughter and bookish conversations, with fans asking about my writing process and inspirations, each question as light as the evening air. But then a young woman in the back raised her hand, her eyes bright with the weight of something unsaid.

"*Dev,*" she began, her voice trembling a little, "*you wrote about Ahaana, about the two of you... and everything you went through. The way you described her, it was like she was the heart of everything.*" She paused, her gaze softening. "*Did you ever... Did you ever see her again?*"

The crowd went silent, leaning in as if holding their collective breath. I was still, the question hit me in a way I hadn't anticipated. I looked down for a moment and gathered myself before finally meeting her gaze.

There was a heaviness in my eyes, as though I was reaching back through years of memories to love and a life that no success had ever managed to erase.

"Years," I started in a low voice, almost a whisper, *"years have passed since I last saw her. Ahaana... She was my everything. But the universe,"* I paused, swallowing hard, *"the universe had other plans. Her family left town without a word like they wanted to erase every trace of her. I searched... God, I searched everywhere, clinging to any hope, any rumor, any clue of where she might be. But she was gone like she'd never even existed."*

My fans sat spellbound as my words sunk in, haunting the air around them. *"I thought I'd made peace with it, that maybe some part of me could move on. But it was a lie. Every book, every page... they were all just shadows of the words I wanted to say to her, all the things I thought we'd have time for."*

I hesitated but continued in a trembling voice. *"And then... one day, I saw her. Just like that. In a crowded street, after all these years. My heart... I swear it forgot how to beat. I didn't even believe it was her at first. But there she was, my Ahaana. She was smiling, laughing, wrapped in this light I'd never seen before, holding the hand of a man standing beside her. She looked... different. Softer, like the sharp edges of our youth had worn away. And she looked... happy. God, she looked happy."*

I clenched my fists and a flicker of pain crossed my face. *"I wanted to believe that I was part of that happiness. Maybe she'd look at me and remember every stolen moment, every whispered promise. So I walked toward her, feeling like I'd been waiting a lifetime for that single step."*

I drew a shaky breath, each word heavy with the weight of unspoken pain. *"I called her name. 'Ahaana,'"* My voice trembled, my gaze fixed on the memory that had haunted me ever since.

"She turned to me, and for a fleeting moment... I thought she'd remember. I thought her eyes would light up, that she'd smile the way she used to. But instead..." My voice faltered, raw emotion slipping through. *"Instead, she gave me a soft smile—polite, almost apologetic—and said, 'I'm sorry, but... do I know you?' Her voice was gentle like she was afraid of hurting me."*

My hands clenched briefly at my sides before I let out a shaky exhale. *"I told her, 'It's me, Dev.' My voice was barely above a whisper, like saying my name could bridge the distance between us. She blinked, her smile fading as her brows knit together in confusion. Her eyes... they searched mine, uncertain, hesitant. She didn't look away immediately. It was like she was trying so hard to remember, but... there was nothing. She turned slightly, glancing at the man beside her as if looking for help. Then she looked back at me, her lips parting as if she wanted to say something, but no words came. Just... silence. Her expression stayed soft, but there was no recognition, no spark. Nothing. She looked at me like I was a stranger she wanted to understand but couldn't."*

The room was utterly still, the weight of my words sinking into the silence. My voice grew quieter, almost breaking. *"And then... the man beside her stepped forward. He was holding her hand. His tone was kind, almost hesitant, like he didn't want to make it worse. He said, 'She had an accident... she lost some of her memories. Maybe... she doesn't remember you.'"*

"And in that moment, as her eyes held no spark of recognition, no trace of the life we'd shared, it hit me like a storm—I had lost her, not to time or distance, but to a place I could never reach. The Ahaana I knew, the one who once knew me, was gone. And all I was to her now... was a shadow of someone she might have once known."

The words hung in the air, laden with heartbreak, leaving the audience with a crushing silence that spoke louder than any sob.

I looked down, my voice barely a whisper now. *"I wanted to scream. I wanted to shout that I was the love of her life, that she was mine. I wanted to shake her, make her see me, make her remember the promises we made. 'Ami thakbo, mone rakhish,' she'd once told me, promising she'd always be there. But she didn't even recognize her own words. That promise? It was gone. Lost in the corners of a mind that had forgotten me."*

My voice broke, trembling under the weight of my words; I struggled to speak. A tear slipped down my cheek, unbidden. And then... I said that they were married. I didn't say it cruelly; my tone was soft, almost careful like I knew it would destroy me. *"She had built a life, her happiness, without me... without us."*

My breath shuddered, and my gaze dropped, the memory cutting through me like glass. *"And when she turned to him, the way she looked at him... it was like the universe lived in her eyes for him. Like he was the home she'd found when I wasn't there. She looked at him with a love so complete, so absolute, it broke something in me I didn't even know could still break."*

I paused, my voice dropping to a whisper, heavy with despair. *"And in that moment, I realized... I hadn't just lost her memory. I'd lost every piece of her—her heart, her laughter, her dreams, her soul. She was his now, entirely his. And all I had left... was the ghost of what we used to be."*

"I stood there, frozen, watching them walk away, her hand in his, like it belonged there—like it was always meant to be. I wanted to shout, to make her remember, to remind her of who we were, but I knew, deep down, even if she did, it wouldn't matter. She wasn't just moving on from me. She was walking into a life I'd never be a part of, and I... I was just standing there, lost, watching her slip further away, with no way to bring her back."

I swallowed hard, and as I looked out at the crowd, a single tear slipped down my cheek, catching the light. I didn't bother to brush it away; I let it fall. My gaze was distant and filled with sorrow that fame could never quiet. The silence in the room was heavy, each listener holding onto their words as if they were witnessing the raw, broken heart of the man behind the stories.

I lifted the stethoscope, the one thing I'd clung to all these years. *"She left this behind once, just a small mistake,"* he murmured, his voice thick. *"And I held onto it, thinking maybe one day, she'd come back for it. But she never did. All these years, it's been the only heartbeat I've ever heard from her—a reminder of a promise that was never meant to last."*

I placed it gently on the table, as though setting down the weight of all I'd carried. I looked at my fans; the tear still fresh on my cheek. They could feel the finality, the deep ache of a love that would forever be etched into my soul, yet remain unreachable. And in that moment, Dev Mukherjee wasn't the celebrated author they'd come to see—he was just a man, stripped bare, haunted by the memory of a love that had slipped away.

"She's living in a world where we never happened, where our story died before it could ever find its ending. And for me... that's the cruelest kind of forever."

– Dev Mukherjee.

AUTHOR'S BIO

Sneha Sengupta is a storyteller who weaves raw emotions into intricate narratives, crafting tales that leave readers questioning their own hearts. A writer by day and a dreamer by night, Sneha finds inspiration in life's quiet moments—half-spoken promises, fleeting glances, and the stories that linger between the lines.

Known for their evocative prose and haunting narratives, the stories blur the line between fiction and reality, inviting readers into worlds that feel achingly familiar. Heartbeats & Stethoscopes is the most intimate work yet—a tribute to the stories we carry and the ones we leave behind.

When not writing, Sneha is often found lost in films, photography, or wandering through places with untold stories, and staring at blank pages, waiting for the perfect word to arrive. This is Sneha's ode to everyone who has ever loved, lost, and dared to remember.